THE CHASM

THE MADION WAR TRILOGY

S. Usher Evans

Sun's Golden Ray
Publishing

THE MADION WAR TRILOGY

THE ISLAND
THE CHASM
THE UNION

Line Editing by Danielle Fine
Madion War Trilogy logo designed by Anita@Race-Point.com
Phoenix and Lion Icons courtesy of VectorPortal.com
Copyright © 2016 Sun's Golden Ray Publishing

ISBN: 0986298166
ISBN-13: 978-0986298165

CONTENTS

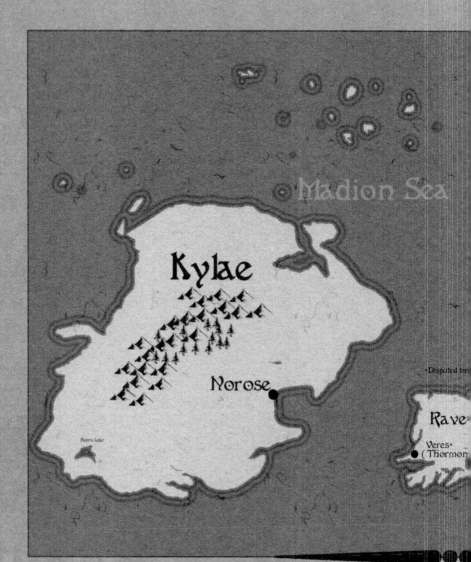

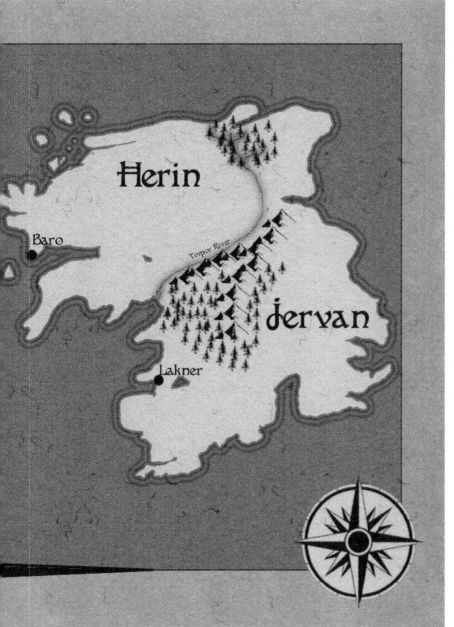

ONE

GALIAN

"Fellow Ravens, my countrymen, my 'neechais *and* 'nichais. *In the fifty years since we've reclaimed our independence from the Kylaens, our great nation has struggled. Great sacrifices have been asked of every Raven man, woman, and child, and we, as a people, continue to rise to the occasion."*

"Sacrifices, of course, being the conscription of twelve-year-old children," the Kylaen announcer said, cutting off the rest of the speech. *"It's just sickening how Tedwin Bayard continues to be heralded as a savior when he's responsible for tens of thousands of deaths a year—"*

I tuned out the rest of the conversation, too tired to get my blood pressure up at either Bayard or the announcer. As far as I was concerned, both were liars. Like most of Kylae, I couldn't give a rat's ass about the so-called president of our disputed colony and would've completely ignored the minute-long segment...

...if not for the beautiful Raven woman sitting just behind Bayard.

Her eyes were locked on some unseen point beyond the

cameras. When I was marooned with her on an island in the northern Madion Sea, she'd been fiery, full of life and passion. Now, there didn't seem to even be a spark in her. Compared to Bayard, who swayed and gestured on the podium, she looked like a wax doll.

I ran a hand over my face. The Kylaen news had moved on to another story—the trade agreement with Jervan—and I was left with my guilt and a half-eaten sandwich. It was midday, and I'd finally been able to spare a few minutes out of my busy shift at the hospital to eat lunch. Seeing Theo had stolen my appetite.

I couldn't blame it all on the news report as I'd already been in a foul mood. After working the late shift two nights ago, I was now on an early shift. The back-and-forth shift-switching had been going on since since I'd returned to my residency, and I could barely tell if it was morning or afternoon anymore.

To make matters worse, my mother had been hounding me to attend some stupid function at the castle for some person who'd done some thing for Kylae—I couldn't care less. Aside from state functions being my least favorite princely activity, I hadn't set foot in the castle in over four months. I'd stormed out of a family dinner and told the king of Kylae to kiss my ass. It was a miracle I wasn't in Mael, our prison to the north.

I glanced at the television again and wished they'd replay the Bayard segment. Days like today, when I was tired and miserable, all I wanted was to talk to her. In the two months we'd spent together, I'd become addicted to her counsel. Hers was the only opinion I cared for anymore, though I was pretty sure I knew how she'd feel about my progress so far.

Theo was home and she was safe, but the larger issues—the war and the Kylaen death camp at Mael—remained nagging issues in the back of my mind. I was no closer to finding a solution to either of them than when I'd started. To make matters worse, the days were passing too quickly for me, and the more time that slipped through my fingers...

"Helmuth, break's over," came a disgruntled voice from behind me.

Dr. Hebendon was my new attending physician. Dr. Maitland had either been asked or forced to take a six-month sabbatical to a hospital in the country of Herin. In his place, they'd sent Hebendon. Like most Herinese, he was tall and pale with jet-black hair that hung in a curtain around his face. I was pretty sure that despite not being Kylaen, he'd been given a royal decree to make my life miserable whenever I set foot in the hospital. Thus my skewed schedule and, of course, the special privilege of having the *best* cases.

"Janna needs you in room fifteen for another impaction," he said, a twisted grin curling around his thin face.

I forced a tight smile onto my face so he wouldn't know how completely *sick* I was of pulling shit out of asses.

Hebendon left, and I pushed myself to stand, tossing my sad sandwich in the trash. When I'd been on the island, I would've done anything to eat so much food.

Now I would've done anything to get those half-starved, beautiful days back.

I took the long way from the doctor's lounge to the patient room where, yet again, I would be dealing in shit. I paused at the window and stared at the Madion Sea. Today it was an awe-inspiring aquamarine, sparkling in the mid-afternoon sun—a far cry from the tumultuous gray water near our island. Although the windows were thick, winter's chill was still pressing in. I tapped my fingers to the icy glass and squinted to the west.

Some days, when I was feeling particularly angry or brave, I considered returning to Mael. I envisioned standing in the center of the death camp, surrounded by prisoners and tabloid photographers, and demanding that my father shut the place down. I'd even gone so far as to mention it to Kader once, but...my resolve had weakened.

The fact of the matter was, without Theo by my side, I was less inspired to be the man she thought I could be. The ever-present ache for her took root in whatever space had been reserved for my courage. Perhaps it was because, deep down, ending the war seemed too impossible even for my own optimistic outlook. And without the war ending, I could never be with her.

I told myself I was making amends here in the hospital, treating both the light-skinned and not-so-light skinned patients who showed up at the hospital. I made extra time for the children, asking about their parents, their health, their eating arrangements, and giving them a stern reminder to stay out of trouble. At the end of the day, I could say I'd done something.

It was a good lie. Some days I even believed it.

"Why do I get to live and they don't?"

I'd no good answer for her then, and I had no answer for her voice in my head now. Some part of me was glad the war raged on. That way Theo would never have to see what a coward I was.

"Helmuth!" Hebendon barked from the other side of the hall.

"Coming," I said, tearing my eyes away from the ocean and pulling my thoughts back into the brightly-lit halls of the hospital.

THEO

The lights blinded me, but I kept my gaze straight ahead, remembering to *look interested, be interested.* That was what Emilie, my public relations liaison, had told me. Recent polling said I came across as bored and unapproachable.

Well, no shit.

I forced a smile onto my face, one I could maintain for however long it would take the media to finish recording this speech. Bayard had said these same words fifteen thousand times already, and he would probably say them another fifteen thousand times more.

"Our Kylaen foes won't take no for an answer, but Rave is better!" Bayard boomed into the microphone. "We will not lie down to those dogs. They cannot come onto our shores and attack, and they will *not* keep us prisoner!"

My cue was coming up. I forced myself to look extra-interested.

"Our symbol of hope, *'neechai*!" he said, gesturing to me. I stood and waved to the cameras, hoping my face didn't convey the awkwardness of waving to a room of disinterested aides and bored camera operators. We always pre-taped Bayard's speeches so the media wizards could edit in the raucous audience. I'd always thought Rave was barely surviving as a nation, but we certainly had a lot of money for Bayard's media campaigns.

I sat down and Bayard continued his speech. He spoke of the great sacrifice of our countrymen, many of them only children. He went on for a good five minutes about how much the Raven military cared for those in its charge. I'd heard whispers of lowering the conscription age even lower than twelve, but even amongst Bayard's staunchest supporters, this idea wasn't very popular. Bayard ended his speech with a call to the *'kaachais* to continue their contributions—code for, "Please make me more children to send to my war."

The lights faded, and Bayard stood, unclipping the microphone from his lapel and ignoring me completely. We hadn't spoken two words to each other since his grand entrance into my hospital room. Not for lack of trying on my part. Before I could open my mouth, another voice cut me off.

"You still look stiff, *'neechai.*"

Emilie Mondra looked like a Raven—dark skin, eyes, and hair—but her speech was laced with the smallest hint of an accent that wasn't ours. Her family was rich (by Raven standards, anyway) and had sent her to a boarding school in Herin, instead of an air force base. She'd joined the ranks of the other wealthy, educated Ravens in the capital city, Veres. Like Emilie, most of the aides and assistants who told me where to be and how to smile had somehow missed the conscription that had sucked me into the Raven war machine at such a young age. They were blessedly undamaged, never knowing what it was to go to sleep hungry, or wonder if every meal was the last.

In fact, there seemed to be a whole world I'd been unaware of from my grungy forward operating base. Some days I scarcely believed I was in the same country.

Bayard walked out of the makeup room, his brown skin shining from the makeup removal. He didn't even glance in my direction, discussing his next meeting with a parade of assistants and higher-ranking officials eager to get an audience with him.

"Emilie is right, you are stiff."

I turned my head slightly to acknowledge the new presence by my side, but didn't respond.

Mark Cannon was the last media darling before me, having survived a particularly nasty battle on the western front where he'd lost nearly three quarters of his squad. And his was the only spot on the president's advisory council that wasn't military- or politically-appointed. If I wanted Bayard's ear, a chance to sway the course of the war, I had to go through Cannon first. And he knew it.

For all of his handsomeness, he might as well have charmed his way into Bayard's inner circle instead of through pure aerial talent. Black hair cropped neatly in the military style, the lines of his face sharp and pronounced, without any trace of a beard. He was the perfect picture of Raven sexiness. Bayard was more than willing to allow him to grace the covers of our very few magazines shirtless and glistening, if only to draw more attention to our own sex symbols than those of our enemies.

For me, Cannon might've been a shade more handsome than a certain prince of Kylae, but I knew where my heart lay.

"Those pants, you should tell Emilie to have them hemmed a bit," he said.

"I'll be sure to let the Raven uniform services know of your tailoring suggestion," I said. "Or have you forgotten what it's like to wear the same thing everyone else is wearing?" I glanced at his designer shirt straight from the front pages of Jervanian magazines. "Or that you should be supporting *this* country's fashion?"

"I simply give our people something to aspire to."

"While you champion their death sentences," I muttered under my breath.

Unfortunately, Cannon heard. "Be careful, Theophilia." I

grimaced at his use of my full name. Emilie said it sounded better than just 'Theo.' "There are those who might think you've allied yourself with those idiot rebels in the slums. Or worse."

I hadn't heard much about the rebels, other than that they existed. I had no idea what end they strove to, but I was fairly sure the Kylaens would pounce if they saw a crack in Rave's government. I lifted my gaze to meet Cannon's and replied, "I'm simply implying that your perceived lack of concern for our brothers and sisters in harm's way is...off-putting."

"Oh, Theo, I'm concerned, trust me," Cannon said, placing his hand over his heart. His brown eyes grew wide and his eyebrows slacked off. "The plight of our brothers and sisters protecting our borders is the most important concern for myself and President Bayard."

I glared at him. "Very funny."

"You see, *kallistrate*," he tacked on a Raven pronunciation, using the Raven word for orphan, "it's easy to pretend you care. I do it all the time with my lovers. They tell me their problems, I pretend to care, and I get what I want." He paused and surveyed me. "Haven't you ever had a lover before?"

I kept my mouth shut, and he took the win and walked away, cackling to himself in victory.

I'd had a lover. Four months before, I'd found myself stranded on an island with the third son of our sworn enemy. And, foolishly, I'd fallen head over heels for him. I'd called him my *amichai*, the Raven word for soulmate. He'd been the best and worst mistake of my life. He'd taken me back to his country, foolishly thinking I'd be safe there, and I'd been arrested and sent to the Kylaen death camp, Mael. It was only thanks to him that I was still alive, a notion that haunted me every time someone mentioned my "two months in Mael."

After I'd returned, I'd told the two intelligence agents debriefing me that my plane had gone down in pursuit of the princeling. I'd told them the Kylaens had taken me from the water and sent me to Mael. I'd escaped while one of the guards was trying to rape me, stolen a prison transport, and made it to an airfield, omitting the part played by my *amichai* and his guard. If it had seemed far-fetched to have completed such a feat without help, they hadn't said anything about it. It had been enough for them, because I hadn't been contacted again, and Bayard just stuck to how resilient I was to have lasted two months in their death camp.

I somehow doubted he would've been so eager to parade me around if he knew the truth.

As it was, I only saw my *amichai* in photos from Raven intelligence. His movements were barely reported in the Kylaen media, possibly due to his resignation from the military. He'd moved to an apartment building fortified with extra security, including the guard who'd assisted in my escape from Mael. He worked twelve hour shifts at the hospital, varying between night and day shifts, and, I supposed, he was happy.

I was happy he was out of the castle, doing what he loved, but I still wondered if he meant what he'd said on that airfield. He'd promised me he'd find a way for us to be together. I wanted to believe that more than anything in the world, but his actions thus far had been...underwhelming.

Then again, I hadn't made much headway either. Being a symbol of Raven toughness had saved exactly zero Raven lives. We were still conscripting the poorest children; we were still at a political stalemate with Kylae. Nothing had changed in my country, as it hadn't for over half a century of war.

Some days, I wondered if it was time for me to move on from Galian. It would only be a matter of time before someone started hinting that I should start doing my part to keep Rave populated. There was no shortage of handsome Raven men (Cannon not withstanding), but I couldn't even force a smile for them.

As Emilie pointed out, I couldn't even smile for the cameras.

GALIAN

A camera flashed in my face, and I grimaced, grasping Martin's arm as he yanked me inside our apartment building. Once we were safely out of view, I took a moment to blink in the dark lobby.

"Did they get you?" Martin asked, walking over to the mailboxes and retrieving our mail. He opened each one, tossing out three pink envelopes I assumed were fanmail or offers of engagement then joined me while I waited for the elevator.

"You'd think they'd get tired of it after a while," I said, rubbing my eyes and still seeing spots. "Maybe I'll wear the same thing every day, throw them off. Then they won't know what day it was they photographed me."

"I still say you should wear your scrubs home. Get some blood and smear it all over yourself. Nobody'd take a photo of you then." He cracked a grin. Martin was nineteen, Theo's age, but seemed so much younger than she was. He'd been dishonorably discharged simply because he'd been my guard and it was assumed he'd been involved in

Theo's escape. When I decided I no longer wished to live in the castle, he "offered" to let me move in with him and drive me to and from work.

I was no idiot. Martin was young, but he'd been trained in personal security and hand-to-hand combat and he'd never asked me to pay a dime in rent. Not only that, but the day after I'd moved in, I saw a few new residents carrying boxes—some of whom looked like my mother's personal security contingent.

The elevator dinged, and we climbed inside. Martin opened the magazine he'd received, and I was already thinking about how disgusting I'd have to be not to shower before I passed out in my bed. But all my great scheming came to an end when the elevator doors opened.

Kader, the only bodyguard still officially assigned to me, stood in the doorway to his apartment, glaring at the two of us as if we'd personally offended him with our presence. He and his wife, Rosie, lived next door to Martin and me. I felt slightly safer having the tall, bald, imposing man next door in case of an errant assassin or lovesick fangirl. But it also meant that he was my mother's personal fetcher, and I could read the glare on his face as plain as day.

Kader said nothing to me, and I didn't bother to ask how long he'd been waiting for me. Ours was generally an unspoken hatred of each other. He'd also been assumed complicit in Theo's escape, but since he had a good fifteen years of military service, he'd just been permanently reassigned as my personal bodyguard.

I would feel worse about it if he wasn't such an insufferable asshole.

"You're late," he growled, following Martin and me into our apartment.

"Good morning to you too," I muttered.

"It's not morning, it's seven o'clock at night," he said. "And you had to be at a state dinner ten minutes ago."

I yawned and walked to the kitchen, scouring the mostly empty fridge for something to eat. Martin might've been skilled in personal defense, but my personal kitchen-minder he was not. Still, he usually bought enough food that I could throw something together. After all, I'd been able to prepare a rabbit on the island; sautéing some vegetables wasn't that difficult.

"*Galian.*" Kader sounded like he was about to beat me to a bloody pulp, but I didn't care.

I was sleep-deprived, and had spent most of the day alternating between the aftermath of a spate of stomach viruses and Hebendon's lovely impaction-removals. The very last thing I wanted to do was spend five hours schmoozing my father's richest friends and having to smile for the cameras.

"I haven't been back there in four months. I'd like to keep the streak alive."

"Your mother asked you to be there."

I rubbed my face and felt the stubble under my hands. It reminded me of the beard I'd sprouted while marooned on an island with Theo. "He'll be there."

"Yes, as the king, he will be there," Kader said. "And as your father—"

"Who left me to die, if you'll recall. And therefore, I owe him nothing."

Kader approached right behind me, so close I could almost feel his breath on the back of my neck. "If you don't get into that room and change into the uniform I brought you, so help me God, I will knock your stubborn ass out, dress you, and drag you there myself."

I considered my options and the closeness of Kader. I didn't much like my chances of testing him. So I closed the fridge and plodded back to my room.

I stared longingly at my bed and bypassed it completely. My closet was mostly on the floor, but Kader had hung an officer's dress uniform on the door. The official story was that I hadn't resigned the military, but was simply on reserve duty. Whatever they chose to believe, I didn't care.

"Princeling," I muttered to myself, remembering how Theo used to tease me. I wondered how hard she'd laugh at me wearing this stupid get-up—red coat, black pants, and a set of medals I wasn't sure when or how I'd earned.

I walked over to my bed and picked up the picture frame lying next to it. I'd found a magazine with an official photo of Theo when she'd been announced as the new "thing" in Rave. It was grainy and surrounded by an article about what a terrible monster she actually was (I didn't dare read it as I cut out the photo).

But she was my girl. That's what I'd come to call Theo in my mind, since I still couldn't pronounce that ay-mi-kai thing she called me. Lover, soulmate, she'd described it. I certainly felt like a part of my soul was missing. Then again, I sighed heavily, I hadn't done much to deserve getting it back.

I stared into the grainy eyes and tried to draw strength. I'd need it to put up with all this bullshit tonight.

Two

Theo

My hands ached as they gripped the grainy wood of the shovel. I wasn't sure how long I'd been working that day, scooping the black barethium from one pile into another. The smell that would one day kill me had taken my mental clarity. I swayed on my feet and wished my body would stop the movements, granting me rest.

There was a presence behind me. Hands wrapped around my arms and pulled me backward, away from the pile. I was too weak to fight him, so I let my body go limp. I was taken to an office, but when I glanced up, it was no office. It was a surgery, but the bed had thick, leather straps. But that made no sense. Galian had blown up the laboratory.

I looked up. Dr. Maitland had guided me to the bed and was strapping me in.

"Dr. Maitland, please, don't do this!" I cried. "Please, this isn't —"

"You're my patient, Theo," he said, placing a hand on my bare calf. It was swollen and bruised, much as it had been on the island.

Maitland shuffled out of the room as I thrashed against my bonds.

I saw him, my *amichai*, just outside the room. He wore his bright red uniform, his hair cropped short. And he looked right through me.

"Amichai! Help me!"

The room began to fill with black smoke, and I screamed.

"Amichai!"

My voice echoed around me when my eyes snapped opened, and my hands were tangled in the sheets around me. The stench of Mael remained in my nose, and my stomach came to my throat. I tumbled out of bed, rushing to the bathroom and vomiting into my toilet. I shakily held the sides of the metal bowl, thankful that this time, at least, I'd made it.

I slid to the cold floor and forced myself to remember kinder hands. His gentle caresses up and down my back, the soft whispers telling me he loved me and that everything would be all right. If I focused long enough, I could convince myself that he was there with me, and I could catch my breath.

I pushed myself off the floor and flipped on the light. I rinsed my mouth out and splashed water on my face, patting it dry with a nearby towel. Staring at my reflection in the mirror, I poked at the dark circles under my eyes the makeup artists worked so hard to cover up. Perhaps Bayard wasn't the only one putting on appearances.

I tossed down the towel and left the bathroom and bedroom to the joint living room and kitchen. The Raven government had put me in one of the nicest apartment in Veres, which meant it had running water, a working furnace, and a pantry that was stocked from the government supply store. I felt like I should've been sleeping on a lumpy mattress in a room with two hundred other people. I'd always presumed that only Kylaens lived a life of luxury, but now I wasn't so sure.

My pantry was full of mostly nonperishable rations from the stores, the same sort of shit they'd fed me at my forward operating base, but they did stock one new item. I dug the half-empty bottle of brown liquor—whiskey, maybe—out of the cabinet, gulped a long swig, then carried it with me to the living room. I switched on the fancy radio in the living room and settled onto the couch.

"...*The Vinolas Forward Operating Base suffered heavy casualties yesterday after a Kylaen air strike on the armory.*"

I drank more, wiping the remnants off my lip. Vinolas had been my home for much of my training. After I'd been commissioned as a captain, they'd sent me back there to command a fleet of twenty planes. Taking heavy casualties was nothing new, but it still left me feeling ill for my lack of progress.

I pulled over the decorative map of Rave that had been left in the apartment and traced my hand along the border. Vinolas was on the northern edge of the island, where the Kylaens attacked most frequently. Had I been assigned to any of the bases on the eastern side of the country, those closest to Jervan, I might never have seen battle.

I might never have crashed on that island and met my *amichai*.

I flipped the map over to display the four countries. Herin and Jervan shared a continent to the east of Rave—Herin to the north and Jervan to the south. Rave was a tiny island compared to them, and to Kylae, which loomed over all the other countries in the west. I placed my finger on Norose, where my *amichai* was sleeping tonight.

Tears pricked at my eyes and I let them fall. I traced the distance between him and me. On this map, it was only finger-lengths. In reality, there was so much more standing between us.

I traced the path our planes had taken on that fateful day. North from Vinolas a few hundred miles, to between the coasts of Herin and Kylae. I wasn't completely sure where we'd landed, having been too preoccupied with shooting down the princeling to note my location. At the time, I would have given anything for this luxurious apartment, but now...now I missed it. I missed him.

I missed waking up to the smell of cooking rabbit meat and the proud grin he shared only with me. I longed for the days when we just talked, sharing stories about our childhoods, his family, my life in Rave. I wished for more than the few precious hours after we'd confessed our love for each other, when we'd showed how much we truly cared in the most intimate and breathless ways.

If only my dreams could be filled with *that* instead of the nightmares that plagued me every night. I wanted to dream about his hands, not those of the Kylaen guard. I wanted to envision *his* face, not the man who'd walked into his own execution rather than die the slow, painful death of barethium poisoning. I wanted to dream of how *he* smelled, not the stench of Mael.

It rose from my memory and I gagged, jumping to my feet and running to the nearest trashcan. After my stomach was empty again, I shook on the cold linoleum floor, begging my mind to stop reminding me of things I wanted to forget.

There was no one to offer me comfort, as I dared not mention my nightmares to anyone. I was afraid that if I did, there might be more questions. But if I were truly honest with myself, it was more than just the fear of being found a fraud. A nagging guilt ate at me. I'd survived Mael, but there was no justice in it. My whole life, I'd believed surviving for as long as I had meant I was made for something greater, but I couldn't seem to accept that anymore. I'd survived merely because a man I fell in love with had the resources to get me out of the death camp.

Some part of me, the one that had been so hellbent on supporting Rave even when I knew the battle was hopeless, hated him. Hated him, his father, his country, and how they continued to force Rave into battle. Hated that he'd promised me he'd come for me, that he'd close down Mael, and had done neither.

But another, stronger part of me still loved him. No matter how much I tried to convince myself that I was better off forgetting him, forgetting the island...I couldn't. As bad as Mael was, as much as it haunted me, it was tinged with the beautiful memory of him. The island was our respite from all of that, a place where we'd forgotten about the war and just loved each other.

He was the one good thing I ever had.

More tears slipped down my face and the pain of missing him dragged me deeper and deeper into despair. I grabbed the bottle and took three long gulps, coughing as the liquid burned on the way down.

Tilting my head back, I glanced up at the moon. It was full and bright, reminding me of nights when it was our only light. I took another, less desperate sip, and wondered if he was looking at it, too.

GALIAN

Damn, the moon was bright tonight.

I stared at it longingly when I could spare a moment from the idle conversations about the interests of the most powerful men and women in Kylae. In a perfect world, perhaps, they'd be concerned about the number of planes my father sent to bomb Rave every week. But most of the conversations revolved around art openings and which socialite was found in the wrong bed. The only topic I was mildly interested in was the upcoming trade agreement with Jervan. This party was celebrating the commissioning of a huge shipping frigate to carry Jervan's wheat across the Madion Sea, paid for by one of Kylae's wealthiest shipping magnates and my father.

The man of the hour, Silas Collins, was a national hero, so the conversation went. Collins would lower the cost of food and strengthen Kylae's economic engine. Collins was single-handedly bringing trade and jobs to the port city of Duran. Collins was...I downed my champagne because I just couldn't stomach much more of this.

"Smile, Gally, it's a party." Rhys, my oldest brother, joined me on the fringes of the party, replacing my empty glass with a fresh one. He wore a uniform similar to mine, and his brown hair cut closer in the military style. We both resembled our mother, whereas our late brother Digory had been thick and brutish like my father.

"Careful, Rhys, the media'll get wind of you serving drinks and they'll call it a new career," I said lazily, examining the drink he'd given me. "Your part-time job at the radar tower is boring them."

"I think they'll be more shocked that you returned to the castle," Rhys replied. "Is your great feud with Father over?"

My gaze darted over to the front of the room, where my parents sat on their thrones receiving guests. My mother was radiant, smiling and graciously greeting all the richest bastards in my country, whereas my father seemed more distant. I hadn't as much as inched in that direction since I'd arrived half an hour before, and I had no plans on going any closer.

"I was threatened with bodily harm if I did not attend."

"I do like that Kader," Rhys said with a grin that quickly disappeared. "It's damned good to see you, regardless." His eyes remained focused on the crowd, but his voice rose a bit with emotion. "We pulled you off that island and...it's like we lost you all over again."

I looked at my champagne, considering how much I'd have to drink to not regret it in the morning. "Anything happening up that way?"

"Nothing—Raven or otherwise—has passed the airspace over your island," Rhys said with a loud sigh. "Do you realize this is the first time I've seen you in almost four months? We haven't even had a conversation."

"Work's been keeping me busy."

"Bullshit."

"What do you want me to say?" I said, glancing at the front of the room again. "I can't stand to live under his roof. I can barely stand to live in his country." I wrenched my gaze away. "Not after what he did to me. To *her*."

"Gal, one of these days, you're gonna have to let her go," Rhys said. "She's Bayard's now. Maybe she had feelings for you at one time, but now...now the Ravens are probably pumping her head full of lies."

My grip tightened on the stem of the glass, and I downed what was left of my drink. "Whatever, Rhys." I placed the empty glass on the tray of a passing waiter and strode toward the thick crowd of people.

"Galian..." Rhys called after me, but I lost his voice in the conversations around me. My appearance at a palace event was somewhat of a conversation topic, and no less than four people stopped me to remark on it.

All were young women, dressed in their finest low-cut gowns

with painted faces and coiffed hair. From their expressions, I guessed my mother had informed them I would be in attendance, which had prompted them to line up around me. In my younger days, I might've continued drinking and taken my time choosing which I'd be taking back to my room.

"Was that between your debauchery and socialite girlfriends?"

Theo's voice in my mind took me out of the room and back to the island. A waiter walked by with skewers of meat on sticks, and I could taste charred rabbit on my tongue. The roaring fires burning in the hearths reminded me of the way the firelight used to flicker in her brown eyes. The green of a socialite's dress was the same shade as the forest that was our home. Our sanctuary.

"Your Highness, is everything all right?" Olivia Collins, Silas' very eligible and very beautiful daughter, stood in front of me, resplendent in her sky blue dress. Her strawberry blonde hair was pulled back in a twist, and delicate diamonds hung from her ears. My eyes briefly drifted down to her bust, noting that she wasn't offering her breasts to me like the rest of these girls.

Then again, Olivia didn't have to try very hard. She was the current frontrunner to be my girlfriend—I wasn't sure if by her hand or the media's. She played the part admirably, taking tea with my mother and nearly gluing herself to my side whenever we were in public together. Part of the reason I kept myself *out* of the public's eye.

"It's just lovely, this event your father has thrown for Daddy," she said, looping her arm through mine. With so many eyes on me, I didn't have the heart to remove it.

"Lovely, yeah."

"I do hope that Daddy will take some time off now. He's worked so hard on this agreement for nearly half my life. I don't recall a time we weren't at the shipyard."

I resisted a snort. Like this girl would ever set foot in a shipyard. I found myself comparing her to Theo, as I did with every woman who flirted with me. Theo would've mopped the floor with her with one of her signature "are-you-kidding-me" looks. God, I missed those looks, even if they were usually directed at me.

"...the trade agreement has just been ghastly. Father is, of course, loyal to Kylae, but the Jervanian representatives have given him the runaround. They want twenty crowns a bushel for wheat, can you believe that? Cheaper to grow it ourselves."

I stifled a yawn.

"You don't know why your father is so dead-set on this trade agreement, do you?" she asked with a sly look.

"Nope. I'm too busy pulling shit out of people's asses at the hospital."

She laughed, and I could practically feel her forcing it out. This girl didn't think I was charming or attractive, but she was trying her best. I caught my mother's eye across the room and she nodded her approval. Swallowing my annoyance, I turned back to the young woman in front of me and struggled to find something intelligent to say to her.

The only thing I could come up with was that I used to be so much better at all this.

"Your Highness—"

"Galian," I said. That was a start, at least. "I prefer Galian."

She blushed demurely, almost as if on cue, and took a dainty sip of her drink. "Very well, *Galian*, I was wondering if you were planning on attending the latest Kaines play in the theater district?"

"I..." Plays made me want to gouge my eyes out. "I hadn't

thought about it. Getting good reviews?"

"Oh, the best, you must see it soon," she said, with a flirtatious bat of her eyelashes.

I stared at her for a moment before realizing she wanted *me* to ask her to the play. I suppressed a groan and scrambled for an excuse. "Unfortunately, the hospital keeps me busy. I have a few late night shifts."

She sighed and shook her head. "You have a good heart, serving your countrymen. Kylae is lucky to have such a thoughtful prince."

That wince I couldn't keep hidden. I wasn't thoughtful or kind, or any of that. Not really, not when the children from Kylae's slums were working in a death camp sanctioned by the very people in this room. Not when I'd promised Theo I would come for her, and...

"If you'll excuse me," I said, placing my now-empty glass on the serving tray and walking toward the open balcony on the other side of the room.

The fresh air hit my face, and I unbuttoned my tight collar in relief. Straining my eyes in the darkness, I looked for any sign of Rave in the distance. But just like my girl, her country was out of reach.

I pressed my head against the cold stone railing and sighed.

"Not having a good time, my darling?"

My mother had joined me on the balcony. She looked beautiful tonight, with her regal gold gown and the delicate crown atop her head.

"I saw you with Olivia," she said. "Charming girl."

I grimaced, sensing where this conversation was going. "Mom, I've had a long day. I'm not in the mood—"

"Do you remember Mr. Gumbles?"

"My old teddy bear?"

"When you were four," she said, gently placing her perfectly manicured hands on the railing. "You wouldn't let him out of your sight. You even made me put him on the sink while I gave you a bath."

I gave her a dubious look appropriate for a man my age talking about a teddy bear, but she shrugged lightly.

"On your fifth birthday, we had a big party for you—do you remember?" she asked me with a nostalgic smile. "And Digory, rest his soul," she looked up at the moon when she mentioned my late brother, "Digory was so jealous of the attention that he stole your teddy bear and threw it into the ocean."

I turned away, remembering how I'd told this same story to Theo once on a rainy day. The ache in my heart returned with a vengeance.

"You were *inconsolable*," she said, emphasizing the word so I knew just how much of a fuss I'd made. "You didn't want any of your toys, or any of your friends. We had to cancel the party altogether because you refused to come out of your room."

I blushed as she grinned at me.

"Is there a point to this embarrassing story?"

"Yes, son," she said, patting my arm. "You asked if we'd found Mr. Gumbles every single morning for a year. Every morning, you would come into the playroom and say, 'Momma, did he come back?'" She cooed at me. "It was precious, and it broke my heart."

"Point?"

"One day, you just...stopped asking," she said, sounding like the idea surprised her, even two decades later. "You found some other toy to play with, and you were back to my beautiful, happy baby boy."

I nodded, finally seeing her point. "And so you think that this is the same?"

"I think that you loved that girl very much," she said and my heart hurt at the thought of it. "But I also think that one day you'll forget about her the same way you forgot about Mr. Gumbles."

I pushed myself off the balcony.

"Gally," she called after me.

"One question, Mom," I said, turning to look at her. "Did I ever love anything as much as Mr. Gumbles again?"

She opened her mouth, and nothing but a sigh came out.

"Can I go home now? I have a long day at the hospital tomorrow."

"Of course, son." She smiled lovingly. "It was very good to see you tonight. I miss you."

"I miss you, too," I said, but she didn't ask me to come home. For that, I was grateful. I hated saying no to my mother.

THREE

THEO

The car rolled to a stop, and I rubbed my face to wake up. My head pounded and my mouth was dry, but there would be photographers at this event—yet another commissioning ceremony for a crop of young pilots—and I needed to look presentable. Running my hands along the top of my head, I smoothed the stray hairs into my bun. I rubbed under my eyes, feeling the puffy dark circles and the concealer I'd added to mask them.

The door opened, and the light made me wince. I pulled my sunglasses over my face and stepped out, searching for the newspaper reporters and saw none. That was concerning. My first event had been swarming in photographers, but ever since, there'd been fewer and fewer. In order for me to maintain my status at Bayard's side, I needed to draw attention to myself. Unfortunately, I was at a loss on how to do that.

The airfield was similar to the one where I'd flown before the island. Most Raven airfields, I'd come to learn, were vestiges of Kylaen rule. While Veres had seen upgrades and new construction, the rest of the country, the parts where I'd grown up and learned to fly, remained stagnant. Even the hangar where I'd be "inspecting" our newest aviators and pinning on their wings still bore the shadow of the Kylaen crest. At one time, I'd have thought the crowned lion was meant to remind us of who we were fighting against and what for, but now I knew better.

"Major Kallistrate!"

A harried-looking teenager wearing captains' bars rushed up to me. He looked barely sixteen; perhaps he'd become the favorite and ascended rank as I had done. I could see myself in him, the worried bags under his eyes, the youth that clung to him while he struggled to remain in charge. This was a new assignment for him, and he was carrying the weight of twenty souls on his shoulders.

"Captain." I nodded my greeting to him when he half-heartedly saluted me.

"We are so honored you've agreed to attend our first flight demonstration," he said, as he'd been instructed to say.

"Has the media arrived yet?" I asked, peering around hopefully.

"N-no, I don't think anyone is coming. Were they supposed to?" He ran his hands through his short-cropped hair.

"No," I said, swallowing my own disappointment to keep him from thinking he'd done something wrong. "Shall we?"

The captain, named Govine, took me on the same tour I'd been on six times already at different bases, and the same one I'd had to give when I was a young captain in Vinolas. We started in the hangar, where the line of Raven planes had been lined up in almost perfect formation. They were the same models I used to fly, and seeing them always twisted my heart a little. I missed the thrill of flying, but I hadn't as much as sat in a plane since my crash.

"How many mechanics do you have on staff here?" I asked,

walking up to one of the planes.

"Ten," Govine replied. "We've asked for more, as we've got near two hundred planes here, but—"

"I know how that goes," I said, shedding my jacket and tossing it on the wing of a plane. I wasn't supposed to do more than just look at the planes, but I couldn't help myself. I knew the risks of flying planes that weren't well-maintained.

I opened the hatch to the engine, calling for Govine to hand me a socket wrench. I checked the oil and tightened a few nuts that had come loose. It wasn't a full inspection, but I felt like I'd done *something*.

"Major," Govine said, holding his hands nervously. "Major, I don't want to keep you from the rest of your schedule. The pilots are ready, if you'll join me outside."

I was about to argue that I could be much more useful working on the rest of the fifty planes, but I heaved out a breath. That wasn't what I was there to do, and I had my orders.

I followed the young captain out of the hangar to the small seating area that had been set up for me. A group of twenty pilots in identical uniforms stood facing me, their hands pressed behind their backs and their feet hip-width apart at attention.

But as I got closer, I saw what my heart already knew. They were children, the lot of them. If this was their commissioning ceremony, they would've just completed their flight school after six months of training. Most of the heads barely came up to my shoulder as I passed them.

I wished I didn't have to see the fear in their eyes, the nervousness that came with commissioning. If they were lucky, they'd be assigned to bases in the south and west. Or even to protect Norose, which hadn't seen an attack in over a decade. If they were unlucky, they would be sent north, to a base like Vinolas.

I finished walking the length of the assembled group and turned, clicking my heels together as I'd been taught.

"Fellow Ravens, today marks the end of your training. The—" I swallowed, struggling to keep my brain on track. If I just spat out the words quickly, I could get through this. "There is no greater honor than defending Raven independence. You are..." Another hard swallow. "You are the lucky ones. You will be celebrated and honored for your sacrifice. On behalf of President Bayard, thank you for your...service." I forced my hand from my side to the top of my brow in salute.

The young pilots saluted me in return, then were dismissed by their captain to retrieve their planes. I had a small moment when their backs were turned to exhale my disgust at myself. I'd never been comfortable with the official speeches handed down from headquarters, but now that I was smarter, the sentiments made me even sicker.

Most of these children were from poor families, or orphans whose parents were killed in action, as mine probably had been. But now that I had some money and prestige, if I ever had a child, they would be exempt from the conscription that had sucked up these children. Just as Emilie had been.

The hum of the planes grew louder as they left the hangar then queued to take off. I sat next to Govine and slid my sunglasses over my eyes. The pilots were supposed to show that they could take off, perform basic aerial defensive and offensive measures, and land. It was a very low bar, but then again, we needed more pilots to help defend our country.

And yet, there were hundreds of children in Veres that—

No, I wouldn't think about that.

To my eyes, these pilots were untrained and sloppy, but what else could be expected after only six months? They would either get better or they would die. That was why I still lived.

I winced as two planes clipped each others wings, forcing myself to stare at the ground.

Twin whistles.

Boom.

"Oh...oh God," Govine whispered beside me. He stood and rushed to the wreckage, but I remained where I was.

I said a quick prayer for the two pilots who'd most assuredly lost their lives, and another for Govine. He was still young, and these were the first pilots he'd lost. They wouldn't be the last.

My leg twinged, and I remembered my own nearly fatal crash. I remembered waking up, seeing his face for the first time up close. How he'd saved my life, how I'd hated him for it, how much I missed him in that second—

I swallowed and forced myself to look up at the sky to keep my tears from falling.

I was doing nothing by following orders, and yet following orders would get me to my end goal: Bayard's office. It was endlessly frustrating—made more palpable by the two lives that I quietly added to my tab. If I'd been successful in finding a way to forge peace between Kylae and Rave, these two kids would've still been alive.

"Major." My driver was behind me. "If we don't leave now, we'll be late for the next ceremony."

I nodded and exhaled loudly. It would be a long day before I could reach the safety and privacy of my apartment and properly mourn the two children. And the however many others who would lose their lives today.

GALIAN

Now that I was getting paid a resident's meager salary by the hospital, I liked to do normal things with it. Today's excursion with Martin was to the corner grocery, because there was nothing left in our pantry but beer and molding apples.

I'd been to the store with him three times already, but the sheer amount of food that greeted me when I walked in the front door never ceased to amaze me. Fresh fruit imported from far-off countries, spices, breads, chocolates. If I'd known such a bounty existed whilst on the island, I might not have made it.

I spotted a girl giving me the side-eye from across the apples and I ignored her. Martin was three aisles over, probably filling our cart with the unhealthiest junk food he could find. It was usually up to me to pick out the real stuff.

A gasp of surprise echoed across the empty market, and a middle-aged woman pressed her hand to her mouth, blushed, then disappeared down an aisle. I chuckled and tossed citrus fruits of different sizes and shapes into my basket. The handwritten sign marked them as from Jervan. I let my mind wander to Theo, and wondered if Rave got imports from other countries, or if they only ate the food they grew.

I was being watched, and I spun around to find the source. A girl, who couldn't have been older than seventeen, sauntered over, swinging her hips.

"Do you need help with anything?" she asked, eyeing me from

beneath her lashes.

"Er...do you work here?" I asked, feeling the heat rise on the back of my neck.

"I do if you want me to—"

"Ah, there you are, Jem," Martin's voice was a Godsend as he forced himself between the girl and myself. He looked at her and shook his head. "Did you confuse my idiot friend for the prince? Happens all the time. He gets laid three times a week with it."

The girl frowned then huffed away, throwing glares at me.

Once she was out of sight, I breathed a sigh of thanks to Martin, who seemed to find the whole thing funny.

"This is why I can't take you anywhere, Jem," Martin said, taking the empty basket from me and filling it with fruit. "But seriously, don't wander off."

I nodded my agreement and kept close to him while we continued filling our bags with food. I spotted a little dark-skinned boy hovering near a big pile of apples. He was maybe six or seven, barely tall enough to reach the first row. I watched in slow motion as he grabbed one from the top, sending the pile of apples tumbling to the ground.

He locked eyes with me then dashed away when the manager of the store came running in.

"Stop thief!"

"Thief?" I said, quirking my brow.

My question was answered when the little boy was dragged back in by one of the other store workers. The apple hung from his little fingers, and his eyes were wide and terrified.

"It'll be to the death camps for you, creature," the manager snarled, slapping the apple out of the boy's hand.

"Hey!" I barked, stepping forward. "Don't talk to him like that."

"And who are..." The manager spun on his heel, but recognition dawned on his face and his pale skin turned whiter. "O-oh, Your Majesty, I'm s-so sorry, please forgive me for my rudeness." And he dropped to the floor, probably ready to kiss my shoes if I hadn't stopped him.

"Stop," I said, my hand firmly on the black-haired boy. "I'll take him. You forget this happened."

"Y-yes sire. Right away, sire." On and on he went before he disappeared behind the aisle.

"P-please don't send me away," the boy whispered, shaking under my hand.

"I won't," I said, handing him the bag of food that I'd been gathering. "Here. Take it. And..." I fished out a bank note from my pocket. "Take this too."

His eyes grew wide, and he stepped back.

"I know what it's like to be hungry," I said, knowing he might not believe me. "Nobody in this kingdom should ever have to."

He clutched the note in his hand then his eyes widened as a shadow fell across his face.

"Big, bald guy?" I asked the boy. He nodded fervently, and I shook my head. "Just my shadow. Don't worry, he's harmless." I put my hand over the boy's small one. "Get home. Make sure you give that money to your mom to buy food, okay?"

"She'll probably use it for drugs," Kader observed as the boy dashed out of the store.

"That's awfully presumptuous of you," I said, walking forward to start reassembling the apples onto their stand. I noticed that I'd gathered a crowd, and did my best to ignore them.

"It's awfully presumptuous to think he has a mother in the first place," Kader shot back. "More than likely, he's got a handler who sends him to be a distraction while he cleans up. You just made his month." He glanced at the manager, who had reappeared. "You might want to check your registers."

Despite my optimism, my face reddened slightly. There was truth in what Kader said, even if was only that I'd presumed the child had parents. My face grew warmer when I heard the manager cawing about empty registers.

"Would've been better to let the kid get caught. At least then he'd be out of the dealer's hands," Kader said, bending down to pick up an apple, then placing it atop the pile.

"Don't kid yourself. He'd be sent to Mael."

"You aren't going to get back to Theo by saving every half-Raven kid in Norose," Kader replied softly.

I winced at her name, but continued stacking the apples. "What choice do I have? I can't just... I can't do anything else."

"You could try forgetting her."

I clenched my jaw and glared at him.

"I don't doubt that you both felt something, and I don't doubt when we took her from Mael, her intentions were pure. But it's been four months, and she's..." I looked up at him; his face was stony and severe as usual. "She's Bayard's new puppet."

I hated every single person who called her that. "Theo's no puppet. Trust me, she's capable of making her own decisions."

"Exactly. And once this Mael story dies down, she's going to be shopped around to marry whomever Bayard thinks would make the most sense from a public relations standpoint, if she doesn't already have someone in mind herself. That fool who was there before her, I forget his name already, but he'd make a good candidate."

The idea of Theo with anyone else churned my stomach.

"But most importantly, there's no way you could ever actually be together," Kader said with a gentle tone that surprised me. He actually sounded concerned for my emotional wellbeing. "Not now, anyway. Not with her face nearly as well-known as yours. Not with the story they told."

"I told her I'd figure it out."

"You've done nothing but go back to the hospital and avoid your father," Kader said. "And now, you've made an ass of yourself by getting involved in a petty dispute with a shop owner, who'll most likely talk to the press."

I clenched my jaw. "What's your point?"

"If you're so hell-bent on getting back to her, stop half-assing it and do it. Otherwise, quit making a complete fool out of yourself."

I was about to respond when I saw the shop owner making his way over to me. I could already tell I would have to pay a *lot* of money to make up for what I'd allowed to happen. A flash caught my eye, and I groaned. The crowd of photographers had assembled on the perimeter of the store, unwilling to come inside, but waiting for the moment I stepped out.

With all the ruckus at the market, Martin and I came back to our apartment empty-handed. To boot, I was now half a month's salary lighter to repay the money the man had lost. As Prince Galian, I could've taken it from my family's coffers. But since I was now just

Galian, the money had to come from me. But I was glad to do it; I felt responsible for his losses.

Lucky for Martin and myself, when we arrived back at our apartment, Rosie was waiting for us with a bright smile on her face.

Where Kader was tall and lanky, Rosie was short and shapely, with light brown curls that accented her round, rosy cheeks and a smile that could make me forget whatever troubles weighed me down. What she saw in Elijah Kader, I had no idea, because she was as kind and gracious as he was rude and gruff.

"You boys hungry?" she asked, wiping her hands on her apron. "I just made a big pot of stew, and Eli and I won't be able to eat it all."

Martin and I exchanged happy smiles.

"C'mon in." She held the door open for the two of us, and we filed into her apartment. If I hadn't seen her and Kader's wedding photo on the mantle, and seen the man himself come in and out of the door, I would never have guessed that he lived in such a warm and inviting place. Reds and yellows accented the small living room and a squishy, dark brown couch sat in front of the television, where Martin made himself comfortable. I followed Rosie into the kitchen, hoping for a bit of guidance and to avoid hearing about what was being said about the day's events.

As if she'd read my mind, Rosie nodded to the fridge. "Have a beer, honey."

"Is Kader coming?" I asked, realizing that he hadn't come in the door yet after driving Martin and me back to our apartment.

"No, sweetheart, he had some business to take care of at the castle," she said, taking the second beer from me. "Sit down and keep me company while I finish dinner."

I sat on the small kitchen table and watched Rosie bounce

between the stove and the fridge. "I can't drink too much. I'm working in the morning."

"Poor baby," Rosie replied. "Is that attending still giving you off and on schedules?"

"I think it's my father's doing."

"Oh, honey, not everything that happens to you is the king's fault," Rosie said, walking up to me with a spoon. "Taste." I did so and nodded appreciatively. "Sometimes, life's just unfair."

I thought of that little boy in the grocery store, just as I heard Martin calling my name. When I leaned out of the kitchen, I saw a photo of myself talking with the grocery manager. The headline read, *"Prince Galian helps local merchant, defeats five thieves."*

"You've got to be kidding me," I said, leaning back into the kitchen.

"Oh, I saw that earlier," Rosie said with a smile. "Elijah told me it was a little boy you were trying to help."

She placed a bowl of chunky meat and vegetables in front of me and patted my cheek. "Such a good boy." I didn't have the heart to remind her I was twenty-five. Martin appeared in the doorway to the tiny kitchen and made himself a plate, shoveling the stew into his mouth as he walked back into the living room, pausing only to offer a garbled "thank you" to Rosie.

I ate as much as I could, more than usual, so Rosie wouldn't fret over me.

"How are you doing, sweetheart?" she asked after a moment.

"I'm..." Fine would be the word I'd use with my mother, but today I couldn't bring myself to say it again. "I feel like I'm spinning my wheels. I haven't done anything but go to work and come home. Mael still burns. Bombs still drop. And Theo..." I closed my eyes. "I miss her."

"I know how you feel. Every time Eli left for another mission, I couldn't sleep until he was back home. I hated feeling helpless."

"But you knew he was coming back home," I said. "I don't know if I'll ever see Theo again."

"I didn't, though," Rosie replied, glancing at the front door for a moment before returning to me. "Eli never went into details, but I know... I could tell every time he came home and held me that he'd been close enough to not making it back."

I glanced out into the living room again, still wishing I knew more about my bodyguard's past. "So you asked him to quit?"

"He quit himself," Rosie said. "He said he was tired of...of the strain. Wanted a better job." She smiled sadly at me. "He was beside himself with worry when you disappeared."

"I find that hard to believe."

"Eli takes his job very seriously. And he knew you didn't want to be out there. He thought it a...." She trailed off and glanced around for a moment before dropping her voice. "He thought it a travesty that someone as good as you was forced to give up your medical career to fight in that stupid war."

"And here I thought he hated me."

"Eli's used to a different sort of cohort. All his old special ops buddies are a riot. I had to take care of them all. After a mission, they'd all crowd around in here, drinking themselves silly and eating whatever I put in front of them."

"Does he still talk to them?" I asked, hoping I hadn't really ruined Kader's life.

"Heavens, yes!" Rosie said with a laugh. "They meet up once a week to get rip-roaring drunk." She added quickly, "On his off-duty nights, of course."

At that moment, I saw the man in question walk through the door. He took one look at Martin, then shook his head, barging into the kitchen.

"Hello, dear," he said, bending down to kiss Rosie on the forehead. He grunted in my general direction before helping himself to the food on the stove.

"How did it go?" Rosie asked.

"Fine." He sat down and dug into his meal.

"Fine? Elijah Kader, fine is not the answer I wanted to hear from you."

Kader paused mid-chew, then looked at me. "I'll tell you more once the boys are gone."

I would've bristled at the use of the "boy" but I was more curious. "Why? What's going on? What can you tell Rosie that you can't tell me? What's going on at the castle?"

Again, he glanced at Rosie, who looked awfully smug.

"Rositanna," he grunted. "You know I'm not allowed to talk about it with him."

"Why can you talk about it with her and not me?" I asked, nearly pulling the 'I-am-the-prince' card out of my pocket.

"Because unlike her," he nodded to Rosie, "I'm under express orders to keep *you* out of it. If you want to know, go talk to your mother."

"M-Mom?" I blinked. "What does she have to do with anything?"

Kader snorted and picked up his plate. "In case you didn't know, I work for her."

FOUR

THEO

The one bright spot in my otherwise dreary life was the weekly meetings with Bayard's public relations staff. It was arguably the biggest support staff in the Raven government, which made sense considering how much bullshit he had to peddle.

The meetings usually allowed me a glimpse into world beyond my own involvement. Walking around their office had netted me a wealth of information about ministers, officers, and other power players in Bayard's government. I stored the personality quirks, jobs, and passions away on the off-chance I'd be able to use it one day when I made it past commissioning pilots.

I considered what new information I might glean from today's briefing as my car sped through the unpleasant parts of Veres. My apartment was in the wealthy district, but there were at least ten blocks of slums between it and the seat of government. These slums reminded me of the Rave I knew: a grungy, poor place that was just barely surviving.

My car approached the iron gate surrounding the Raven

government complex. In the distance, far away from where I spent most of my time, was the presidential office. We called it *Platcha*, a Raven word that meant something like the village meeting house. It was the most beautiful building in the country, colored a unique pink, and was the former Kylaen governor's mansion. One day, I promised myself, I'd go there.

But for today, my destination was the set of buildings that bordered the stone walls around the complex. Three levels of concrete with square windows, they'd once been barracks for Kylaen soldiers. Now, the building housed the support staff for the president and his cabinet. Building three was the home of not only the public relations group, but also trade and agriculture departments. I didn't think we had trade or agriculture, but there was a sizable staff regardless.

I slammed the car door shut behind me and squared my shoulders, walking past the two soldiers standing guard out front, and making my way toward the small office space where Emilie shaped the hearts and minds of Rave.

I bypassed the central bullpen of desks, heading for the conference room. I took a seat at the back of the table, hiding myself as much as possible while the rest of the meeting attendees filtered in. Already in the room was Wesson, one of Emilie's two aides, gathering folders from the previous meeting. I noticed the *Secret* marking atop them and ached to know what they said. If I'd only been a few minutes earlier, I could've swiped a look before Wesson gathered them up.

Cannon strolled in, glancing at Wesson. "So when are we scheduling that trip to Malaske?"

I stiffened, straining my ears. Malaske was a secret facility on the western edge of the country, far away from the prying eyes of the Kylaens. Thormond, Galian's great-grandfather, had been the first to realize the potential of the mineral barethium. It was present in the Kylaen mountains, but had been easier to extract in Rave, and Malaske had been one of the largest processing plants. Until recently, I'd thought it had been destroyed. Over the past few weeks, I'd been hearing more and more whispers about a secret project there. But as there was no media invited along, it wasn't necessary for me to accompany Bayard on his visits. After all, there were young pilots to "inspire."

Wesson shot a glance at me and then Cannon. "I'll talk with you later."

I didn't let my annoyance show on my face, as it would only embolden Cannon. Then again, with his ego doing most of his talking, perhaps it wouldn't be so bad to let him know I was agitated. He might let slip something truly interesting.

His attention was diverted as soon as a pretty girl with curly hair walked into the room. She was the public liaison for our trade department, and she and Cannon were rumored to be flirting or sleeping with each other, even though she was engaged to another aide of a top general. Then again, perhaps Cannon was just perpetuating that rumor for his own media gain. He, at least, was still followed around by photographers even after being in the spotlight for two years, whereas I was failing miserably at it.

I let a cloud of annoyance settle on my shoulders. *None* of the ceremonies I'd attended in the past week had any media. This was a bad sign; once Emilie caught wind of my ineffectiveness, she would most likely stop sending me, and the door to Bayard's inner circle would shut forever.

I didn't have time to consider this further as Emilie walked in, followed by the rest of her of aides and office workers. A few of them, like me, had survived in the military long enough to get a promotion to safer places. But most of them were daughters and sons of the wealthiest Ravens. Their smiles and idle conversations were a stark contrast to the haunted eyes of the children I saw at our air force bases.

"Good morning, good morning," Emilie said, placing her coffee directly in front of her. She picked up a stack of papers and flipped through them quickly. "From our Kylaen *friends*, Grieg threw a party for Silas Collins, the man behind the new shipping line between Kylae and Jervan."

"Jervan was supposed to be negotiating that treaty with us, weren't they?" a young woman beside Emilie said.

"Indeed they were," Emilie said, pointing to Wesson. "We need to update Bayard's trade speech with this."

"Yes, ma'am."

Emilie went back to the paper and clicked her tongue against her cheek. "Oh, this is interesting. The princeling even showed up. Says Silas' daughter, Olivia Collins, was getting cozy with him."

I wanted to smile, but something sharp twisted under my ribs. I was grateful for the pain. It kept my face from betraying all the questions rising in my mind. Why, after all this time, had Galian decided to return to the castle? And who the hell was Olivia Collins? And why hadn't he...

"What else has the princeling been up to?" Cannon asked, breaking my train of thought. I could always count on him to goad Emilie into saying more about my *amichai*, but I didn't know if I wanted to hear more. I hated the reports on who was trying to sleep with him. My fear was that one day, I'd get confirmation that he'd actually done it.

Emilie scanned the pages and her eyes lit up. "Turns out he was in a bit of a scrap with a storekeeper. A child was shoplifting, and he intervened."

I pinched myself to force a scowl onto my face instead of the smile that threatened. Idiot princeling.

"He paid for all that the child stole," Emilie said, and it took a lot not to grin like a lovesick idiot. My excitement dampened when Emilie frowned. "Oh, but the child was caught and sentenced to sixty days in Mael."

The forced scowl turned into a real one. The conversation dulled and my mind returned to the mines, the stench. My stomach churned and I swallowed hard, breathing in deeply. I didn't want to have to leave this meeting early because I couldn't control my reflexes.

"Are you all right, *'neechai*?" Emilie asked.

I glanced at her and nodded fervently. With great effort, I released my iron grip on the chair, pulling my hands into my lap.

Emilie continued the meeting, assigning me three more commissioning ceremonies next week and another two taped speeches. She said nothing about Malaske, or anything else that I found useful. It was another day of keeping the Raven people's morale above water.

When the meeting dismissed, Emilie asked me to stay behind so she could speak with me. She took the seat next to me as the last of the stragglers left the meeting.

"How did the ceremony go? Did you have to give a statement to anyone?" she asked.

I winced. "Nobody from the papers showed up."

"Ah," she said lightly, turning away from me.

My fear returned. "I don't know what I'm doing wrong. Cannon still draws a crowd and he's been around for years."

"Cannon is...well, he's Cannon," Emilie replied. "He's

charismatic, he's handsome."

I tried not to feel insulted by the comparison.

"Theo, we've talked about this. You just...you don't have any emotion. The entire Raven citizenry sees you almost weekly, and you barely draw attention to yourself."

"It's hard to do that when Bayard's the one speaking," I said with a frown.

"Cannon managed to capture the attention of the country, and I didn't let *him* speak for nearly two years. Words are only part of it. You need... Theo, you look positively robotic. Here in the office, out there with the people." She paused and her brow furrowed. "The only emotion I see from you is whenever anyone mentions Mael. And maybe it's time we capitalize on it."

I swallowed hard, tempering my expression. I'd been dreading this conversation for weeks.

"We don't want to ask you to do anything you aren't comfortable with, of course. But..." She shook her head, her gold earrings dancing in the light. "There might be an opportunity to use what happened to you. If you feel up to it, of course."

I forced myself to respond, "I would be. If it meant I could be useful. But...I don't see how my display of emotion *helps* anyone."

Emilie opened the manila folder holding the intel reports, and my breath caught in my throat. My *amichai* had been photographed at some fancy party. He wore a bright red jacket and black slacks, his brown hair trimmed and combed. He stood with his brother, who wore a similar red jacket. The resemblance between the two was more pronounced than I'd seen before. Galian's face was tense, as was his brother's. They must've been arguing about something.

But, damn, he did look handsome.

"Two things sell in this world," Emilie said. "Passion and sex. These two and Cannon," she pointed to the photo, "have the latter. Unless you want to make some serious personality changes, you are going to have to find your passion."

I stared at my *amichai* and envisioned him sitting next to me, the sound of his voice, the lame joke he would try to land after hearing Emilie call him sexy. It curled a smile onto my mouth.

"I'll try," I said. As she picked up the photo, I stopped her, "Can I keep that?"

She quirked a brow at me. "Really? You're one of *those* girls?"

"I'd like to burn it," I said, thinking quickly. "Maybe it will help me find...my passion."

"Fair enough," she said, sliding the photo over to me.

When she was out of the room, I made sure to fold it up and stuff it in my back pocket, out of sight.

I had the next day off, so I sat in my apartment, clutching a cup of coffee and considering Emilie's words. I didn't need her to tell me that I was dispassionate and detached. I hadn't felt like myself since I'd left the island, and although my heart ached for my *amichai*, missing him wasn't the only reason for restlessness. I looked around the apartment that wasn't mine, the breakfast I'd made with food that wasn't mine, the coffee in my cup that wasn't mine...and I suddenly needed to get out of the apartment. I put the cup near the sink and fetched my thick winter coat, hoping a long walk would clear my head.

Rave was too far south to get the snow storms that were plaguing Herin and Kylae, but it was still frigid. I wrapped my scarf tighter around my neck and zipped up my jacket, stuffing my hands into my pockets. Veres sat on a peninsula that stretched out into the Madion Sea, and the wind could be merciless as it blew through the buildings.

No stranger to daily physical training and with the whole day to myself, I decided to walk down to the shoreline. Rave had no money for parks or betterment, so there were no sidewalks, nothing but the natural rock and the sea splashing up against them. The water was a dull gray, churning and frothing with the wind. It reminded me of our island.

I let my memory return there, hoping to find the spark that would bring me back to myself. There certainly hadn't been any lack of passion there—not when I'd fought him on everything from his medical degree to his father's war. For those first few days, I'd spent more time being angry than not, until I'd realized that survival depended on us working together.

I snorted. There certainly hadn't been a lack of passion when we'd made love in that cave either.

But—I opened my eyes to the gravel stone beneath my black boots—Galian and I had failed. We hadn't rescued anyone but me, and Mael continued to stay open. The war that raged in my heart whenever I thought about it threatened to rise to the surface of my mind, and I gently patted it back down. I loved him, but I was disappointed in him, but I loved him. And around and around it went until my head began to hurt.

On the island, I'd decided that there wasn't enough space in my heart for Galian and forgiveness for his country, so I'd turned a blind eye to his involvement or lack thereof. The more time that passed, however, the more I began to wonder if my love for him was blinding me to all his faults. He'd made me a promise that he would go back for those prisoners and now he was back attending events at the castle and flirting with girls.

But I really hadn't done much better. When Bayard had appeared in my hospital room and offered me a place beside him, I'd had great visions of using my newfound fame for good. Demanding closures, improvements in the military bases. Perhaps even convincing Bayard to raise the conscription age to something reasonable like fifteen. Instead, all I'd done was smile and wave and sit behind the president, saying and doing nothing. How could I possibly be angry with Galian for not doing anything when I was guilty of the same thing?

But I could change that, a voice whispered in my mind.

Emilie was giving me the opportunity. But what would talking about Mael entail? And could I really stand in front of my country and *lie* about how long I'd really been there? The guilt which had settled on my heart the moment I'd escaped returned with a vengeance. I felt dishonest, like I was taking credit for something I hadn't done. I was no hero, and I was no savior. I was alive purely because of Galian and who he was. Would it be right to help when the only reason for getting the opportunity was sheer dumb luck?

My footsteps stopped abruptly and another pair continued behind me. The hair rose on the back of my neck and I turned, glancing behind me. A man stood there, his black hair hung around his eyes and blowing in the wind. He wore an old winter jacket, too rough to be new, but too patched up to have belonged to someone with money.

"Can I help you?" I asked, trying to sound stern in case he was after trouble.

"You're that *kallistrate*. The one Bayard's been carrying around with him."

I nodded, sensing it would be better to remain distant from him. Emilie had warned me that now that I'd become the new face of Bayard's media campaign, there might be a bit more attention, and to be careful about walking alone. Then again, I was a seven-year veteran of the air forces and had survived two months on an island. I was pretty sure I could handle myself.

I waited for him to ask me for an autograph or rob me; instead, he came to stand next to me and watched the churning ocean. "Pretty, isn't it?"

"What?"

"The Madion Sea."

I turned to face the ocean, and a big wave sprayed salt water on my exposed skin. "It's a bit rough today."

"Seas are always rough. Even when they look calm, there's always something dangerous beneath the surface."

I glanced at him out of the corner of my eye. "Poetic."

His smile was enigmatic, and the creases around his eyes deepened. It had taken me a moment, but I realized who—or what—he was. The first day I'd shown up in the public relations office, Emilie had mentioned there was a small rebel movement in Veres. She and everyone else had dismissed them as a joke—Bayard's approval rating was through the roof—but she'd said they might come to me eventually.

As if he was reading my mind, the man turned and handed me a small piece of paper. "If you get tired of shilling for Bayard's bullshit farmers, let me know."

"I won't," I said, not taking his card.

"Ah, loyal to the president?" He surveyed me and I didn't like the tone of his voice.

"I am loyal to Rave," I replied. "And right now, he's the Raven president. That's why we're a democracy. We choose the president."

His throaty laughter made me feel like a child. "Spoken like a true brainwashed child soldier. How old were you when they took you for flight school?"

My jaw clenched.

"I don't blame you for being so ignorant. Most of Rave knows what it's told. They think every decision Bayard makes is for the betterment of our country."

I couldn't force my mouth open to argue with him.

"Why, then, are all the children picked for conscription from orphanages and the poorest cities? Why are hundreds of Veres-born children educated and sent to non-combat bases in the south and west of the country? There are more *kallistrates* in the Raven air forces than those with real names."

My cheeks began to heat up. "What do you suggest then? Kylae bombs us—"

"Kylae bombs our arsenals, not our cities. If they wanted us back in the fold, they would bomb our cities and break us quickly." He turned to look behind me at the skyline of Veres. "Not a single bomb has reached Veres in fifteen years. But I suppose it would look different in Vinolas."

I almost refuted his comment, saying that Kylae still considered us very much at war, but that might've insinuated that I knew more about Kylae than I let on. Besides, I was fairly sure that speaking with this man at all would be frowned upon—or worse.

"I have nothing to say to you," I replied as curtly as possible.

"For now, perhaps. But I think a few more months in Veres

will change your mind," he said, nodding slightly. "Until we meet again, Major."

I waited until the footsteps on the gravel were gone before I turned to hurry back to my apartment, promising myself to listen to Emilie's advice on walking alone.

FIVE

GALIAN

Growing up, I'd known my parents to disagree more than agree, but my mother usually kept her comments to herself. Hers was more a passive rebellion, working to achieve progress in the places my father didn't care so much, and treading carefully where he did. I supposed I'd never considered who exactly Kader had been working for, but to find out he was sneaking around on my mom's behalf was odd. Kader wouldn't have been involved in something frivolous, so whatever he was doing had to be important.

But what vexed me the most was he was under strict orders not to include me.

I pondered this question whenever I had downtime over the next week, in which Hebendon had me do a morning-to-evening, then an evening-to-morning, then another evening-to-morning, rounding it out with a morning-to-evening. I barely even knew my name by the end of it, let alone why my mother was keeping secrets with my bodyguard.

But when I'd had a few nights to catch up on sleep, I made the decision to seek out my mother. To do this, I had two options. The first was to go to the castle. But unless Kader was breathing down my neck, I wasn't going to go back there. The second option was to meet her for coffee somewhere in the city.

And by meet her, I meant meet her and the hovering photographers.

Kader kept them away from me as I crossed the street. My mother already sat in the window, chatting with the owner of the shop with a smile on her face. She was blissfully ignorant of the cameras; maybe one day I would be as unbothered by them as she was.

"There's my boy," she said, standing and coming to hug me. I noticed how her hands lingered on my shoulders, but then she stepped back, an overly cheerful smile on her face. "You look tired, honey."

"I've had a long week," I said, sitting down.

The owner placed a steaming cup of coffee in front of me. I smiled and reached for the wad of bank notes in my pocket.

"Don't be silly, dear, I already paid for it," Mom said with a wave of her hand.

The owner bowed once more and left us alone to talk. The cafe was mostly empty, save a few interested girls and one very self-absorbed man leaning over a notebook.

Exhaustion took my tact. "What is Kader doing with you that you can't tell me about?"

She smiled and stirred her coffee. "I don't want you involved in that."

"Mom, seriously," I said, leaning forward.

"I am serious, Galian, *I don't want you involved,*" she answered with a tired look. "I've only just gotten you back, and I don't even *have* you back. This is the first time we've spoken in weeks. Thank goodness

Eli has been keeping me informed."

"Then you're talking to Kader about me?" I pressed. "Is that what you're—"

"Is that Hebendon still working you to death?" She clicked her tongue disapprovingly. "I should really see to having someone step in."

"Have you heard from Dr. Maitland?" I asked.

"Oh yes, dear, he's having a lovely time in Baro," she replied brightly. "The Herinese are treating him wonderfully, though he said he could do without the blizzards."

"Are you sure?"

"Why would he lie to me?"

"I'm not saying he's lying, I'm just..." I heaved out a breath. "Are you sure he's still alive? Father didn't...off him, did he?"

She placed her cup down on the table. "Let's just say that Sebastian thought it might be best if he left the country for a while. But he went of his own volition."

I shook my head. All these lives upended to appease one man. "Well, lucky me, I get to deal with his replacement. Father's just not content to see me happy, is he?"

"You think Hebendon is your father's doing?" She tutted and shook her head. "Son, your father has much more pressing things to worry about than torturing his son."

"Like what?"

"The upcoming Summit of Nations," she said, looking out the window. "We've received word that Jervan has invited the Ravens."

I almost choked on my coffee. The Summit of Nations was an annual gathering of leaders from Kylae, Jervan, and Herin. Kylae had hosted the summit almost every year, and had made it clear that none of the other countries was to invite Rave. But this year, Jervan had offered to host and, apparently, expanded the invitation list.

"Wow," I said, wiping my mouth with a napkin.

"Wow is right," Mom said, distractedly watching the street. "Your father is considering not going."

"Oh, come on," I scoffed. "It's about time we at least sat in the same country as them. Might change some things."

"Speaking of changes, I want you to take Olivia Collins on a date."

"I... What?" I blinked. "No, Mom."

"How will you know if you don't try?"

"I don't want to try."

"Son, you're miserable. You survived the island, but you don't live. You just mope around that apartment and go to work and get into fights at grocery stores." The corners of her mouth twitched when I groaned. "It made for a good story, Gally."

"I'm not going out with Olivia."

"And why not? She's a lovely girl."

"She's not Theo."

Mom was silent then asked, "And you think Theo still feels the same way about you? Are you so sure she hasn't fallen out of love with you now that you don't have the threat of starvation hanging over your heads?"

I shifted in my seat and had no answer.

"All I'm asking is that you take Olivia on *one* date," Mom said, taking my hands. "Not for her sake, but for yours. Galian, you can't waste your life hoping for something that might never be yours again. Go on this date and see if you find the spark with this girl that you found with Theo."

I stared out the coffee shop window at the crowd that was doing its best to jostle for a glimpse of Her Majesty and myself.

"One date, Galian, please. As a favor to me."

I tilted my head back and said a silent prayer. I hated saying no to my mother. So I didn't. "Fine. One date. But I don't have to like it."

She beamed at me.

It wasn't two days later that I found myself staring in a mirror. My attire was semi-formal—crisp black pants, ironed button-up shirt (Thank God for Martin), dinner jacket. My face was a mixture of sheer terror and disgust that I was actually doing this. With a heavy sigh, I walked out into the living room. Martin gave me a once over and thumbs up, his mouth crammed with chips. Kader, who was the lucky one to accompany me on this farce, simply snorted in my direction.

"You're going to be late," he said.

"Yeah, yeah, one second," I said, going to the kitchen and locating the bottle of alcohol Martin always left in there. I took a long swig, then another.

"It's not that bad," Kader said.

"How can you be so sure? Have you done a background check on this woman?"

"She's a socialite. I doubt she's got skeletons," Kader replied lazily.

"She could be a sleeper agent."

"As if Rave has enough resources for something like that."

I closed the freezer and sighed. "What if I just don't want to go?"

"As much as I don't care about your dating life, I think this is good for you," Kader said. "Try and forget about Theo for the night."

It was hard to think about anything *but* Theo as the photographers had a field day with my dapper outfit as I left the apartment, and nearly wet themselves in excitement when my destination wasn't the hospital, but the fanciest restaurant in Norose. I could just imagine Theo's face when she found out.

My palms grew sweaty and I tried to quiet the voices reminding me that I should've been anywhere—Mael, or even the hospital—but this restaurant.

"Ah, Your Majesty, welcome to my restaurant." The hostess was beaming, although she looked a bit old to be a—She owned the restaurant, I realized with a small grimace. "Your date has not yet arrived, but shall I show you to your table?"

"Sure," I said, tossing one final, pleading look to Kader, but he'd already returned to the car. Unless I wanted to brave the photographers by myself, I was stuck.

I didn't have to wait long. Olivia arrived in a dress that was somehow refined and elegant (dare I say, princess-like) and yet still drew my attention to her breasts, her hips, and the shape of her calves in her heels. Her long hair was perfectly curled at the ends, and her perfect smile accentuated the perfect amount of makeup. I stood to greet her, aware that my photo was being taken by the flashes just outside the window.

"You look great," I said, gently kissing her cheek. I gestured to the madness outside. "Sorry about all that."

"It's part of it, I suppose." *Ah, test number one failed.* There were usually two types of women who dated me—those who hated the spotlight, and those who relished it. Judging by the way Olivia's gaze kept darting around the restaurant in satisfied superiority, I guessed she might be the latter.

Immediately, I heard my mother's voice in my head. *Give her a shot, Gally.* Her disembodied voice was right; what good was it to meet people if I never gave them more than five minutes?

"I have to admit, I was really surprised when you called," Olivia said, oblivious to my worry. "You didn't seem so interested at my father's party."

"In my defense, I'd just finished a twelve-hour shift," I said, not really hungry for the salad that was placed in front of me. "And I was dragged there against my will. State dinners aren't my thing."

"Not since your time on the island?" Olivia asked. "What was it like there?"

I grimaced. The island was the last thing I wanted to talk about on a date with another woman. "Uh...cold," I said, my gaze sliding over to the crowd just outside the restaurant.

I jumped when her unfamiliar hand covered mine.

"Galian, I know that it was an ordeal, but you can trust me."

Her eyes glittered, and I caught myself wondering if it was another act. If she was simply there because I was Galian and a prince and she wanted the prestige. I opened my mouth to tell Olivia how it felt to be a piece of meat, but I couldn't force out the words. Would she even understand? Would she care or simply take the tale of woe out to the tabloids waiting outside?

"That sounds lonely." Theo's voice echoed in my head. When we'd talked about life under the spotlight, she'd understood immediately and hadn't judged me. And she, above everyone else, had the right to judge my complaints.

I looked at the fine wine in my glass and the green salad on my plate and I considered all the children at Mael, which continued to crank out weapons as sure as it killed the workers there. I had promised Theo I would save them and I'd done nothing—I didn't even bother to check up on what had happened to the prisoners who'd been there when I'd broken her out.

"Why do I get to live and they don't?" Why indeed, I wondered, gripping my knife with all the anger I felt toward myself. I wished I was the man Theo wanted me to be, but I was too cowardly. There I was on a *date* instead of standing in the middle of Mael and demanding it be shut down—

"Galian?" Olivia's voice cut through my near breakdown.

I released my grip on the knife and forced a smile onto my face. "Dessert?"

She smiled, but I saw it—that moment of nerves and pity. "You haven't even touched your dinner," she said softly. She thought me to be damaged.

Good, I thought, *maybe now she won't want to be with me.*

"Right," I said. "It's been a while since I've done this."

"I've made the prince of Kylae nervous. Well, isn't that something!"

We descended into awkward silence, and I began to fidget with the edge of the tablecloth. I had one move left to salvage this horrible dinner.

"So, tell me about your day?"

"Oh, well, it was just exhausting." I doubted that. "I spent all morning with my father, helping him finalize the trade agreement."

"Really?" I said, picking at my salad. "I didn't think you worked with him."

"Oh, Galian, did you think that I simply flitted around and went to art openings and fashion shows all day?"

"Er..." In fact, that was *exactly* what I thought she did all day.

"Daddy is growing older, and he's starting to groom me to take over the Collins empire in the next decade."

It was odd, then, that my mother was pushing me toward her. When she'd become queen, my mother had to give up her career at the university, as her duties as queen took most of her time. Then again, perhaps the wife of a spare prince was less busy than that of the queen of Kylae.

"This trade agreement has been the result of ten years' worth of work," she said, excitement lacing her voice. It was nice to see some sort of humanity from her for once. "We will be transporting five thousand tons of Jervanian wheat across the Madion Sea every year. Your father has spent millions of crowns on improvements at the port in Duran. It's created hundreds of jobs there, you know."

I nodded. Duran was a shithole of a port city last time I'd checked, so I was glad my father had invested in them.

"Unfortunately, the Jervans have seen fit to throw all that away," she said, her face growing darker. "They've invited that falsehood of a government in Thormondia—"

"Veres," I corrected quietly.

"Veres, Thormondia, whatever they wish to call their capital. It's a sham government. Corrupt as the day is long."

"Uh-huh." If I sounded anything like this when I was on the island with Theo, it was a small miracle she hadn't shot me dead with our flare gun.

"But now Jervan has *invited* them to the Three Nations' Summit," Olivia replied, placing her fork down. "As if they belong there like some real country. Your grandfather started that summit, you know. And for them to spit in our face like this is just..."

"I don't think that inviting Rave is spitting in our face," I mumbled, unable to keep my opinions to myself.

"Oh..." Her eyes widened, and a blush crossed her face. "I didn't realize you were one of *them*."

"Them?"

"You're right. It's not a slap in the face." Her face was a mask, but I guessed she was weighing whether being a princess was worth having to pretend she cared about the lives of a few hundred thousand people.

"You're free to have your opinion, Olivia," I replied. In fact, if she differed from me instead of acquiescing all the time, I might actually consider dating her. "You were saying something about the trade agreement going to hell?"

"Y-yes. We had planned on finalizing the agreement between Kylae and Jervan at the Summit. But now we have to make alternate arrangements. Your father is...well, he has *mentioned* he might scrap the entire deal. We might make the agreement with Herin instead. They don't have as much wheat, but they're willing to compensate in wood."

"Seems a bit of an overreaction."

She barked a laugh, then quickly covered her mouth with her hand. "You can't be serious, Galian. By inviting our colony, Jervan is giving them *legitimacy*. That's... They can barely keep their country together as it is."

"Maybe that's because we keep bombing them."

Again, her eyes widened. "Because they won't come back—"

"But why do we want that land in the first place?" I asked, sitting back. "Barethium? My father's ego?"

"Because it's *ours*."

"It was theirs first. And don't even start that line of thinking that they can't possibly be trusted to establish their own government. That's some Kylaen media bullshit to make the war easier to stomach."

Her mouth opened and she stared at me for a minute. "I see. It's no wonder you aren't speaking to your father."

"That and other reasons."

I was sorely tempted to tell her the truth, that my father had left me on the island to die. But I didn't. For one, I was fairly sure she was so far up my father's ass she could see out his nose. And for another, our argument had attracted the attention of some of the nearby tables. If I didn't want the media painting me as an abusive date, I needed to salvage this and fast.

"Olivia, I'm...sorry. This isn't really great date conversation," I said, sitting back. To smooth things over even more, I added, "I'm a little rusty at this."

Her eyes softened a little. "I understand."

"Why don't you tell me more about this art gallery your mother is opening?"

She graciously took the conversation change, and we spent the rest of our dinner in the realm of the civil. The further we veered from the war, the happier she looked. By dessert, she was back to the gaga eyes that might grace the front page of the papers tomorrow.

I was thankful that our dinner plans included a play, because it meant I didn't have to talk to her. I would've napped during the whole thing, except that Olivia seemed keyed into every move I made. She wrapped her arm around mine and rested her head on my shoulder. I almost imagined Theo by my side, but then I realized that Theo would never drag me to a play. She would consider it a complete and total waste of time.

"So what is this play about?" I whispered to Olivia as the

orchestra began warming up.

"Based on an old Kylaen legend," she replied with a smile. "A story of two lovers from disagreeing families."

"Of course it is," I replied.

"Relationships are hard enough without even more complications," Olivia said, tightening her hold on me. "I'm so glad our families get along."

So we were in a relationship now? I prayed she wasn't expecting a ring at the end of our first date.

Thankfully, the play began and our conversation ended. I watched it for a bit, two Kylaen actors bellowing flowery words of love and longing. In my opinion, it didn't hold a candle to breathless lovemaking in a cave and the quiet whisper of *amichai* on her lips. The conflict was that their families didn't see eye-to-eye, which elicited a hefty eye roll from me. If only our problem was simply our families and not two entire countries, life would be so much simpler.

"Oh, it's romantic," Olivia said, catching my expression. She laid her head on my shoulder and sighed loudly enough for those around us to know she was happy.

Olivia was the definition of a wealthy Kylaen—poised and well-educated, with an undeserved sense of ownership over Rave. What would it take to change her mind, and the minds of the rest of the Kylaens of her status? She spoke about Rave like it was nothing but a petulant child, digging its feet in and demanding dessert. She had no idea about its fierce patriotism, its culture, the country's beautiful brown eyes shimmering in the firelight.

And yet, I wondered: if I'd never met Theo, if I'd never crashed on the island, would I have married Olivia? Would I be on this date with Olivia, wondering if sitting through this play would result in a hefty sexual favor?

I gave myself a little more credit. Even before Theo, the war hadn't sat well with me, and I doubted pre-island me would've stood for what Olivia had said.

Pre-island Galian would've sat quietly and let her talk, simmering in silent anger and not doing a damned thing about it. So the only change was that I'd learned how to speak my thoughts to those who had no power to change anything.

Pathetic.

When the play was over, the tabloid photographers were there when we walked to my car, but Martin was the one waiting for me instead of Kader. I didn't ask why the sudden change in guards, as I didn't want to arouse Olivia's suspicion and Martin was too busy keeping the photographers back.

I slid in next to Olivia and heard Martin slam the driver's door. He'd been nice enough to raise the divider, and I wondered if he truly thought that this date was going to go that well. Or maybe he was just encouraging me.

Either way, I knew that look on Olivia's face. She'd snuggled up right under my chin and was batting her lashes like I was the most handsome thing she'd ever seen.

So I kissed her. She tasted of wine and of mint, and she was soft and supple and would probably do anything I asked. I could show off my medical degree, and Olivia would fall at my feet. She would laugh at every joke I made and do her best to make me the happiest man in the world. She would never call me princeling or roll her eyes at me.

She wasn't Theo.

I shook my head and moved away from her. "I'm sorry, I can't do this."

"Is there a problem with me?"

"No, you're... You're just not..."

"Not what?" Olivia said, her face turning red with embarrassment.

"Not her," I whispered to myself as the car rolled to a stop.

Olivia said nothing to me when she exited the car, but I figured the flashing lights of the tabloids was payment enough for my lack of passion. At least she'd get attention.

Martin slid back into the car, lowered the divider, then drove. Once we were a ways away, I clambered into the front seat, my feet landing on cans in the bottom.

"Thought you might want a drink after all that," he said, cracking a grin. One of the six was missing from the pack.

"Where's Kader?"

"Beats me. Was supposed to be my night off, but he told me I had to come get your ass."

I frowned. "I'm surprised he left me alone at the theater."

"Nah, we had three guys watching you," Martin said.

I laughed and cracked open the beer, sucking down half of it. "Thanks for not thinking I'm an idiot."

"Oh, I still think you're an idiot. But I'm not going to lie to you." The car rolled to a stop. "It really went that badly?"

"She'll make someone else a great wife."

"You think she'd be interested in me?"

I took another sip. "I think she'd find your lack of royal pedigree a problem."

"Damn," Martin said with a chuckle.

"Maybe she'll marry my brother," I replied, watching the streetlights pass by. "But you know, I think I'd have a hard time being married to someone with views I'm diametrically opposed to."

"I think your mother does it admirably."

I snorted and glanced over at him. He shrugged and turned the wheel as we took a left to head back to our apartment.

But I didn't want to go there. "I want to go to Cinzia."

Martin made a noise, but didn't disagree. Instead, he turned the car around to get back on the main road in Norose.

We drove in silence for an hour, and I drank another beer to forget my disastrous date. The streetlights grew sparser the farther out from the city center we drove. Soon there was nothing but my headlights on the road. I glanced behind the car to look for dark shadows of cars with their headlights off. But the photographers had their story, so maybe they'd leave me alone for the rest of the night.

Martin pulled the car over and turned it off. I opened the door and stepped out onto the soft sand. The cold winter wind cut right through my jacket, and the salty air bit at my face. In the brief moments when the wind died, I heard the lapping water against the beach, but thanks to the overcast sky, I couldn't see the Madion Sea.

It was too cold to remove my shoes, but they made walking in the sand difficult. After a long trek, I made it to the shoreline. Water slipped over my shoes, soaking them.

Within a week of being back, I'd found this beach. I'd done the math and measured four different maps to make sure.

Right where I stood was the closest I could get to Rave on Kylaen soil.

Theo was sleeping a mere three hundred and seventy-two miles from where I stood. Sadness tugged at my heart, and I closed my eyes, whispering my feelings to the wind and hoping they landed in her dreams.

I stood on the beach until my hands and wet feet had grown numb then turned to walk back to Martin, who was drinking a beer inside the car. I sat down in the passenger's side, feeling as numb as my hands.

After a moment, I asked, "Do you think I should give up on Theo?"

"Fuck, no." Martin drank more of his beer. "You love her, right?"

I nodded.

"Then you need to figure out a way to be with her," Martin said, looking out into the darkness. "I mean, you survived a plane crash *and* two months on a deserted island, yeah?"

"She helped."

"So? You did it."

"Yeah, I did do it." I sat up, feeling pumped. "I killed rabbits and made fire, and I save lives and I am gonna get my girl back."

"That's the spirit," Martin said, raising his beer in solidarity.

"I just hope she wants me back," I said quietly, looking at the time. The papers were probably printing their wildly inaccurate stories about my date with Olivia. I just prayed none of that would reach Rave.

SIX

THEO

Prince Galian Finally Courting Collins?

Could there be royal wedding bells? Last night, Prince Galian was seen dining with Olivia Collins, heir to the Collins shipbuilding empire. The two dined at Freihof before taking in a play. Witnesses confirmed seeing the two holding hands and speaking quietly during the performance.

"Olivia has been taking tea with the queen regularly, and it's no secret that the two were close before the prince's disappearance," an inside source confirms. It seems the party-boy prince is finally ready to settle down.

I put down the paper and stared out into the street. I had decided to get breakfast at the diner at the street level of my apartment building to kill some time before my car arrived, and someone had left behind the gossip section of the paper. My eyes had been drawn to the title, and as I read, my hopes sank lower and lower.

Galian had never mentioned another woman—he'd told me point blank that he'd never been in love before. I remembered every piece of that conversation, how lonely he looked when he'd said no one knew the real him. He'd also mentioned—many times—how much the tabloids liked to make up stories.

Yet there was a photo of him with this girl, and he looked...happy. He'd smiled at me like that countless times on the island. That was the look of a man in love, or one trying very hard to be. There was a photo of the girl just below. She was the picture of Kylaen beauty. Strawberry blonde hair, a white smile that seemed nearly painted on. She carried herself with much more grace than I probably ever could.

"Taking tea with the queen," I muttered to myself.

I doubted Galian's mother would ever take tea with me. I tried to picture myself wearing a fancy dress and sipping on some acrid brew while trying to keep my opinions to myself. The idea was laughable.

I ran my finger along the printed visage of my *amichai*. He looked happy, at least. If I couldn't be there with him,all I wanted was for him to find happiness without me.

That was what I told myself, anyway.

For today, I had bigger things to concern myself with than if my *amichai* had found a new love. Today, I was meeting with President Bayard.

I'd found out just as I was leaving a commissioning ceremony the day before. Emilie had radioed my driver to pass along the news that I would need to be ready in my dress uniform at 0700 to arrive at the presidential palace in plenty of time. Of course, I'd slept little and was showered and dressed in my black dress uniform, checking the ribbons and buttons three times to make sure they were right. I was much more at home in my flight suit, but for today, it was imperative I make a good impression.

I'd paced in my apartment for an hour before deciding it was smart to eat something. This small diner sat at the bottom of my apartment complex and was sometimes frequented by other military elites. It was convenient enough for me that I ate there a few times a week, but this morning, the eggs and bacon were unappetizing—and it had nothing to do with the meeting I'd been hoping for.

I glanced at the paper on the table again and thanked God when my car pulled up outside. It did me no good to wallow over some possibly fabricated story about a man I might never see again. I left the paper and the photo of my *amichai* behind. I already had a photo of him looking striking in his red jacket. I didn't need another with a vapid, perfect princess in it.

I shook my head. That sounded awfully jealous and catty.

I continued to oscillate between mental preparation for my meeting with the president of my country and worry that Galian had moved on. I'd convinced myself that she was better than me in every way, then practiced my talking points on how raising the conscription age would actually result in *more* Raven pilots, because less would die, then considered what Perfect Princess would say about that—

I closed my eyes and took a deep breath.

"Focus, *kallistrate.*"

The car stopped at the wrought iron gates and they opened slowly. We bypassed the normal route to Emilie's office and my heartbeat quickened as we drew closer. Thick, expensive trees lined the driveway—no doubt placed here by the last Kylaen governor—forming a beautiful archway of foliage that sheltered us all the way to the mansion. A working fountain spouting crystal clear water sat in the circular drive as we parked in front of a carved archway over the entrance, where two guards stood at attention.

My driver opened the door to the car, and I stepped out,

nodding my thanks to him. Up close, *Platcha* was much more ornate that I'd previously thought. Much like Bayard himself, it seemed out of place in a country that conscripted children at twelve.

A tall, thin man came out to greet me, introducing himself as Agustin and informing me that my morning meeting with Bayard had been pushed to this afternoon on account of other priorities.

"Oh," I said, my heart sinking.

"But I have been asked to take you on a tour of the grounds, until he's available."

A tour was the last thing I wanted to do, but I smiled grimly and allowed him to walk me around. The inside of *Platcha* was even more beautiful than the outside, with high, arched ceilings, detailed columns, and portraits of Raven heroes adorning the walls. I barely paid attention to the poor tour guide, even though he was obviously very interested in what he was saying.

He led me out into a garden filled with the most beautiful flowers and plants I'd ever seen. It was winter, so I was surprised to see flowering plants. Agustin pointed to a particularly striking purple plant in the center.

"That is the phoenician plant, the official flower of the nation of Rave," he said. "It blooms even in the harshest temperatures. Every six weeks, it sheds its flowers and grows new ones, just like the symbol of our nation—"

"The phoenix," I murmured.

It really was a beautiful plant, but as my gaze traveled around this green, lush oasis of beauty, I considered the disparity. I'd known nothing of this in my youth. I'd known cold nights and cramped spaces and meager foods. I'd known work and hardship.

"How long has this garden been here?" I asked.

"Since independence. It was the prized jewel of Lady Leonia, the wife of our first president. She spared no expense to make sure it was properly maintained."

I swallowed. "Oh? Seems like a bit of a frivolous expense...considering the circumstances."

"She wanted every person who walked through the front doors of *Platcha* to know that Rave was a true country, worthy of their trade and assistance." He seemed a bit cold to me now. "Appearances are everything."

"Indeed, but the *kallistrate* hasn't quite learned that lesson."

"Cannon," I said, turning to face him as he approached.

He nodded to Agustin and the other man quickly turned and scampered away. I got the feeling he was happy to be free of me, and that bothered me a little. I wasn't *that* bad company, was I?

"I hear you have a meeting with Bayard today," he drawled.

"Happen to know what it pertains to?" I asked. Cannon did have a higher clearance than I, so I figured it might be good to stroke his ego a bit.

"Not in the least," Cannon replied, but the smirk on his face told a different story. "Such a peaceful garden. I often come out here to think after my meetings with Bayard."

"I still think it's wasteful," I replied, glancing at a placard sticking out of the ground. In fact, all the plants had placards detailing their origin and importance to Raven culture. I knew the phoenician plant was integral to a summer festival called *Prima Anela*, but the rest of the plants I'd never heard of before.

"And that, Theo, is why you will never make it as a politician," he said.

"I didn't say I wanted to be a politician."

He smiled. "Then why are you here?"

"Because I want to make a difference," I replied, lifting my head higher.

Cannon snorted as if my sincerity was amusing to him.

After several hours wandering around the presidential gardens, Agustin found me and brought me to the presidential offices. It had been two hours since he'd dropped me off, and I was still sitting on an uncomfortable antique couch in the antechamber of the president's office.

I didn't see how Bayard's office could be any more ornate than the rest of this silly, pointless house, but this antechamber was awe-inspiring. Blue velvet drapes hung from large windows, the carpets were meticulously cleaned and intricately designed. The chandelier that hung above my head sparkled like diamonds and I prayed to God they weren't real. Everything in this room could've fed my whole squadron for a year.

I put aside my concerns for my country's fiscal responsibilities and returned to my mental checklist of topics for Bayard. I was intent on demonstrating that I was more than just a pretty face that smiled and sat next to him. Intent on showing that I hadn't attained the rank of captain for nothing—

"Major," I whispered to myself.

People came and went through the large doors leading inside, but I wasn't allowed to follow. His private secretary had attended to my needs for the first fifteen minutes, but the more I asked about the meeting, the terser he became.

I began to fidget. The sun was hanging low in the sky, painting the clouds pink and orange. I wasn't sure what kind of hours the president of Rave kept, but I was sure he'd probably send me home instead of staying later than usual.

Finally, the doors opened and three ministers strolled out. I knew one was Breen, for he'd spent some time in the public relations office with Emilie. The other two, I didn't know.

"Ah, it's the famous 'neechay!" Breen's face split into a smile as he approached me. I was surprised when he pulled me into a familiar hug, as if we were old friends. But I also couldn't help but notice the odd way he pronounced 'neechai.

"Minister, how are you?" I replied.

"Splendid! Tedwin and I were just discussing you, in fact."

"Albric." Bayard, the man I'd been hoping to speak to for four long months, stood in the doorway of his office. He held an unspoken conversation with Breen, who held up his hands in surrender.

"Fine, fine. I'll let you two get to your meeting. Be seeing you soon, 'neechay!"

"Come in, 'neechai, come in," Bayard said, waving me into his office. I stood, feeling like a child who'd been sent to the headmistress's office for acting out, but held myself upright as I followed him inside.

If the outside of Bayard's office had been beautiful, the inside took my breath away. I lingered in the doorway, admiring everything from the gold-plated lamps on the wall to the even *more* ornate chandelier above my head to the beautiful rug, to the dark mahogany desk—

"Have a seat, Major," Bayard said, interrupting my thoughts. "Unfortunately, most of my meetings have run late today, so I'm afraid I don't have as much time as I'd like to chat with you."

I swallowed a comment about how he'd sat next to me for four months, and took a seat at his engraved table.

"This is just...beautiful," I said, running my hands along the dark wood.

"Finest Herinese wood right there. I had it commissioned upon winning my third term as president." He sighed, seeming to revel in the memory of his victory, before he joined me at the table. "Tell me, Theophilia—"

"Theo is fine, sir," I replied hastily. To his quirked brow, I replied, "I'm not the biggest fan of my full name."

He surveyed me carefully. "You're what, nineteen, twenty?"

"Just passed my twentieth birthday," I said, leaning forward. Now was my chance to prove my worth to him. "And while I am grateful for the opportunity to be present at your news conferences, I..." I swallowed, carefully phrasing my words. "I feel like I could be more useful to the cause if I could..." I let out a breath. "Speak."

"And what, my dear, would you like to speak about, hm?"

I felt emboldened; he didn't seem to hate the idea. "I would like to talk about what the war is doing to our people. I want to talk about how it felt to fight off Kylaens every day of my life, to make a plea to the international community to intervene."

Bayard chuckled to himself and reached into the small drawer under his table, rolling a small ball down the table. I picked up the item and realized it was candy—chocolate. We'd receive a ration of the sweet during *Prima Anela* to keep up morale, but smelling the sweet aroma in the winter felt...wrong.

"Your idea is a tad problematic, though. You see, if we were to shine a light on our own struggles, it would reflect poorly on this nation and my leadership of it. Now we don't want that, do we?"

My face grew warm, and I shook my head. Why hadn't I thought of that?

"Major, do you understand the importance of an image?" Bayard began before pausing and looking at the chocolate expectantly. I quickly unwrapped the treat and stuck it in my mouth. When he was satisfied, he continued, "An image, a brand, tells people who you are in a few words. When they look at Mark, they see a man who has defended his country, smart and savvy, and roguishly handsome. Do you know who he was before we got a hold of him?" He snorted. "He mumbled and couldn't look into the camera. But Emilie did what she does best and look at him."

I kept my thoughts about Cannon to myself.

"We made Mark into what we needed at the time, the picture of Raven strength and resilience. And you, Theo, I want to turn into a symbol of Mael."

My hand tightened around the empty chocolate wrapper.

"Instead of telling the world of our troubles, let's focus the story on Kylae and their death camp. After all, it exists to bolster their arsenal to kill Raven citizens, does it not?"

I focused my gaze on my hands, on the my knuckles turning white. "Sir, I'm not sure... I don't know if I can speak about it."

Bayard's face slipped, and I worried I was making my case worse. I scrambled to find that girl who would take orders blindly, knowing that those above me had the best interests of the country at heart. Or at the very least, I forced myself not to speak any more.

"Theo, I don't trust you," Bayard said.

My gaze shot upward to him again, and it took all my willpower not to respond.

He chuckled and stood from the table, walking back over to his desk and procuring more chocolate, which he handed to me with a tight smile. "Oh, don't get me wrong, I believe you're dedicated to this country and the cause of independence. But I don't trust that if I put you in front of a camera, you won't say the wrong thing. You're too honest for your own good."

I took the chocolate, and allowed myself a small nod of thanks. "I'm sorry, sir."

"You see? That's what I'm talking about," he replied. "But no matter. I'm willing to look past all that and put in the effort to really make you shine. Because I need you, Theo. I've been handed a golden opportunity for Rave and I need your help."

I edged forward in my seat. "Anything, sir."

"I've received confirmation that we've been invited to the Summit of Nations."

He appeared pleased, but I'd never heard of such a thing before.

"The summit is an annual gathering of the Madion nations," he explained without missing a beat. "It's where the major treaties are discussed and signed. The only time all the heads of state are in the same room, able to come to terms on the topics most important to our countries."

"And we've never been invited before," I guessed.

"Right you are," he said with a curt nod. "But thanks to some of our friends in the intelligence division, we've finally been able to secure an invite. It hasn't been completely confirmed or announced, so please keep this to yourself." He paused and smiled. "But I would like you to give a speech about your time in Mael."

Again, my chest seized. It was one thing to have others talk about Mael and use my face; it was quite another to stand in front of the international community and lie. I stared at the veins in the wooden table, considering my options. If I said no, I would effectively lose my spot on Bayard's team. I'd be reassigned somewhere else, or worse, they'd send me back to Vinolas. But if I said yes...

"You see, *that* is the kind of palpable emotion I want to see from you!" Bayard said, pointing at my stricken face. "Our country doesn't want a stoic stalwart. We need someone to show strength and *passion*."

That word again. I was starting to hate it as much as *'neechai*.

"I've asked Emilie to draft a speech for you herself and to work with you over the next two weeks. She's the best of the best, and I know she'll be able to bring out the best in you."

As I sat in Bayard's office, the taste of chocolate odd on my tongue, the president's voice in my ear, and a sick feeling in my stomach, I considered whether the best in me was really what they were after.

GALIAN

As had been the case for the past four months, the fiery inspiration to get back to Theo was quashed by Hebendon's mad scheduling—this time, four night shifts in a row. As if the hours weren't bad enough, the cases were all difficult ones. A rash on a young boy that took me several rounds of medications to dissipate, a cough in an old woman that was too watery for my liking, and a pregnant woman who didn't even realize she was carrying—even though she was several months along. Not to mention that people just kept coming in with impactions. After the third one, I considered asking Rhys to make it mandatory for Kylaens to eat more fiber.

The fourth night was quiet enough that I could sneak away for a quick catnap in the doctor's lounge. Someone else had grabbed the mattress already, so I had to settle for a lumpy chair. I leaned back and closed my eyes, breathing deeply to calm my racing mind. It was no use. I hadn't yet mastered the instant-sleep technique second-nature to the older, more experienced doctors.

My mind filled with thoughts of Theo, the usual questions of how she was doing and if she missed me, then immediately moved on to "what the hell am I going to do next?" I stared at the light above my head and drew a blank—and it wasn't because I was solely running on caffeine.

I sat up and rubbed my face. There was a days-old newspaper on the ground, and I picked it up, thumbing through the articles about the setbacks in the Jervan trade agreement, another damned gallery opening (how many of those did we need?) and...a story about Rave, buried in the bottom corner of the last page.

Raven Interim President Bayard has been invited by Jervanian President Kuman to attend the Summit of Nations, the first time the disputed territory has been asked to appear to the international meeting. His Highness King Grieg has declined to attend, citing the need to remain at home to deal with the Kylaen economic crisis.

I snorted. So my father *had* decided to stay out of it. Idiot. At that point, I nearly put down the paper, except that my gaze landed on a familiar name.

Also attending the summit is Major Theophilia Kallistrate, who will speak on the horrible conditions of Raven airmen.

"Oh my God," I whispered, sitting up straight. Theo was going to be in Jervan. Theo was going to be out of Rave.

This was my chance.

"Helmuth, break's over," Hebendon said, opening the door. "Time to get back to work."

"You bet your sweet ass it is," I said, standing and rushing out the door.

SEVEN

THEO

"Louder and slower."

I clenched my jaw and tried to remember where I was in my speech. Emilie stood at the back of the empty conference room, sipping on expensive tea and leafing through the strategy documents her staff had put together. I would've thought she wasn't paying attention to me, except that she constantly called out critiques of my speech.

She'd insisted I memorize it, stating that it would be less obvious that I was reading prepared remarks. Once I knew the words, we'd work on "the rest."

"Mael is a blight on the nose of civilization, a horrible reminder that..." I closed my eyes, struggling to remember what came next. Something about how Kylae remained as heartless as when they'd enslaved Ravens.

"Theo, if you aren't going to take this seriously, you won't get to speak," Emilie called out to me.

"I am taking this seriously," I said, thankful she wasn't calling me that infernal *'neechai* anymore. "But public speaking isn't exactly on the list of things taught in flight school." That was something of a lie; they did teach us what to say when commissioning or comforting the families of our fallen pilots.

"If you memorize the speech, it will come easier and you'll be able to focus on everything else, like speaking louder and slower," she said, for probably the fifth time. "Now take a deep breath, calm down, and try again."

I nodded and closed my eyes, inhaling and exhaling loudly.

"Good morning, President Bayard, President Kuman, Prime Minister Bouckley, esteemed members of the Jervan and Herin parliaments, and the delegates from the great, independent nation of Rave. Thank you for allowing me the chance to speak with you today. Rave is grateful for this opportunity to have a seat at the table at the Three Nations' Summit, and I am proud to represent her in this very important assembly."

So far so good.

"I come to you as a daughter of Rave. As you know, fifty years ago, after our nation was ruthlessly sacked of resources and enslaved by the Kylaens, we declared our independence. Although we have considered ourselves to be a sovereign nation, our former colonizers believe they have a claim to our land and our peoples. This cannot and must not stand in the international community any longer."

I swallowed, my pulse quickening and the cool coil of dread growing in my stomach.

"But Kylae is not without blame within its own borders. They have a prison in the mountains north of Norose. Their scientists claim it is safe, but the high death toll tells a different tale."

"I think... I think this was a secret testing laboratory. There are other binders of experiments with animals. That's where all the rabbits came

from."

"What could they possibly have been testing that would have warranted this kind of...horrifying..."

I looked down at the podium, taking a long breath as Emilie had instructed when my thoughts began to wander.

"Kylaens use the mineral ore barethium to strengthen their buildings, and their weapons—"

"Louder, *'neechai.*"

"Barethium is the ore they're mining out of the mountains, the same ore found in Rave. This lab was to test how much a human could take before it was fatal."

"Ravens...they were testing on Ravens."

"T-their weapons which they use to kill Ravens in a...blight on the civilization..."

"Wrong, *'neechai.*" Emilie sounded exasperated and I didn't blame her. I was exasperated with myself. Every time I started on the details of Mael, I began to recall the laboratory Galian and I had found on the island. We'd discovered the Kylaens knew the dangers of barethium, had been testing the effects of it on Raven slaves before they'd built a single processing plant. The photo of the deformed Raven with purple blotches and tumors was permanently burned into my memory.

As were the faces of every single person I'd left behind in Mael that day.

"Theo."

I jumped; Emilie had crossed the room and stood below my podium, a curious look on her face.

"Do you realize what sort of golden opportunity has been placed in your lap here?" she asked.

"Yes, I do. I'm sorry. I'll try again—"

"No, I think we're done for the day," Emilie said in a tone of voice that didn't bode well for me. "Come down here for a moment."

I stepped off the podium, and the weight left my shoulders as I slumped in a chair. Emilie handed me a glass of water which I gulped down thankfully.

"What's really going on?" Emilie said. "You breeze through the first part of the speech without a problem, so I know you aren't afraid of public speaking."

"I don't know," I whispered.

"I think you do."

I gulped more water and said nothing. I was so exhausted of all the lies that it was better simply to be quiet.

"Theo...listen to me," Emilie said quietly, placing a hand on my shoulder. "Do you know why Bayard chose you?"

I shrugged. "Because I was newsworthy."

"Because anyone else who went through what you did would've gone insane," she said. "But you arrived and sat in the hospital room and spoke about how grateful you were to be home. You saw the worst of Kylae and *survived*."

I swallowed hard, guilt gnawing at me again.

"I think you know this speech. You have one week before we leave for Jervan. I want you to spend it figuring out why you can't seem to get past your demons. I think once you work that out, you'll be able to deliver this speech as expected." She paused, and I almost saw pity in her eyes. "Perhaps a trip back to your old base would do you some good."

"Vinolas?" I asked.

"It's something Bayard suggested, actually," Emilie said. "You were preoccupied with the plight of our brothers and sisters there."

"It was stupid to even bring it up," I admitted, embarrassed at the memory. "I have a lot to learn about when to ask for things."

To my surprise, she smiled. "It's something you're passionate about, *'neechai*. Which is why a trip might help you refocus on what this speech could do for your country."

I didn't see how talking about a death camp in Kylae equated to helping young pilots at Vinolas, but...the idea of going back and seeing Lanis was appealing. I never really had a home to speak of, but if I had to pick one place, it was there.

GALIAN

Even though it was my childhood home, Kernaghan Castle was always imposing. When I'd come to Silas Collins' party, it had been dark, and the courtyard hummed with the cars and servants of Kylae's two hundred richest sons-of-bitches.

But today was void of all that excitement. The sky was a drab gray, with small flakes of snow spiraling down. Not enough to blanket anything, but enough to keep everyone but the two main guards inside the castle.

Martin drove my car through the gates into the cobblestone courtyard as he'd done a thousand times when I'd lived there. He pulled right up to the doors and turned off the car.

"Well, good luck," Martin said, looking over.

"Thanks," I said, feeling less sure of myself now that I was actually doing what I'd said I'd do. I fingered the photo of Theo in my pocket for good luck, and opened the car door, immediately doused in the bitter chill.

I squared my shoulders and closed the car door behind me, nodding my greeting to the two guards.

I noted the pinkness of their cheeks and asked, "How long's your shift?"

"Until noon," one responded.

"Stay warm," I replied with a half-smile.

"Thank you, Your Highness," the other replied, returning my smile as he pulled the door open.

The castle was toasty warm compared to the outside, a few fires crackling in the hearths lining the entrance hall. I shrugged off my thick, black wool coat and almost immediately, a servant appeared to take it from me. I snorted; I'd forgotten how much power I had in this place.

"Shall I inform your mother that you're here?" he asked.

"Actually, I'm headed to the other side," I said, amused at his widening eyes. The palace staff were the biggest gossips, and, undoubtedly, the source of much of the "inside information" leaks to the press. I was sure they knew every detail of the fight between my father and me. What surprised me more was the rest of the country remained ignorant of it.

Then again, knowing my father, it didn't surprise me at all.

The south wing of the castle was our private residences, but the northern side was dedicated to the business of ruling Kylae. Our parliament met in the basement, and my father's offices spanned the top level. When I was a boy, I used to stand in one of the giant windows and stare at the Madion Sea. But a new memory tainted that old one; I'd been in his offices when I'd found out he'd sent Theo to Mael.

I wasn't planning on breaking my promise never to speak to him again, so instead, I headed to the second level of the north wing, where most of the support staff worked. Including the heir to the throne, who was apparently deemed as important as my father's social secretary.

I approached the small, nondescript door and leaned against the frame, waiting for him to notice me. Rhys' office was simple, the walls covered in detailed maps of Kylae. It was no accident he'd chosen radar operator for his mostly-ceremonial military assignment. He'd always been obsessed with map-making and the boundaries of the countries.

His small desk had stacks of paper and a single lamp that illuminated the concentration lines on his face. He didn't look up from the paper he was scrawling on and had even begun mumbling to himself as he read over what he'd written.

"Hard at work, I see."

He glanced up, shock evident on his face. "G-Gally!" He jumped out of his chair and crossed the room in three steps to embrace me. He stepped back and gripped my shoulders. "This is a surprise!"

"I had a day off, decided I'd pop in and see my brother," I said, and took the seat in front of his desk. "You've done...absolutely nothing with this place."

"Father keeps me busy," Rhys said, pointing to a stack of papers on the desk. "Trying to detangle this Jervan issue. They've really stepped in it."

"Yeah, so why aren't you going to the summit?" I asked, cutting right to the chase. "And don't give me the same bullshit reasoning you give the press."

Rhys stared at me, processing my question for a moment then

sitting back. "She's going to be there. Of course you're interested."

"I'd like to offer my services to go in your stead," I said.

"No way."

"Why not?"

"Because, in the first place, last time I checked, you wanted nothing to do with this family or its policies regarding Rave," Rhys said. "And in the second place, Father said no one from Kylae may go. He's trying to send a message."

"Uh-huh." I kept a comment to myself. "Then I'll just go as a private citizen."

His eyes flashed. "Galian, don't you dare."

"Are you gonna stop me?" I asked. "Your Majesty?"

"And what, you're just going to waltz into the summit and ask Theo out? Announce your intention to marry her right there? Bring her back to Norose to share that tiny little apartment with you and Martin?"

"I wasn't going to be that direct, but if you think it would work..." I said with a grin.

Rhys put down his pen and sat back in his chair. "It doesn't matter what I say because you're going to do what you want. Why did you even bother to come ask me?"

"Because my preference is to go on Father's behalf so that we can make some headway with peace between Kylae and Rave," I replied. "But since that's about as likely as the Madion Sea freezing over..."

"Gally, this is not a fight you want to get in the middle of," he said, looking out the window for a moment.

"I want to be in the middle of it," I replied. "I'm already in the middle of it."

"You have no idea..." Rhys let out a long breath.

"Rhys, I can't... I miss her," I said after a moment. "I have to see her again. This is my only chance."

He stared out the window, unmoved by my speech as the concentration lines appeared between his brow.

"For fuck's sake, Rhys," I said, throwing my hands down. "Do you even—"

"Shut up," Rhys said suddenly, placing his hands on the table and leaning forward. "As the crown prince of Kylae and your brother, it's my job to tell you that you are not allowed to leave Kylaen airspace and you are absolutely not allowed to attend the Three Nations' Summit on behalf of Kylae."

I rolled my eyes and prepared to leave.

"But if *I* were the third prince of Kylae and I were hell-bent on going to Jervan, I wouldn't make a big spectacle of myself."

I opened my mouth to argue, but realization dawned.

He tapped his fingertips together. "I might ask my guard, who has a really good track record of sneaking into and out of countries, to help me get into Jervan without being followed by the media. Because if Father got wind that his son was meddling in the summit, it might cause a lot of problems."

I nodded. "Sound reasoning."

"And also, if I were the third prince of Kylae, I would remind myself that I was still a member of the royal family and I still had duties and expectations of my position. I would think long and hard about whether this woman, who is a sworn enemy to the crown, was worth all the potential trouble that this theoretical visit would cause."

I stood, but there was a smile on my face. "And if you were the third prince of Kylae, you'd know there was no other option than to go. Because she's the best thing that ever happened to you. And you love her."

"Just...be *careful*," Rhys called after me as I left his office, a new plan forming in my mind.

"No."

"Kader, you didn't let me finish!" I cried.

Upon my return from the castle, I'd gone straight to his apartment. I'd bounced my ideas off Martin, who seemed on-board with the idea, especially as Lakner, the city in Jervan where the summit was being held, was a known resort town and at least twenty degrees warmer than Norose.

Kader had been at home, thankfully, drinking a beer with Rosie, who'd excused herself as soon as I walked in the door. But if I'd assumed he'd be in a good mood, I was sorely mistaken.

"There are a thousand reasons why this is a terrible idea, most of which you don't know about," Kader barked. "So no, your ass is going to stay here in Kylae."

"Eli, don't be so mean," Rosie chided from the kitchen. "I think it's romantic."

"Romantic and a good way to get the boy in hot water with his father. Not to mention with other players *he doesn't even know about.*"

"Rhys said I could go," I said. I didn't care what Kader said. If he refused to take me, Martin had already said he and I would figure something out. The trick would be to make travel arrangements without letting the media (and, by extension, my father) know.

"I highly doubt..." He stopped, and his eyes flickered for a moment. "Your brother wasn't opposed to the idea, you say?"

"He's the one who told me to talk to you!" I plopped down in the chair across from him. "He said you were well-equipped to smuggle people into and out of countries."

"He did, did he?" Kader said, scratching his chin. "Anything else he mention? Did your mother approve this idea?"

I shook my head, unsure why my mother had any say in this. "I didn't see Mom. But Rhys said that if I went, I needed to fly under the radar and not make a big deal about being there. And I figure, once I get there, I won't even leave the hotel room—"

"We're leaving in four days," he said abruptly. "Tell Martin to be ready."

My mouth parted in surprise. "Just like that?"

"Do not speak a word of this to anyone else," Kader growled at me. "Do you understand? Not your mother, not your brother, not even in your sleep."

I nodded fervently, willing to do whatever it took. His abruptness was extremely curious, as I'd never known Kader to change his mind about anything. But I didn't care why or how it happened, because only one thing mattered in that moment.

I was going to see my Theo again.

THEO

Now entering
Vinolas Forward Operating Base

The familiar rusted iron sign greeted me as my military car drove onto the base. Everything was as I remembered it, though the armory seemed to have suffered some more recent bombing. But the hangar, the barracks, the supply buildings. It wasn't home, but I felt a piece of myself returning when I stepped out of the car. Especially when I saw Lanis waiting outside for me. I hadn't seen him since my official promotion ceremony, so I meant it when I told him it was damned good to see him.

"You as well," he said, patting my cheeks. "*neechai*."

"Don't call me that," I groaned, rolling my eyes.

He laughed. "I was surprised to get your call. Didn't think you ever wanted to set foot in this place again. Most don't once they leave."

My gaze drifted towards the hangar. "I felt like working on some planes. Got any?"

Again, he laughed, slinging an arm over my shoulders and walking me into the cavernous space. I found the spot where I used to leave my girl after missions, my heart twisting when I saw an unfamiliar plane instead.

"Who's the new captain of my squad?" I asked.

"Name's Avanti Kallistrate," Lanis replied. "She's pretty good. But the attacks been a little less frequent lately, so we haven't been as pressed. I wonder if the Kylaens have run out of bombs."

I smiled but then I stopped, attention diverting to our glory wall. It held photos of the Kylaen Royal Family. Before my time on the island, I'd known these people as abstract things that I had been taught to hate from a young age. Now, this was my *amichai's* family, and, of course, my *amichai* himself.

I walked up to the wall and placed a hand on Galian's photo. It was a different photo than I remembered. I lifted the edge of it and saw the familiar one with a big red 'x' on it.

"We were so pissed they found that bastard alive," Lanis replied with a shake of his head. "I still don't believe he was on that island for two whole months."

"Where do you think he was?" I asked, a smile tugging at my face.

"My theory? After your plane went down in the ocean, he turned tail and ran. Took him two months to scrounge up the courage to return home. So to save face, his father told everyone he was stranded."

I turned away from Lanis to hide my smile. "That sounds...plausible. Knowing the princeling."

"Especially considering he went back to the hospital after that. Might've been a power play with his father."

"Let's talk about something else, please. The princeling pisses me off."

So Lanis and I went to work, and the feel of metal and smell of oil was calming. Besides the major's gold star where my captain's bars had been, I felt like the old me. The engines were known entities that didn't have hidden agendas. Fixing planes, at least, I could do without feeling like I was venturing out onto a ledge by myself.

"So tell me about this trip to Jervan," Lanis asked.

"That's part of why I'm here," I said, pulling out the dipstick to check the oil level. "Emilie, Bayard's public relations lead, doesn't think I'm... She's not very impressed with me. I don't think Bayard is either. He said I was too...honest."

"I guess it's true, you gotta be a liar to be a politician," Lanis said. "Not like a king."

"Kings have to be political, too," I said, tightening a nut that had come loose.

"Not Grieg. Anyone disagrees with him and it's a one-way trip to Mael."

I didn't respond, my thoughts drifting back to Galian. He'd said that same thing, and at the time I'd thought it cowardice. Now that I'd had a taste of politics in Veres, I'd begun to see our conversations in a different light.

I pressed my hand against the engine and allowed the lonely to well up inside me. Glancing at Lanis, I wished I could confide in him. He was the closest thing I had to an ally in this country, but I still couldn't bring myself to tell him the truth. Not when he'd pulled me out of the Kylaen plane when I'd returned, nor in the hospital, and not now.

"How's that engine coming?" Lanis asked, wiping the oil off his hands. "Don't tell me you forgot how to fix it?"

"She's gonna fly great," I said, slipping off and down to the floor. "I'd fly her myself."

"Maybe you should come back here after Bayard's done with you," Lanis said. "We could use another mechanic."

I beamed at the compliment then faltered when I saw two small children wander into the hangar. They approached the ships that were three times as tall as they were and opened the hatches. The little boy crawled inside his engine bay while the girl climbed into her cockpit, the spoilers and ailerons on the wings moving up and down as she tested their functions.

"They get younger every year, it seems," Lanis said behind me. "Those two, Ranj and Elisha, they're pretty good about checking their engines. Wish the rest of them would more often."

"Those two want to survive," I replied.

We were silent for a moment, watching the young teenagers work on their planes. A heavy feeling settled on me.

"How do you do it?" I asked.

"Hm?"

"How can you work here, year after year, watching kids like that when you know they're..."

"They've offered me jobs in the headquarters over the years," Lanis said, his gaze still on the pilots. "Turned 'em down."

"Why?"

"I can't stop the Kylaens from attacking, and I can't help every kid whose plane goes down. But what I can do is fix as many planes as possible," Lanis replied, gripping my shoulder. "That's all I can do, all I can control in this crazy world. You just have to do what you can and leave the rest up to God. There was a reason why you survived that death camp, 'neechai."

There was a reason, and yet again, the weight of my undeserved survival hung around my neck, made heavier by the two child pilots who might not be as lucky as I was.

EIGHT

GALIAN

Even though I'd never seen Kader make a joke in the two years I'd known him, some part of me still wondered if his acquiescence to my pleas was his idea of a laugh. True to my word, I hadn't said a thing to anyone other than Martin, and he'd only gotten the bare bones of, "We're going to Jervan in four days. Don't tell anyone." I hadn't even asked for the time off at the hospital, hoping to beg for forgiveness.

At the stroke of midnight, Kader arrived with a knock on the door, and my butterflies turned into a firestorm of nerves. I went to fetch Martin, who was taking a nap before our departure, and when I returned to the living room, the lights were all off. Kader looked at the small black bag in my hand—all I had been allowed to bring—and nodded his approval before silently opening the door.

We slipped out into the empty hallway and padded to the back staircase of the building. Even though I wanted to, I didn't ask questions, simply thankful that Kader was taking me out of the country. He picked the lock on the back door of the stairwell leading out into the street and opened it. A cold blast of air hit me and I shivered, wishing I'd brought my thick coat. I'd figured it wouldn't be needed in Jervan and the less I brought, the better. Besides, I'd spent eight weeks wearing the same t-shirt and pants on an island; I could handle a few hours being chilled.

We must've walked for an hour. The streets of Norose were quiet, our three sets of footsteps echoing off the dark buildings. Kader kept to the shadows, leading me and Martin without ever checking to make sure we were still there. I understood that we needed to fly under the radar, but this level of secrecy seemed a bit extreme to me.

I'd been focused on trying to stay warm while putting one foot in front of the other, but when I glanced up, we were in a different part of town. In the city center where I spent most of my time, the barethium-laced buildings were tall, sleek, and modern. But here, the dark shapes here were shorter and bulkier. We must've ventured into the slums.

There were more people braving the cold, windy night, but I doubted they were there by choice. They, too, wore flimsy jackets and shivered around small bonfires that reminded me of myself and Theo on the island. They had sunken faces and dead eyes, and didn't even acknowledge us as we walked by.

Kader took a sharp left down a dark alley then stopped in front of a door. He knocked three times, paused, then knocked twice, four times, then once more. The door clicked and he held it open for me and Martin.

The lights were low, but it was still a change from the near pitch black of the streets. And it was warmer, but not by much. Four people sat around a table illuminated by a single light. I immediately felt their eyes on me, and took a step back, bumping into Kader.

"They're expecting you," he said, patting me on the shoulder and brushing past me. He walked up to the first figure, a woman who stood nearly as tall as Kader himself. They spoke in quiet murmurs for a moment before grasping arms.

Kader turned and placed a hand on the woman's shoulder. "Galian, this is Sayuri Johar, one of my oldest friends."

The woman walked closer to me, holding out her hand. I shook it, noticing the black tattoo that snaked up her arm, the buzzed haircut, the gold earrings that dotting her lobes. She surveyed me in the same cold, calculating way Kader always did. I wondered if I'd do any better with her than with him.

"Nice to meet you," I said, without anything else to say.

She released my hand and walked back to the table, leaning over a map of the Madion nations.

"Here's the plan, Highness: we'll be leaving here from Calandra airfield, that's a forty-minute drive," she said, pointing to a space north of Norose. "Kylae has an informal agreement with Herin to transport airplane parts every week. We'll leave from Ider Airfield and land here, in Gamar." She pointed to a spot on the northern coast of Herin. "From there, we've made arrangements to hop onto a Jervanian passenger plane that will take us right to Lakner." She pointed to the city on the coast.

I couldn't help but notice that we would cut out a good thousand miles if we flew directly over Rave to the capital of Jervan, but I kept that comment to myself.

"Listen up, Highness," Johar said, surveying me again. "This plan is predicated on us moving without attracting attention. Can you handle that?"

I nodded. I never wanted to attract attention in the first place.

"Once we get to Jervan, we'll figure out how to get you to your girlfriend. But first, we have to get there. Understood?"

Again, I nodded, a little awkwardly. This was a lot of effort just so I could see Theo.

But then again...

I glanced around the room at the others, who were murmuring to each other. This all seemed awfully convoluted to have come together so quickly. There were many players in the room I'd never seen before. Kader's excessive secrecy, the hour-long walk to the slums, flying all the way to Herin before getting to Jervan...

I said nothing, did as instructed, and kept my nose down. But I couldn't help wondering if I was simply a hanger-on to a much larger plot.

THEO

As jittery as I was to be leaving Rave for Jervan, especially as I still felt no better at delivering my speech than when Emilie had sent me to Vinolas, I was actually calmed by seeing the presidential plane in the airfield. Even though I wouldn't be at the helm, the idea of flying put a little smile on my face.

Our transport to Jervan was a repurposed cargo plane. Twin propellers sat on either side with blades bigger than my whole body. Inside, there were two sections I could see—rows of seats in the front, and a back room I presumed I was not allowed into. I took an empty seat next to a window and leaned back into the seat cushions.

I heard Emilie's voice before I saw her, and she boarded the plane with Wesson and another aide in tow. She hadn't asked to see me again, and I didn't know if that was a good thing or bad. She paused by my row as her aides passed her to disappear in the back.

"It will take a few hours to get to Lakner, so if I have time, please be ready to deliver your speech to me."

I nodded, secretly hoping we wouldn't have time. Emilie left through a divider in the center of the plane. Bayard's private office, I supposed.

A few minutes after I'd settled in, Bayard boarded the plane, followed by his most trusted aides, Ministers Breen and Lee, and Cannon. Bayard stood in the front of the plane, surveying the group in front of him with a pleased smile.

"Ravens, today is a monumental day for our country," he began, and I couldn't believe he was giving *another* speech, especially to those of us who already followed him blindly. "To meet with our Herinese and Jervanian siblings on equal footing. To have a seat at the table." His gaze landed on me, and I wished I could disappear. "To be able to speak about the horrible atrocities in our enemy's backyard." All I could do was half-smile at him. "Carry on, *'neechais and 'nichais*!"

He and his entourage walked through the center aisle, smiling and nodding at me as they passed. All except Cannon, who stopped at my aisle and leaned over the seat to whisper, "So don't fuck this up, *kallistrate*."

A woman much smarter than I could've retorted with something savvy, but I turned away from him. He took his victory and followed Bayard into the back of the plane.

I released a sigh and sank further into the cushion, focusing on the vista of the Raven airfield. The pilot radioed and signaled that we were ready to take off, and a few minutes later, the plane rolled forward.

I closed my eyes, imagining that I was back in my girl, taxiing out for a routine surveillance. The days we weren't fending off Kylaen attacks, I used to take a few planes out with me to patrol our zone. With no threat of danger, I was free to practice my aerial defensive maneuvers, and just take my girl as far as I knew she could go.

The plane picked up speed, and I flattened against the seat as the nose tipped upward then we were in the air. I opened my eyes and pressed my face to the small window, watching the airfield grow smaller and smaller beneath us. After a few minutes, the land below was nothing but dark brown squares. Every so often, we'd pass over an airfield or small city, and I'd try to guess which it was based on my limited knowledge of Raven geography.

I grew tired of this game after a few minutes, and glanced around at the others seated near me. Most of the important people were in the back with Bayard, but Wesson sat two rows behind me, reading through a docket and writing notes in the margins. He caught my gaze and offered no kindness.

"I do hope you're ready to give this speech, *'neechai*."

I nodded and turned around. I retrieved the weathered paper with my speech on it and read through it several times, if only to appear like I was preparing so Wesson wouldn't tell Emilie otherwise. What I was going to do when I stood in front of the international community and couldn't speak was beyond me.

Who knew, maybe I'd be dead by then?

I snorted at my joke and glanced out the window again. Blue ocean lay beneath us—the Madion Sea. This water that had surrounded Galian and me on the island. The water that lay between his country and mine.

Yet again, I wished to see him so badly it ached. It would be enough for me to hold him, to breathe him in for one moment. To watch him smile for me. I wondered if the Kylaens would replay my speech for him. Maybe I would add a line for him, to let him know I still waited for him. I still loved him.

I glanced down at the paper again. It wouldn't do much good to add a line if I couldn't choke out the speech in the first place, so I attempted to focus.

We landed in Jervan a few hours later, and I'd spent most of the flight looking at my speech but daydreaming about my *amichai*. Those seated in the front half of the plane disembarked first, crowding around Wesson as he told us which of the fine Jervan cars we would be riding in. I was assigned to cram into a leather-seated car with no less than six others from the security detail. Our car left first, as the detail needed to set up and sweep the hotel before Bayard's arrival.

The car drove through fields of sunflowers and vineyards, and the guards talked about wanting to taste fresh Jervanian wine while we were there. But when we crested a rather large hill, everyone in the car grew silent.

Even though I had to crane my head to see, the sight of Lakner took my breath away. White plaster houses with thatched roofs spread all the way to a turquoise bay. As we drove into the city, I drank in the new architecture, the blues and greens and browns that sprang up at me from every direction. We even passed by a building covered in lush green vines, and another with flower pots adorning the walls. I craned to look closer—there were actual flower pots built into the white-painted walls of the house.

We entered a main road, and I turned my head to see more. A bubbling fountain, a marketplace filled with people and things, gardens and parks and everything I'd never known to be in a city, free for everyone to use.

An ornate building lay in front of us, even more beautiful than *Platcha*. The car drove underneath a large stone awning and came to a stop.

"Where are we?" I asked the man to my right.

"Ginger Finn Hotel," he replied. "Nicest hotel in all the four nations."

I nodded my agreement and clambered out when I was allowed. I stood in the doorway, looking at the murals painted onto the walls, the carving of the stone columns, absorbing the pure luxury and richness.

And I was spending two nights there.

I covered my mouth to suppress a giggle, and turned to the security detail, who were unpacking their gear from the back of the car.

"I'm going to take a walk," I said.

"We're under orders not to leave the hotel," the head security guard said, throwing down a bag. "Sorry, *'neechai.*"

I frowned. I was in this beautiful city with so much to explore and I was trapped in the hotel? But then again, if the rest looked as beautiful as the lobby, perhaps this place wasn't the worst prison.

GALIAN

Jervan and everything about it could burn in a fiery hell.

We'd arrived in the city that smelled like a dead fish after nearly nine hours of flying and traveling with the world's worst people. I was obviously the odd man out, being told to sit and shut up and not make any sudden moves more times than I'd ever been in my life. I'd caught a catnap, but we'd hit rough turbulence over the mountains between Herin and Jervan, and I spent nearly an hour praying to whatever God was up there that I wouldn't die in a plane crash.

Then, after we'd landed in some barely-passable landing strip, we piled into a rickety car that stank of gasoline, and drove for another three hours before finally reaching Lakner. The only good thing about reaching the city was that Kader and Johar dropped Martin and me off in a raucous marketplace, telling us to stay within the square until they finished whatever they were actually there to do. I assumed they would be back for us, since I doubted they would let me come up with a plan to get to Theo on my own.

The marketplace was full of people jostling and pushing us around as they filled wicker baskets with goods. I kept close to Martin, who seemed more at ease and struck up easy conversations with some of the patrons. He'd even figured out where we could grab some breakfast, though the coffee was weak as hell.

"Cheer up, Jem," Martin said, noting my scowl. "You're gonna see your girlfriend today. And," he leaned in close, "there ain't one of those Goddamned photographers around."

I let my bad mood fall away. I was sure someone would've caught wind by now that I was out and about, but so far, my cap and sunglasses were working. Or, more likely, the Jervanese weren't as keyed into the Kylaen royal family as others were.

Martin had stopped in front of a small booth where an old, wizened woman was selling wood carvings, taking his time to examine each of the figurines. I picked up a fish and marveled the artistry of it, and the talent that must've gone into it. It almost looked alive in my hand.

"These are beautiful," I said to her, and she nodded her thanks with a wide, toothless smile. I turned to Martin and held up the small fish. "Do you think Theo would like this?"

He crinkled his nose. "Nah, she's not into that kind of stuff."

"Oh?" I chuckled at his familiarity. "You know her so well?"

"Just from what you've told me," Martin said, glancing around the street. I wasn't sure if it was to check for assailants or because he was bored. "She doesn't strike me as someone who likes a whole bunch of trinkets. She'll just be glad to see you."

A knife twisted in my heart. That was the other reason for my sour mood. After we'd left Kylae, I'd begun to worry that, perhaps, Theo *wouldn't* be happy to see me. After all, there was no reason she should still love me. I hadn't closed Mael or saved any of the prisoners there. As easily as this trip had come together (for whatever ulterior motives there were), my gut told me I didn't deserve to see her again—and I was worried she'd agree.

The old woman was watching me carefully, so I turned to Martin. "Can you spot me some gold? Maybe I'll get this for my mom."

Martin dug in his pocket and tossed the woman her price. I pocketed the small fish figurine and thanked her with a smile.

We wandered around the marketplace until Kader and Johar found us again. They wore neutral expressions, so I supposed that whatever they'd gone to do had gone well. They said nothing, but motioned for us to follow them.

We left the busy marketplace and found an even busier outdoor cafe where Kader and Johar ordered large plates of eggs, bacon, some Jervanian delicacy with pork fat and corn meal, and coffee. It was so loud I could barely hear myself think, but perhaps that was the point.

"We found your girlfriend," Johar said, leaning over the table. "Staying at the Ginger Finn with the rest of the delegates. The place is crawling with security and media. It's gonna be difficult to get in there unnoticed."

I furrowed my brow and stared out at the street. A wall of flower vases peppered with red buds stared back at me.

"Why don't I just make my grand appearance?" I asked. "Pretend like I'm on vacation, oblivious to all this bullshit going on."

"Do you really think your father will believe that?" Kader asked.

"It's not him I need to convince, it's the media," I said. "I'll go to the pool, flirt with a bunch of girls. Play stupid. It wouldn't be too out of character."

Kader didn't look too opposed to the idea, but glanced at Johar, who frowned. "Eli, a word."

As they walked away from the table, Martin shrugged and leaned over to take a piece of bacon from Kader's plate.

I turned to watch the Jervanians eating and talking loudly. Many of them wore easy smiles and lacked the tension most Kylaens had. Their skin was brown from the ever-present sun, but not as dark as the Ravens'. The atmosphere from the hundred-year-old cafe was infectious, and my mood improved somewhat.

Kader and Johar returned, the latter looking apprehensive. "How were you thinking of announcing your presence?" Kader asked.

"Just walk in the front door?" I said with a shrug. "I'm pretty recognizable... I think? It might take a minute for the media to get wind of me, but—"

"And you're willing to accept whatever punishment your father metes out because of this?" Kader replied. "I'll remind you that he left you on an island."

"Do you really think he's going to be *that* pissed at me for sneaking into a country just to get laid?" I asked, adding hastily, "I mean, that's not really why I'm here. But that's what *he'll* think. I won't attend the summit. I won't even act like I know what it is. He already thinks I'm an idiot—"

"Actually, he thinks you're quite smart," Kader interrupted.

I paused, considering the many layers of deception. "But does he think I'm involved in whatever you two are here to accomplish?"

Kader and Johar shared a glance.

"I doubt that either of you would've agreed to ferry me across the Madion Sea just to see Theo," I said dryly. "I won't ask what it is, or why you're doing it. But whatever it is, my father doesn't know that I'm involved, correct?"

"That is...correct," Kader said after a long pause.

"Therefore, me being here does nothing to put your mission in jeopardy. In fact, it might actually help you two provide a cover *if* you're found out. As far as what my father will do to me, as long as I act like an idiot, he'll have no reason to punish me. He's more concerned with what people think than the truth anyway."

Johar actually looked impressed. "I underestimated you, Galian."

I tried not to look too smug.

NINE

THEO

The weather was pleasant, not too hot, but not too cold that the water was uncomfortable. I dipped my feet in one of the three outdoor pools, watching the tourists from Herin, Jervan, and Kylae enjoy themselves. To my eyes, I was the only Raven there, but I felt just as welcome as back in Veres. I supposed no one was eager to perpetuate a war while on vacation.

My time was cut short when Emilie spotted me and beckoned me inside. The rest of the Raven delegation had arrived, but when I joined the crowd sitting in the hotel bar, Bayard and the ministers weren't there. They'd taken a meeting at the Jervanian palace with the president, or so I gleaned from conversations.

Emilie seemed a bit on edge as she gathered the attention of the ten people sitting on antique chairs in the bar. She told us she'd demanded a meeting space in the hotel, but there was none to be had at the moment. Something in her tone of voice told me that she'd ordered the hotel staff to *make* space.

"Bayard won't be back for at least two hours," Emilie said,

glancing at her watch. "We will probably need to tweak his talking points based on his discussions with the Jervan president. Wesson, take the lead on that."

He nodded and scribbled in his book.

"Aruna," Emilie said, nodding at a younger girl I'd seen in a few meetings. She paled at being called on, but held her pen ready. "Find Cannon and tail him. Make sure he stays on message and doesn't dally in anything...embarrassing." She paused, a disgusted look crossing her face. "And if he does, make sure nobody knows. Talk to Wesson for crowns if you need it."

She nodded with a small smile. She might take that mission a little *too* seriously.

"And *'neechai*," Emilie said, grabbing my attention. "You and I will spend the afternoon working on your speech. I trust that you've resolved whatever...issues you were having."

I dipped my head, even as dread coiled in my stomach. Emilie moved on to someone else, so I pulled the speech out from the calf-pocket of my jumpsuit. I'd practiced it once or twice while sitting in the pool, reading quietly to myself and envisioning what it would be like to speak in front of the Madion nation leadership.

But even in my head, I still stumbled through the parts about Mael. Stumbling wouldn't cut it for Emilie, so I prayed for a miracle.

"What's going on out there?" Emilie said, squinting to her left. I followed her gaze and saw a crowd of people standing at the hotel's entrance, craning over each other to get a look at whatever was outside.

I stood with the rest of the Ravens and walked into the lobby. The crowd grew more frenzied and then the front doors of the hotel opened.

The crowd pushed in then parted, and in strolled the last person

I'd ever expected to see again.

"Amichai."

He was beautiful, a wide smile on his face and his gait confident. His brown hair was clipped shorter and he no longer wore the beard I'd grown accustomed to seeing on our island. He paused in the middle of the lobby to talk to two journalists who'd approached him, then threw his head back and laughed.

Then his eyes locked with mine.

It was as if everything and everyone disappeared. The corners of his mouth turned up and I suddenly forgot how to breathe. Electricity crackled in the hundred steps that lay between us, and I could've sworn I knew exactly what he was thinking. If I'd had any doubt about his reason for arriving in this city, in this hotel, on this day, it vanished in that moment.

As desperately as I wanted to run to him, for some reason, my legs wouldn't move. Something was keeping me from going to him, but for the life of me I couldn't remember what it was...

"What in the world is the princeling doing here?" Cannon's voice pierced my bubble, and I wrenched my eyes away from Galian's. Where I was, who I was with, and my purpose rushed back to me like waking from the best dream into a nightmare.

I found my voice. "I have no idea."

"I doubt he's meddling in the summit. He'd be stupid to disobey his father." Cannon shrugged mightily. "Then again, the princeling's never been too smart."

"Right, he's an idiot," I said.

Stupid, *stupid* princeling. How could he be so irresponsible as to come to Jervan? Especially after his father had forbidden anyone from Kylae to attend, or so Emilie had told us in a meeting earlier that week.

And he just walked through the front door, announcing to the entire world that he was there.

I realized I was still watching him when Cannon's voice again interrupted my thoughts. "Come now, *kallistrate*, don't be star struck. He's *just* a prince."

I nodded hastily and turned away from him so I wouldn't be tempted to stare. "Just a prince, right."

And my *amichai*.

GALIAN

She was the most beautiful thing I'd ever seen.

I drank in the sight of her: the way her velvet lips parted, how her big brown eyes widened slightly. Her hair pulled back into a bun, her Raven uniform immaculate. The shape of her body. How her dark skin had grown pale.

"If you're trying to pretend you don't know her, perhaps you shouldn't stare," Martin snickered beside me. "I'll stare at her for you. She's a lot cuter than I remembered."

"Right," I said, turning away. "So do you think it worked?"

I had just finished talking to a reporter, feigning ignorance about any sort of summit or why the leaders from three of the four Madion nations were in this city. I'd made sure to talk about my plans to drink heavily and meet some hot Jervanian girls, just to play the part.

I attempted to keep the giddy smile off of my face as I checked into the hotel. When I snuck another glance at her, she'd turned away from me, but the rest of the Ravens kept staring at me, pointing and discussing amongst themselves. I wondered what they were saying.

"I apologize, Your Highness," the clerk said with all the sincerity of a wet mop. "All of our suites have been reserved by delegations to the summit. The only rooms I have are the basic rooms."

"I doubt I'll be sleeping in my own room anyway," I said with an overly confident grin.

The clerk, predictably, rolled his eyes in disgust.

I caught Martin's eye, and he snorted.

"Your keys, *Your Highness*," he said, sliding over two access cards. "Please be advised that there is a two hundred crown cleaning fee for any...destruction."

I winked at him then motioned for Martin to grab our bags. I would've carried my own, but it would've been contrary to the part I was playing.

"You sure faked that well," Martin said, tossing my bag to me once we were safely in the elevator.

"I wish I could say I've never been that much of an asshole before," I said with a small grimace.

We got to our room and Martin went out on the balcony to alert Johar and Kader of our room location. I sat on the edge of the bed, tapping my foot nervously. It was very hard to know Theo was so close and I couldn't hold her yet. But all my worry that she'd be upset to see me had disappeared when I locked eyes with her. For whatever reason, my girl still loved me as much as I loved her. And that, more than anything, was a huge weight off my shoulders.

Kader and Johar arrived in our room a few minutes later, and we crowded around one of the two beds to make our plan of action.

"The Ravens have a block of rooms on the fifth floor," Kader said. "I'm not sure which one belongs to your girlfriend, so you'll have to wait until she goes back to her room to find out. I wouldn't recommend knocking on the door, so you might have to go in through the balconies. The sun should be setting soon, so you'll have cover of darkness."

I stared at Kader, a little worried that he would let me crawl across balconies five stories in the air just like that. "You really think I can do that?"

"I'm going with you," Johar replied. "But you're going to do your own climbing."

"What if we get caught?" I asked. *Or fall?*

"Then we'll just chalk it up to the dumb princeling looking to get laid," Kader said, shooting me a knowing look. "Speaking of which, you'll need to go back downstairs and do some more *convincing*."

"Why?" I said, still considering how I was going climb up balconies.

"In the first place, your girlfriend seems to be working with Bayard's public relations aide," Johar said. "So we won't know which room she's in until she's dismissed."

"And in the second place," Kader said, cutting her off, "the word downstairs is that you're here to fuck up the summit. If that becomes the narrative, you're the one who's fucked, understand?"

I nodded. "So what do I need to do?"

"Martin'll keep an eye on Theo and give you the signal when she returns to her room. Until then, go be your usual charming self."

THEO

I stood in the bathroom for nearly half an hour, staring into my own wide eyes.

Galian was there. Galian was in this hotel, perhaps on a floor above or below me. Galian, the man I'd been dreaming of, the man that I'd been aching for, was now close enough to touch. It would be impossible for me to speak to him in plain view; it wasn't as if I could simply walk up to him and strike up a conversation. A public relations nightmare.

I couldn't touch him. I couldn't even act like I knew him. He was just an idiot. A stranger. My mortal enemy.

My soulmate.

I splashed water on my face and left the bathroom. With the appearance of the third prince of Kylae, Emilie's demands for a private meeting space grew loud enough to hear from across the lobby. The hotel staff, eager to prevent the Madion War from erupting next to the front desk, provided her a room on the first floor. The ten of us, plus Cannon, were crowded around a small bed.

Emilie was leading a discussion on which Herinese minister to press about what topic, so I took the opportunity to slip out through the sliding glass door that faced one of the pools in the hotel and sat in a chair. The courtyard was open to the blue sky above, and the air was warm and sticky thanks to the glittering pool in its center.

Facing away from the Ravens, I bit my lip with a smile on my face. I couldn't help it; as dangerous and risky as it was for either of us to be seen together, I was giddy with excitement to see him again.

I didn't have time to dwell on Galian, because the door behind me opened and Emilie joined me on the patio. Wasting no time, she said, "I want to hear your speech."

A speech? Oh, right, I was supposed to be remembering a ten-minute diatribe against Galian's country. How did it begin again? "P-president Jervan..." My eyes widened, and no more sounds came from my mouth.

My *amichai* had entered the pool area, bare-chested and pale, with a charming and sexy grin on his face. On his arm were two Jervanian girls, both flustered with red faces. There was a second, younger man, who I believed was the guard Galian lived with in Kylae. He carried an armful of drinks. The four of them took lounge chairs and Galian's guard passed the drinks out. The girls paid him little attention, more focused on the handsome prince who'd decided to flirt with them.

"Theo," Emilie said, snapping her fingers in front of me. "I don't know what the princeling is playing at, but we won't let him distract us. Your speech, please."

She handed me a copy of the words I was supposed to be saying. They made no sense, and I couldn't concentrate. Not with my *amichai* mere feet from me, and hanging on other women.

He sat between the girls and they cozied up under his arm the way I used to. I knew it had to be a farce, but jealousy roared inside me as I watched them paw my *amichai*.

Fat chance, girls, that man is mine tonight.

"*Theo*," Emilie said. "Theo, you need to focus."

"I'm sorry," I murmured. "I can't concentrate. I'm too...nervous." I hoped I looked nervous and not murderous. It would've helped if I'd been better at concealing my emotions, but even then, I wouldn't have stood a chance with him so close.

"I understand that," Emilie said, sitting back. "But this is important. This is your chance to speak in front of the world and tell your story. To make a difference. Remember?"

I nodded, arguing with the part of my brain that wanted to run across the courtyard. I had wished for him to come to me, but now, realistically, his timing couldn't have been worse. I had a speech to give, one which I continued to stumble through. And he'd probably come to my room, we'd make love all night long and...I kept the lovesick smile off of my face before it appeared. *That* was precisely why him being in Jervan was a terrible idea.

Across the pool, his gaze locked with mine. Then, to my horror, he blew a kiss my way.

"That son of a bitch," Emilie growled, standing up. "Disgusting pig. Foul creature. Let's go inside."

"Horrible," I said lightly, following her inside and sneaking a look back at Galian. I hoped he saw the smile on my face.

My focus was effectively shot, as I attempted to deliver my speech five more times and couldn't even get the opening remarks right. I just kept envisioning Galian's bare chest, his handsome smile, and then my mind began to spin wildly sexual fantasies of us meeting in my room later. Eventually, Emilie threw her hands up in disgust.

"I can tell that you're tired from the trip," she said. "Go to your room and get some rest and *please* be ready tomorrow."

Wesson walked into the room at that moment, interrupting us. "Emilie, the Herin delegates have invited us out to dinner tonight. They especially want to meet her."

"I...uh..." I swallowed hard. "I'm not sure that's such a good idea tonight."

Emilie's head swiveled around. "'*neechai*, your speech is just one part of your campaign. If you want to change people's minds, you'll have to talk to them. Get to know them. Show them that you're human."

"Perhaps she's right," Cannon said, lounging on the chair behind me. "*Kallistrate* is wooden at best, and at her worst...you might as well send the princeling instead. He might do a better job."

I would remember to thank Cannon later. "Emilie, this speech... I want to practice it more before tomorrow. As you said, I only have one chance. I'd be better off if I just...spent all night practicing it."

"Fine, fine," Emilie said. "But I want you down here first thing in the morning to give the speech *in its entirety.*"

I nodded and walked as casually as I could out of the room, then, once the door was closed, ran for the elevator.

GALIAN

I'd found two willing participants at the now-deserted bar, and they'd been eager to fawn over me. I felt kind of bad for leading them on, but maybe once I made my exit, Martin could entertain them. He seemed up for the task.

I'd been at the bar when I saw her appear near the pool, and, although I knew it was a little risky, I wanted to be out there. I had no idea what she was thinking, but I hoped she knew that I would be there soon.

I'd convinced the girls to go to the pool, but by the time we'd gotten there, Theo had been joined by the pretty Raven woman who had been screaming in the lobby earlier. By her posture and Theo's submission to her, she must've been the aide Kader was talking about. The woman had noticed me staring, so I'd done the only thing I could— act like an ass and blow her a kiss.

Still, the look of shock and amusement on Theo's face was worth the fury on the other woman's as she pulled Theo back inside the room.

But I had to be careful. This was about drawing attention to myself, and not Theo. I didn't know what they'd do to her if they found out about our relationship, and I was damned if I'd mess anything up for her.

"Oh, quit antagonizing our colonists," Martin said, his arm slung over the shoulders of the girls as Theo and the other woman went back into the room.

"Stop," the girl on the left said, swatting him on his stomach. "Rave should be left alone. Galian, why does your father keep bombing them?"

"Who cares?" I said, hating myself. I could barely see into the room Theo'd disappeared into, but I saw Kader appear around the side of the pool. That was my cue. "Martin, I'm going to get a beer. Keep the girls warm for me, will ya?"

"Yes, sire."

I snorted at Martin's overt bow, and hurried over to Kader. He handed me a shirt and we walked through small walkway to the back of the hotel where Johar was waiting for us. She wore a black tactical suit that left me feeling woefully underprepared in my shorts and t-shirt.

"The rest of the Ravens are in their meeting room, so now's the best chance to get to her room," Kader said.

I glanced upward, my vision swimming. "And you don't think anyone will notice a guy climbing up balconies?"

"Getting cold feet?" Johar asked.

"N-no," I said, shaking my head. "Just...if I splatter on the ground, know it was in pursuit of love."

I followed Johar around to the back of the hotel and could see why she was unconcerned about being spotted. A river cut the ground mere steps away, presumably flowing down to the inlet at the bottom of the city. On the other side was a park shaded pink by the setting sun.

"Let's go," Johar said, pulling herself up onto the first balcony. She had a good five inches on me, so I had to jump and pull myself up, wishing I'd spent a bit less time at the hospital and more time doing pull-ups. By the time I'd scrambled over the first railing, she was already hanging from the one above.

"Slow down!" I hissed to her.

"Hurry up, Jem."

I scowled; so now I was Jem to everybody.

My hands, arms, and shoulders ached by the time we reached the fifth floor. Johar tossed me a small tool.

"Use it on the doors," she said, walking toward the glass of the guest room.

I stood, watching her for a moment, and she glanced at me over her shoulder. "Well, get going."

"Aren't you searching the rooms with me?" I asked.

"Nope." She clicked her own tool into the lock and carefully slid the door open.

"But what if this is Theo's room?"

"It's not. Trust me."

Not wanting to know which Raven room Johar was breaking into, or why she was so sure it wasn't Theo's, I lifted myself onto the railing between this balcony and the next and slid over. With one more glance at Johar and the mystery room, I stuck the small tool into the lock on the glass door and heard it click. I slid the door open and walked insidee.

There was nothing to mark it as occupied except for one black bag in the center that hadn't been unpacked. Conscious of what Kader had said about making sure no one knew I'd been there, I unzipped the bag and carefully pawed through it. Men's underwear—definitely not Theo's room.

I zipped the bag back up and made sure nothing else was amiss before returning to the balcony. As I exited, Johar was out of the room, a disgruntled look on her face. She saw me on the other balcony and saluted me before climbing over the edge.

So I was on my own now. Perfect.

I climbed over the balcony to the next room. This one had several bags on the ground, dresses in the closet, and the person had already unpacked hair brushes, makeup, and jewelry.

Definitely not Theo.

I was turning to leave when I heard a key slide into the door. Panicking, I dove outside onto the balcony and closed the door, praying no one had heard me or could see me. The thick blinds that kept the light out of the room were mostly closed behind me, but I could still hear the conversation inside the room.

"...just don't know about her. She's got some kind of mental block." That sounded like the woman who'd been screaming before.

"I could deliver my speech, you know." A man.

The woman sighed. "Yes, Mark. But Theo deserves a chance to try."

"She's been trying, and she's been failing miserably. She's going to embarrass the country tomorrow."

I glared at the other end of the balcony.

"You know I won't let that happen. If Theo can't give her speech tomorrow, you're up. Now get to your room and get dressed. And *please* don't embarrass us on this trip. The last thing we need is another sex scandal from you."

I heard the door close behind him and glanced into the room. The woman sat at the desk and was applying makeup. I slid to the other side of the balcony and hopped the railing, making sure to listen carefully before picking the lock on the next balcony.

TEN

THEO

The elevator doors opened, and I walked out onto the ornate carpeted floor, feeling both exhilarated and exhausted.

I'd accepted the fact that he *wanted* to see me, but how was he to know where I was? There were hundreds of rooms in this hotel. Would he be stupid and just knock on every one? What if he happened upon Cannon's room? Or Emilie's? Emilie would probably call hotel security, but Cannon might hurt him. I approached my door and held my breath as I unlocked it.

It was empty of everything except the black bag I'd hastily thrown on the bed before returning downstairs.

"G—Anyone in here?" I called, looking around. I opened my closet and checked the small bathroom. He wasn't there.

A cloud of disappointment settled over of me. Perhaps I'd been wrong. Maybe I'd just wanted to see the love so badly I'd imagined it. Or perhaps it *was* just a coincidence that he'd shown up in this hotel.

A knock on my door jarred me from my thoughts. Heart pounding, I slowly approached the door, praying with all my heart that

Galian *wasn't* on the other side—and at the same time, praying that he was. I took a deep breath and unlocked the door.

And came face-to-face with Emilie.

"Hi," I said, my heart still pounding.

"I just wanted to check on you," she said, inviting herself into the room. "Are you worried that the princeling is here?"

I cleared my throat and shook my head, hoping I'd miraculously become a better actress in the next few seconds. "Why would it?"

"The Kylaens weren't even supposed to be here, and now..." She sighed and shook her head. "I doubt he's here for anything other than to get his dick wet."

I coughed into my hand to hide the mixture of amusement and horror.

"I'm leaving to meet with the Herinese delegation," she said. "*Please* be ready for tomorrow."

I nodded. "I will. I promise."

She didn't look all that confident, but she bid me farewell and a good night, and left me alone in my room. I turned and flung myself on the bed, a hurricane of worry and anticipation swirling through me. I began to hate my own mind; I should've been worried about making a speech to the international community, instead I was fretting about whether or not a boy was coming to visit me.

Not a boy, I reminded myself, *My* amichai.

I heard a small click on the glass door leading out to a balcony and I sat up, sure that I'd imagined it except that the drapes fluttered, and a shadow was visible on the other side. Before I could open my mouth to speak, the figure on the other side walked into the room.

It was him. All of him. Really standing there in the middle of my room. His hair, his body, his chest, his lips, his eyes, his...I couldn't tell if I was dreaming or not. Had I wanted him to appear so desperately that I'd hallucinated him?

"Hey." His voice reverberated through me. God, had he always sounded this sexy? I tried to keep my composure and remember that people who wanted him dead were mere walls away from us.

"H-hey..." Was that really all I could say?

He stalked toward me with a strange and hungry look on his face. Words failed me when he pulled me into his arms. I shakily reached up to touch his face, scarcely believing that he was really, truly there. My fingertips pressed into his soft, pale cheek, and the sensation washed over me. His skin, his body, *he was really there.*

"*A-amichai,*" I whispered.

He took my hand and kissed it, and my relief welled to the surface. My lip trembled, and tears splashed down my face. I knew, somewhere in the back of my mind, that this moment was stolen, that it wouldn't last, and soon I'd be back in Rave and he in Kylae. The world that had torn us apart would come crashing back in.

But in that moment, I was willing to endure the pain for this one moment of perfection.

Then his lips covered mine, and I lost whatever semblance of self-control I had left.

GALIAN

A sob escaped her lips as they moved against mine, and she

pulled away, her cheeks wet and her face puffy. She began to speak, l
I couldn't understand between the sobs and the high-pitched whin
She buried her head in my chest and sobbed harder.

"You know, this wasn't how I pictured this happening," I sai
resting my cheek on her forehead and rubbing her back. "I though
there'd be less crying and more ripping off clothes."

She snorted. "Good to know your jokes haven't improved."

I laughed, holding her closer, suddenly overcome with a
tightness in my chest. I'd missed Theo, but to hear her voice, to know
she found me ridiculous even after all this time, struck a chord in me.

She sniffed hard and looked up at me, a smile finally gracing her
beautiful lips. "I can't believe you're really here. You have *no idea* how
much I needed you, *amichai*."

I didn't know if the word had some magical property or if
knowing the intent behind it gave it power, but a chill ran down my
spine. I kissed her again, this time opening her mouth with my tongue
and tasting her. She moaned and grasped my shirt.

"You taste the same," she whispered against my lips.

"Do I? I've brushed my teeth a few more times..."

"Goddamn, I missed your lame jokes," she said with a giggle.
Pulling back, she stared at me like I was the most amazing thing she'd
ever seen, and a light flickered in her eyes. And just like that, she was
my Theo—the girl who'd kept me sane and alive for two months, the
one I'd fallen head over heels for despite all rational thought or the
consequences.

She rested her hands on my chest and kissed the corner of my
mouth, my chin, my neck, and a fire began to grow. It had been four
long months since I'd touched her, and I was eager to make up for lost
time. I slipped my hands underneath her rear and picked her up, loving

...er giggling as I carried her to the bed.

...grinned at me when we plopped down, brushing a stray

...face. "You didn't come all the way to Lakner just to get in

...did you?"

...What can I say, it's a perk," I replied, gazing at her body. I

...she'd been eating better. Even the first day on the island,

...en too thin, but as I reacquainted myself with the shape of her

noticed the change.

"*Amichai*," she whispered in the soft purr that reminded me of

...st night she'd said the word to me.

"I love you," I said, although the sentiment fell a bit flat. I was

...ing to think the Ravens had something with these special words.

She leaned up to capture my lips and pull me on top of her.

THEO

He moved slowly, taking his time unbuttoning my jumpsuit
and kissing every inch of my exposed skin as he went. I was grateful for
his restraint, for I wanted to savor every second with him. He reached
the last button and climbed his way back up my body, covering my
mouth again and wrapping a hand around one of my breasts. I moaned
slightly and he lifted his lips.

"Now remember to be quiet," he said, nipping at my neck. He
pushed the sleeves off my jumpsuit and unhooked my bra. "Or, on the
other hand, don't."

Before I could respond, his mouth had covered the mound of

flesh and I arched my back, letting the sensation roll over me. With his other hand, he massaged the other breast, toying with the sensitive nipple and glancing up at me with inquisitive eyes.

He lifted his mouth and pulled the rest of my jumpsuit off, kneeling over my body with an odd look on his face. His gaze slid over every inch of my body, slowly and deliberately.

"I want to imprint you into my brain," he said with a smile. "Because my memory of you is not nearly as good as you look right now."

"I've bathed a few more times," I retorted, earning a devilishly handsome smile from him. I kissed him again then pulled his shirt over his head to reveal the chest that I'd seen downstairs. The memory made me laugh.

"What?" he said.

"I was just thinking about you down at the pool," I said, running my hands along his bare skin. "Flirting with those girls."

"I had to make it look good," he said, removing my hand from his chest and pushing me back down on the bed. Before I could say another word, he hooked a finger around my underwear and slid them off.

I sat up when he pressed his mouth to the warm center between my legs, the unfamiliar feeling almost overpowering. He looked up at me, waiting for my signal, and I half-smiled at him. Then he went to work, sucking and nipping and licking and all manner of other things I couldn't even begin to describe. My body was no longer my own, twisting and gripping the sheets as he drew me higher and higher, slowly pulling me to the apex which I hadn't felt since our night on the island.

My body seized, and I bit down on my lip to keep from

ming. I came back to myself, although the ecstasy was still flooding
y body. I caught his eye as he kissed the inside of my thigh and
climbed up to join me at the head of the bed.

"You okay?" he asked, running his hand down my side.

I nodded, as words weren't coming. I couldn't even remember
my own name.

"You sure?"

I nodded faster.

"You need a second?"

I nodded again, but cracked open one eye. He looked awfully
smug. And I would be lying if I said I didn't love his smug face.

"I used to think about doing that to you when I saw you in the
news," he said.

"You've been watching me?" I whispered then smiled. "I've
been watching you."

"You mean the tabloid photos?" he asked. "Have you been
getting the magazines just to gaze upon my face?"

I snorted and rolled my eyes. Just because I hadn't seen him in
four months and couldn't keep my hands off him didn't mean I was
going to let him get away with his pompous princeling act.

"Oh, so you've recovered?" he asked, moving his hand to where
his mouth had been. I was still sensitive, and I jumped as he slipped his
fingers inside of me.

"Barely," I whispered, closing my eyes and letting him work his
magic. He knew the right way to touch me, the right movements, and
before I knew it, he was covering my mouth with his as I came again.
He paused a moment before continuing, apparently intent on making
me pass out from pleasure, but I stopped him. I didn't want his fingers,
I wanted the hardness pressed against my leg. I wrapped my hand

around it and he moaned as I gently stroked him. I took my time, exploring the sensitive part of him, until he growled and wrenched my hand away, gasping for air.

"Enough of that," he said, his cheeks flushed. His hand still around my wrist, he grabbed my other and pushed them over my head. He spread my legs with his knees and settled between them, watching my face. I nodded to him and he slowly entered me.

I let out a breath. It was still painful, but not nearly as much as our first night together. Like with everything else, he went slowly, taking his time to make sure I felt every inch of him. I arched my back and moved with him.

"Theo," he whispered, stopping and looking down at me.

I closed the space between us with a kiss, and he pushed me back on the pillow, exploring my mouth with his tongue. I wrapped my legs around his waist to keep him close and he groaned, panting.

Then, in a move that I wasn't quite sure how I managed, I rolled him onto his back.

He frowned and his mouth opened in confusion, but I grinned and moved my hips against him. Almost immediately, his face relaxed into a smile.

"Where'd this come from?" he asked, his voice gravelly.

"Do you like it?" I asked, though the answer was written on his face.

He grabbed my hips and adjusted the movement and a shiver ran up my spine. I continued to move as he'd showed me, and his hands fell away to grip the edges of the bed. His eyes closed, and he groaned, his face turning redder with each passing moment. My own fire was growing and I knew I was about to reach my peak again. I closed my eyes and moved harder, quicker, his soft moans telling me that this was what he wanted as well. I felt myself reach the edge again and let the beautiful feeling wash over me as I slowed my rhythmic movements to a stop.

"God damn, Theo."

I looked down at my *amichai*, his eyes wide, his mouth open and pink, his cheeks and the top of his chest bright red. The light sheen of sweat that glistened on his chest as it rose and fell with great effort. His eyes finally settled on me, and he laughed, running his hands along the sides of my body.

Unable to resist, I grinned down at him. "*That* is what I used to think about when I saw you in photos."

GALIAN

She climbed off me and I pulled her into my arms. There was nothing in my brain but the ceiling and my rapid heartbeat and her resting in my arms.

After a moment, I noticed she was watching me. "What?"

"How've you been?" she asked with an amused smile.

I couldn't help but smile back at her. "You pull that move on me and ask me how I've *been*?"

"You're the one who started taking off my clothes, princeling."

"I missed that—princeling," I said, cupping her cheek. "I missed you. I missed everything."

"Me too," she said, leaning into my hand. Her brow knitted together. "I missed you so much."

Before she got emotional again, I pulled her close to me and held her tight. "Ssh, I'm here now."

She nestled her head in my neck and sniffed hard. "I never thought I'd see you again." My face fell at her words, and she asked, "What's wrong?"

"Just...I haven't done anything I promised you."

"You went back to the hospital. And," she smiled, "you helped that little boy in the market."

I groaned and tilted my head back. "You heard about that?"

"Showed up in our intel briefings about you." Her smile faltered, and she pursed her lips. "And who...is Olivia Collins?"

I groaned again, louder. Of *course* Theo had seen all that. "That was a favor to my mother and nothing more. I hated every moment of it. Wished I was with you. It was awful. She smelled bad—"

Theo leaned forward and kissed me. "*Amichai*," she said, resting her chin back on my chest. "It's okay. And even if you liked her—"

"Which I didn't—"

"It would be a lot easier to be with her than me," she finished.

"She's way too...submissive. I like a woman who can put me in my place." She caught my meaning, and the smallest blush appeared on her cheeks. "So where'd you learn *that* move?"

"Nowhere," she said. "I've been too busy...parading behind Bayard. Being told to look interesting and smile."

"Are you serious?" I said with a small laugh. "Theo, you're..." She cocked her head to the side, curious. "Damn, you're the most beautiful thing I've ever seen."

"That's not what you were going to say."

"I don't want to talk about anything else but how good you look naked and lying next to me." I ran my hands down her back.

"Theo—" Her body shook underneath my hand. "Theo?"

"I'm losing myself, *amichai*," she said, as two thick tears rolled down her face. "You have no idea. I'm so glad to see you... I needed you so much. This speech...and it's a lie...and I can't even do it...and I don't know what I'm going to do..."

"What are you talking about?" I said, rolling over onto my side so I could hold her better.

She rested on the crook of my arm, but wouldn't meet my eyes. "I have to give a speech tomorrow."

"I know."

"And it's a lie."

"So what's new?" I said. Her eyes met mine, but there was no levity in them. "Theo, politics...it's *all* lies."

"I didn't think that Rave lied though!" she exclaimed, nuzzling her head into my arm. "I thought we were better than this. I thought..." Her face grew hard. "I thought we had no money, but suddenly, there are fancy buildings and people who weren't conscripted, and I just wonder...am I still on the right side of things?"

None of this surprised me—not that Rave was corrupt or that she'd no idea. She'd been entirely too patriotic for her own good when I met her, and knew little about the realities of politics. Still, I hated to see her lose her faith.

"And now," she said, moving closer to me, "now instead of fixing planes, I sit behind the president and listen to him give the same fucking speech every day, and wonder why he's not doing more. They tell me 'look interested, *'neechai'* and 'you're too stiff, *'neechai'* and it's all I can do not to *scream*. Then they tell me that the best way for me to help is to stand up and talk about *Mael*. They want me to talk about the horrible things Kylae is doing while they do horrible things to our own people!"

"I know," I said, stroking her hair gently.

"And the worst part is," she said, her voice growing thick again. "*Amichai*, the worst part is that I have to play their game if I want to help people. To change the country, I have to get into his inner circle. To get into his inner circle, I have to be the one everyone wants to photograph. And to do that, I have to...*lie*." She closed her eyes. "I have to lie about Mael. I have to get up there and tell everyone I was there for two months, and I can't even say the words."

"Why not?" I asked. "You were there... Briefly, but you were there."

She sniffed. "It's not...all those other people...Galian, they *died* because of me. Because of what we did. Because you decided to rescue me. And..."

"And you think that means you can't speak about Mael?"

She nodded before her face twisted in anguish again and she buried it into my chest. I held her tight, thankful, at least, that I was there to comfort her. "Theo, do you remember what you said to me on the island when I realized no one was coming for us and we'd run out of food?"

"I said..." She lifted her head to look at me. "I said that we wouldn't have survived as long as we did if we didn't have a greater purpose." Then, almost immediately, her brow furrowed, and she shook her head. "This is different—"

"How?"

"Because I know why I survived Mael," she said. "I survived because I fell in love with you."

"Maybe you didn't survive Mael because you fell in love with me," I said, taking her cheek in my hand and brushing away the tears.

"Maybe you survived Mael because it's your purpose to tell others about it. Falling in love with me just put you on a path to be able to speak the truth. And now you can. Now you can tell the whole world about it."

She swallowed. "But what if I can't? What if I'm not strong enough?"

"You are. You're the strongest person I know." I pulled her face to mine in a gentle kiss. "I love you, Theo."

"I love you too, *amichai*." She swallowed and glanced at the ceiling. "Damn, I am so glad you're here."

"Well, let's not talk any more about that," I said, pushing her onto her back. "Because I have four months of you to catch up on."

THEO

When the first tendrils of waking reached me, I squeezed my eyes shut. I'd had this dream many times before. I'd be so sure I was back on the island with my *amichai* next to me then open my eyes and be all alone.

This particular dream was quite persistent, for I felt his breath on my cheek, smelled his skin. My fingertips rested on his strong chest, which rumbled when he spoke.

"What are you doing?"

"I'm not opening my eyes," I replied with a smile. "Because when I do, you'll be gone. I've had this dream bef—"

He pressed his lips to mine again, opening my mouth with his tongue. Pushing me on my back, he climbed on top of me, traveling the length of my body with his hands.

"Wake up."

"No," I said, jerking when he brushed the tops of my hips where I was ticklish.

"Wake. Up."

"*No.*" I squeezed my eyes together and held in a squeal when he dug his fingers into my hips. My eyes flew open finally, rewarding me with my *amichai*'s sparkling brown ones staring back at me.

He kissed my nose gently. "See? Still here." The unspoken end to his sentence forced a grimace to my face. Galian cooed and kissed the side of my head, then left a trail of kisses down my collarbone. His hand cupped my breast and he gently massaged it.

"Again?" I asked, cracking open an eye to his boyish grin.

"Again and again," he said, opening my legs and entering me gently. After a long night of practice, we now made love without adjustments or awkwardness. He'd been a quick study in my body and where I was most sensitive. And the more I touched and felt, the more confident I was as his partner.

As we rocked together in the early morning light, he attended to my body with a lazy sort of passion, marking each place he knew made me moan with pleasure. When we'd had our fill of each other, he held me close, and we watched the rays of sun creep closer to the bed. Soon I would have to leave this room and this bliss, but not yet.

"After your speech today, you should come with me," he said after a while.

I sighed. Still my naïve princeling. "We tried that, *amichai.*"

"Not there. Here. In Jervan. I'll get us a little apartment and we can start over. I'll get a job at the hospital, and you can do whatever you want."

"And you think the world will just let us? The prince of Kylae and Rave's *'neechai*. Living together in Jervan." I closed my eyes, imagining the furor in both nations.

"I could give a shit about them," he whispered. "I want to be with you."

"And what about the war? All the people in Rave? We'll just let it rage on while we honeymoon?"

"We could end it together, you and me."

"From Jervan?"

"Sure, why not?"

Bam, bam, bam! "*Kallistrate!*"

My entire body went rigid. Cannon banged on the door and called my name again, and I sprang out of bed. Galian sat up, confused.

"*Hide!*" I mouthed to him.

He nodded and gathered his clothes on the ground, jumping into the closet. I grabbed one of the discarded robes and wrapped it around myself, pushing my underthings to the floor on the other side of the bed.

After a few calming breaths, I opened the door to Cannon's angry face.

ELEVEN

GALIAN

I barely breathed in the closet, praying to God that the sour-looking man at the door didn't search the room. That was just what I needed for my tabloid persona: *Playboy Prince Found Naked in Hotel Room with Raven Woman.* I'd never be allowed back into the country. Not to mention what they'd do to Theo.

"You missed your scheduled pre-brief with Emilie this morning. She sent me to fetch you," he said, his words laced with disgust.

"I was taking shower," Theo said calmly.

"Your hair isn't wet." I didn't like this guy already, and I really didn't like him when I found a small slit in the closet door to watch through and he was ogling Theo like she was a piece of meat.

"I was about to get in, but someone was banging on the door." I detected the smallest hint of fear in her voice, and I prayed the other guy didn't know Theo as well as I did.

My alarm bells went off when he stepped into the room, using his size to try to intimidate her. If push came to shove, I would step out of this closet, buck naked, and protect my Theo.

"If you don't mind, I need to get ready for my speech today," she snapped, before adding with a smile, "Tell Emilie I'll be down in a moment."

He paused at the closet, but something she said had pissed him off because he turned around to face her again. With a growl, he stormed out of the hotel room, slamming the door behind him.

Theo cracked a half-smile at me when I walked out of the closet and said, "So that's Cannon."

"He's into you. I don't like him."

"Me neither, but not because of that," she said, looking at the closed door before coming over to stand in my arms. I liked how she leaned into me, as if I could shoulder the weight of the world for her. "He's always been an ass, but now that I'm giving this speech today, he's been horrible. I think he's worried I'm going to take his spot on Bayard's council."

"Do you want that?" I asked.

She chewed her lip. "If it meant I could get the war to stop, I'd do it in a heartbeat. But...somehow it doesn't seem as simple as it used to." She groaned and pressed her head into my chest. "I didn't practice *at all* last night. I am so screwed."

"Nah," I said. "You were just holding too much inside. Now that you've let it all out, I bet you'll get up there and give the best speech of your life."

Her smile warmed my heart. "You think so, Dr. Princeling?"

"And in my professional opinion," I said, cupping her ass under the robe and squeezing it, "I firmly believe that being thoroughly pleasured is the best way to get over stage fright."

She laughed quietly but already her nerves had set in. "I wish you could be there."

"Do you want me there?" I said with a smile. "I'll be there."

Her face twisted into horror. "Don't you *dare* show up, princeling. I'm serious. It was one thing to be at the hotel, but if someone saw you at the summit—"

I kissed her. "I love that you still call me princeling."

"I do when you're being an idiot," she said, and I felt her heart race as her bare chest pressed against mine. "I should start getting ready. Emilie's probably livid."

"You did tell that guy you had to shower," I said, twisting a lock of her hair around my finger.

The corners of her mouth quirked up. "I did, didn't—*Ack!*" She'd barely finished her sentence before I tossed her over my shoulder, heading for the bathroom.

THEO

"You look flushed, Theo," Emilie said, eyeing my reflection in the mirror. "Are you feverish?"

"No, just...had a very good night's sleep," I said with a smile I hoped was genuine. There was a red tint to my cheeks, but also a sparkle in my eyes, and I couldn't keep the smile off my face.

Galian promised me he'd be waiting in my room when I returned for one more night of passion. He'd asked me again to consider staying in Jervan with him, and as much as my mind decided that was a terrible idea, my heart overruled it. Five seconds in his presence, and I was back to the lovesick girl who'd decided it was more fun to daydream about kissing a prince than pay attention to where she was going. On the island, it had gotten me lost and stuck up a tree. In the more dangerous game of international politics, it was much more treacherous.

I struggled to remain present in the room as I watched the stylist straighten my hair. I rarely wore it down, as it conflicted with the Raven uniform codes. But Emilie said that it made me look more approachable.

She'd been furious when I'd finally arrived at her room to practice. But, to her surprise, I delivered the speech without as much as a stutter. To be sure, she had me reciting it every fifteen minutes while the Raven stylists fretted with my hair.

"Remember to pause between the part about the prisoners and that the king does nothing," she said, more visibly agitated than I'd seen her before.

I nodded and smiled at her. "I've got this, Emilie."

In the mirror, I spotted Cannon watching me from the bed. I was fairly sure that if he'd heard Galian, I—and everyone else in the Raven delegation—would've known about it. Still, he knew something was amiss, so I had to be more careful around him.

"That's fine, that's fine," Emilie said, brushing away the stylist and pulling me to stand. She adjusted my uniform and pinched my cheeks. "Since you didn't meet with anyone yesterday, we need to do a quick meet and greet today. Can you handle that?" I nodded with a smile, and she stared at me, cocking her head to the side. "Something's...different about you."

"Took some time to clear my head," I replied, amazed at how easily I could lie.

I almost skipped after Emilie as we entered the lobby of the hotel. I glanced around for my *amichai*, but I was secretly grateful I didn't see him. I wasn't sure I could hide my excitement.

I did, however, see one familiar Kylaen. Galian's guard who'd rescued me from Mael was sitting in one of the chairs with another woman I didn't recognize. I knew enough to feel their eyes on me, and I chanced a small smile to him. Imperceptibly, his head tilted down, before disappearing behind the newspaper again.

I followed Emilie out of the lobby to our car, as I would be riding with her and Cannon today. I was eager to see more of the city—

—*especially since I might be living here*, my brain responded in a singsong voice. But instead of getting mad, I simply smiled at myself. It had been too long since I'd been this hopeful about the future.

"We have two hours before your speech," Emilie said, looking over a page in a leather-bound folder. "Cannon, you will round up some of the ministers for Theo to speak with."

He snorted.

"Don't pout," Emilie snapped. "This is Theo's day. You can't have the spotlight forever."

I didn't relish his disappointment, so I focused my attention on the city as it passed by. More white plaster buildings, more flowerpots on the wall. I considered what my life would be like if I lived there with Galian. Walking the market I'd seen the day before, finding our food and cooking it for him. Just like back on the island.

"Why are you grinning?" Cannon snarled.

"Just excited to finally be here," I replied without missing a beat. "I..." My eyes widened as our car turned and the Jervanian palace came into full view. It rose above us in spires and towers too many to count, each one meticulously carved with detail visible from hundreds of feet below. Our car passed through wrought iron gates that far surpassed those at *Platcha*, complete with marble columns with golden statues that sat atop them.

"Put your tongue back in your mouth, *kallistrate*, we don't want them thinking you're simple," Cannon remarked, looking wholly unimpressed by the splendor surrounding us. I was in too good a mood to glare at him.

"Theo, how are you feeling?" Emilie asked.

"I'm ready," I replied. And for the first time, I was. Maybe Galian was right; perhaps bottling up my feelings had been keeping me from speaking clearly. And the sex hadn't hurt either. God, what that man could do with his tongue. I hadn't believed a person could handle that much pleasure in one night.

Once we were out of the car, the insanity began. Photographers rushed toward us, bulbs flashing, calling to us with questions about Rave and Kylae and my speech. Most of them were Jervan, but I spotted one or two who could've been Herinese.

Emilie pushed me through the gaggle, even managing to wear a flawless smile as she did. Once we passed through the open doors, we were greeted by a surprisingly upscale security screening area. They checked me for every conceivable weapon before letting me pass.

Emilie and Cannon joined me shortly thereafter, and led me down another ornate hallway. We passed a large arena-like chamber already filled with people and chairs, which Emilie pointed out would be the location of my speech. The panic, which had been gone since the moment Galian had first held me in his arms, returned with a roar.

"G-good," I said, wrenching my gaze away.

"It'll be fine, *'neechai*," Emilie said, stopping to place a hand on my shoulder. "Come, we've got to do the meet and greet."

The antechamber was a much smaller room, made more so by the number of people and the loud conversations. I recognized a few Raven ministers, but most of the room was Jervanian, with a few Herinese towering over the rest. Emilie threaded through the room as if she knew exactly where she was going.

"And there's the major of the hour!" Bayard's booming voice echoed over the din, and before I knew it, he'd wrapped his arm around my shoulders and he was introducing me to the leaders of Jervan and Herin. President Kuman of Jervan, a rotund man, was at least a head shorter than I was. His hand was warm and fleshy, and his shake was so vigorous, he nearly yanked my whole body with my hand. Prime Minister Bouckley of Herin was a tall, pale woman whose cheekbones and severe gaze stood in stark contrast to the leader of the nation just south of hers. Her hand was cold as it gently enveloped mine.

Bayard's arm never left my shoulder, but I was not a part of this conversation whatsoever. They picked up on a thread they must've started the day before in their private meeting, tossing out terms that might as well have been in a foreign language.

Except one.

"Minister Breen is the expert on Malaske," Bayard said. "Sometimes I'll read his reports when I can't sleep at night."

Bayard and Kuman laughed heartily, but I quirked my brow. Why was Bayard discussing our secret facility with the leaders of Herin and Jervan? Not that I knew what was going on there anyway.

Bouckley lifted her pointed chin higher, and I got the distinct impression she was not a fan of either Bayard or Kuman. "But we're on track?"

"We've begun testing, yes," Bayard said. "If the Herinese technology does what you say—"

"It does."

"Then we should be on track," Bayard said. I snuck a glance at him. He was smiling, but there was tension behind it.

"Let's hope it doesn't come to that, yes!" Kuman said with a jovial smile to me. "Let's hope those bastards hear your charming major's speech and change their minds."

Bayard agreed with him, but I didn't hear the conviction.

"Ah, is it time? Yes, Emilie's giving me the look," Bayard said, and I noticed Emilie's tight smile and rigid stance from behind the Herinese prime minister. Bayard finally released me and I nodded my goodbye to the three world leaders and hurried after Emilie.

"That man could talk for hours," Emilie snapped. "How are you?"

"Nervous," I said honestly. Even though it would be completely irresponsible and dangerous of him, I hoped Galian might show up to watch my speech. Knowing him, he'd laugh off the danger and just walk in the front door.

Idiot princeling.

Emilie took me to a private room where she made me drink a spicy Jervan tea that soothed my throat. She told me to stay in this room until she came and fetched me. Tea in hand, I curled up on the small divan and attempted to run through the speech again in my mind. But it was crowded out by memories of Galian and the question of whether I should go with him when the day was over.

GALIAN

Once I was sure Theo and the rest of the Ravens were gone, I scurried out of her hotel room and took the stairs to the one I was supposed to be sleeping in. There, I found Kader and Johar huddled around the news, and Martin chowing down a Jervanian breakfast. Blessedly, there was a second one sitting next to him.

"Well?" Martin asked.

"Well, what?" I said, downing the coffee. "You want the sordid details?"

"Yes," Martin said, mouth full of food.

I smiled and shook my head, shoveling the cornmeal dish into my mouth. "I asked her to stay here with me. She's thinking about it."

"Your father's ordered you back to Norose," Kader grunted without looking at me. "A plane will be here in three hours and will leave half an hour after that."

"Then I just won't be on it," I said, throwing my hands behind my head.

Kader turned to look at me. "Rosie would be very disappointed."

"R—" My eyes widened, and I sat up. "Are you fucking serious? He didn't—"

"Not in so many words, but the point was conveyed."

I threw down my spoon in disgust. "So I suppose whatever mission you two were on was a failure?"

Johar and Kader shared a glance. "Your father isn't aware of this mission. Nor should he be," Kader said.

"In fact, the only reason the two of us were here is because a lovesick prince forced us," Johar replied. "And Eli called in a favor to an old friend to get you in the country and into her bed."

I nodded dumbly and my attention drew to the television where Theo stood outside the Jervanian palace. Her face was still flushed and her eyes sparkled. She was a far cry from the soulless woman I'd seen behind Bayard. And now I would crush her again by leaving. I wouldn't even get to say goodbye.

I sat up, a smile curling on my face. "We have three hours right? Can I at least watch her speech?"

"In the Jervanian palace?" Kader asked. "Sure, we'll just walk you in the front door—"

"I don't hate that idea," Johar said, cutting him off. "After all, Bayard's room was a bust. They're talking about Malaske in these meetings, and I don't want to go back empty-handed."

I had no idea what or who Malaske was, but I was onboard with getting me into the Jervanian palace.

Kader shook his head. "Sayuri..."

"I have to bring Korina something concrete. Especially after dragging *him* along with us."

Now I was really confused, but I kept my mouth shut, hoping I could learn something about the true meaning behind this mission. Knowing my mother, not my father, was the originator made me even more curious.

"What's the cover then?" Kader asked.

"Call up Sharif again—"

"We already called in that favor to get us into the country."

"So we'll owe him one. But he's got contacts in the Jervanian palace. We'll tell them that the prince harbors sympathies for the Raven cause, and he wants to meet in secret with a few key players."

"And what if word gets out that Galian went to the summit? Grieg is already furious with him. I have Rosie to think about—"

"We won't *let* it get out. We've still got crowns. Anyone who sees us will get paid off." Johar folded her arms over her chest. "I've got my orders, and they may be different from yours, Eli. But I am *not* going back to the queen of Kylae empty handed."

I was getting dizzy from the back-and-forth conversation, so I was glad when Kader didn't respond for a while.

"And what if we miss our plane?"

"We won't," I piped up. "Theo speaks in—"

"Shut up," Kader barked at me. "Sayuri, this is a big risk you're taking with lives that aren't yours to risk."

"If what I'm hearing is true, it won't matter what Grieg does to Rosie, because there won't be a Norose," Johar replied quietly.

"What in—" I started, but a look from Kader silenced me.

"I've heard the same rumors, but you don't think they're true, do you?"

"After five years of careful negotiation, Jervan pulls the plug on the wheat trade agreement? Herin's ambassador has delayed important discussions on scientific transfers? Greig may think it's just a temporary frosting of relations, but Korina believes otherwise. The Ravens are about to start fighting back, and Kylae doesn't want to find out what *truly* being in a war feels like."

"And what, pray tell, are your orders?" Kader asked.

"Classified, per the queen, my friend," Johar said, before looking at me. "Did your girlfriend say anything about a secret laboratory?"

I shook my head. "No."

"Galian, now is not the time to cover for her," Kader growled.

"I swear, she didn't say anything about that," I said, holding up my hands. "And I know Theo. She's more interested in ending the war than keeping it going through *more* bloodshed."

"It's not her I'm worried about, it's her crazy president," Johar replied with a shake of her head. "Boy, if you're coming—"

I nearly tripped over my feet as I leaped off the bed. "Yes! Yes, I'm coming."

"Then do as I say and keep your mouth shut," she replied.

"Wait, Sayuri," Kader said, running a hand over his bald head. "I'm coming with you."

"What about me?" Martin asked, having eaten the rest of my breakfast as well.

"Go meet the Kylae plane, and if we aren't there on time, *stall them*," Kader replied.

"And give her this," I said, standing and walking to the desk in the corner. There was a pad of paper and a pen, so I hastily scribbled out a note. For her protection, and my own, I was vague, but I still managed to say what I wanted to. I folded up the note and handed it to Martin. "Put this under her pillow. She's in room 509."

"Ah, you three get to go infiltrate a castle, and I get to drop off your love notes," Martin said with a sigh, taking it from me. "Who says this job isn't fun?"

THEO

The roar of hundreds of voices conversing reached me as Emilie and I drew closer to the chamber. Bayard stood at the door, continuing his conversation with the other two presidents, not acknowledging us as we stood behind him.

"Are you ready for this?" Emilie asked for the thousandth time.

I looked out into the room and nodded, though I was sure my nerves were evident on my face. It was silly, but I wanted my *amichai* to be there. I knew he'd be watching, and I knew he'd be there when I got back to sweep me into his arms, but...knowing he was nearby might've done something to calm my racing heart.

A tone sounded in the chamber and the conversations quieted to a quiet murmur. The president of Jervan walked out into the assembly, greeted them warmly then introduced Bayard and the Herinese prime minister. Then I heard him introduce me.

"Do your best," Emilie said with a confident smile.

I stepped into the cavernous room and immediately felt every eye in the room on me. My body moved of its own volition, my hands resting on the wooden podium as Emilie's directions of how to stand echoed in my head. My mouth opened and air rushed out of my lungs to give voice to my thoughts.

"Good morning, President Bayard, President Kuman, Prime Minister Bouckley, esteemed members of the Jervan and Herin parliaments, and the delegates from the great, independent nation of Rave. Thank you for allowing me the chance to speak to you today. Rave is grateful for this opportunity to have a seat at the table at the Three Nations' Summit, and I am proud to represent her in this very important assembly."

What came next? My mind drew a blank, and I began to panic as I looked at the faces around me. I should've practiced more; I should've known what I was going to say. I was sunk. I couldn't do this —they were stupid to think...

I saw him.

He was in the back of the room, pressed against the wall. I almost missed him in my frantic searching, but his stance was unmistakable. He had come, even though I'd told him not to. I had no idea how he managed it, either. It wasn't as if—

"'*Neechai*," Bayard's voice prompted from behind.

I smiled and cleared my throat. "I come to you as a daughter of Rave," I said, my eyes glued on Galian. "As you know, fifty years ago, after our nation was ruthlessly sacked of resources and enslaved by the Kylaens, we declared our independence. Although we have considered ourselves to be a sovereign nation, our former colonizers believe they have a claim to our land and our peoples. This cannot and must not stand in the international community any longer.

"There are many stories about how Kylae's attacks have stymied our economy, our people, and our independence, but today, I wish to turn the community's attention to another blight. There is a camp in the northern mountains of Kylae, known as Mael. The Kylaens use the barethium mined there to fortify their buildings and their bombs. In order to extract the toxic material from the ground, they employ slave labor, usually plucked from their slums filled with Raven refugees. I, myself, was imprisoned for..."

I stared at Galian, knowing the words I should say, but very different ones coming to mind. I felt the tension of the room grow as the seconds lengthened between my words.

"I spent some time in Mael," I said finally. "I saw the people, saw the way they were treated, and what they were forced to do. You can't spend one second there without knowing that it's a dangerous place. The air is so poisonous the guards have to wear masks that cover their faces, and perhaps they wish to hide their faces to remain disconnected from the brutal reality.

"For a long time, I struggled to speak about Mael. Not because I was haunted by horrible memories, though they do visit me in my dreams. I struggled because I asked myself *why*. Why was I chosen to survive and others left to a slow, tortuous death? I have never felt worthy to speak on the topic because...there's no good reason I lived while others died." Galian nodded to me and I took another long breath. "But, finally, I realized that I survived so I could tell their stories.

"When I arrived in Mael, I saw a man who was more willing to be executed by the guards' guns than die the slow, tortuous death of barethium poisoning. I watched children forced to work for hours without breaks, chained together as if they were animals. They'd been sent there for crimes like shoplifting and were sentenced to a life of lung disease. But the worst of it all was...I could see in their eyes how hopeless it was. There was no escaping the poisonous gas, or the whip, or the..."

My stomach was threatening to empty itself, so I inhaled a long breath to calm myself. After a tense moment, I continued. "No country is without it's sins, not even Rave. But what happens in Mael is inhumane. Jervan and Herin have banned barethium usage in their buildings and their economy thrives, why not Kylae?"

I glanced up at Galian, and he was beaming. But I felt Bayard's eyes on the back of my neck and knew I might get a talking to when this speech was over. Might as well say what I wanted to say.

"King Grieg thinks he can do whatever he wishes within his borders," I said, and watched Galian's smile grow bigger. "He would rather continue a fifty-year war and enslave those with Raven blood than try to come up with solutions. There is peace to be had between Kylae and Rave, but it takes the first step. And maybe that first step is closing Mael. Even if we don't find peace, Grieg knows closing the prison is the right thing to do. As do we all." I paused for a breath. "Thank you for the opportunity to speak with you today. God bless the free and independent nation of Rave."

To my surprise, the room erupted in loud, joyous applause that took me by surprise. I glanced behind me and was even *more* shocked to see the presidents and prime ministers on their feet, clapping loudest of all. Bayard was grinning with all the sincerity I'd never seen from him before, and the president of Jervan had tears running down his face.

I turned to look for my *amichai* again and saw him speaking with one of his two guards. The look he gave me spoke volumes. He mouthed, *"I love you,"* then disappeared through the doors behind him.

TWELVE

GALIAN

We'd made it back to the Kylaen plane with only ten minutes to spare, and Martin had looked most relieved when he saw us boarding the plane. Johar hadn't shared whether she'd been successful or not in infiltrating the meetings, and, like Kader, I couldn't read her stoic expression. But Theo had delivered her speech perfectly, and that had been mission success enough for me.

My father's orders only required my two feet to be back on Kylaen soil by sundown, but thankfully, they didn't order me back to the castle. My suspicions about his collusion with Hebendon returned as soon as I saw my schedule for the week—night, night, night, night, night...then two early morning shifts. Hebendon said it was because I'd taken unplanned leave and other doctors had to cover for me, but I wasn't that stupid. This was my father's punishment.

The busy schedule did have one benefit: it distracted me from thinking about how much I missed Theo. Being with her again had reopened a deep wound, and our forced separation was like rubbing salt in it. But watching her speak so passionately, seeing the world leaders from three nations stand and applaud her, had finally inspired me to be the kind of man who deserved her. The kind of man who didn't make excuses about night shifts and exhaustion. The kind of man who followed through on his promises to the woman he loved.

I wasn't surprised that Theo's speech and the summit in general didn't even get a mention on the back pages of the newspapers. I checked for nearly a week, cover to cover, and saw nothing of it, nor a mention of my appearance at the hotel. That, at least, surprised me a little. I'd done my best to show the worst parts of myself to the media. The tabloids usually ate that up. Then again, perhaps my father had let the stories of my youth run because it fit a narrative he was trying to craft. Now the story was better if I just hadn't gone anywhere at all.

By the end of my week from hell, I was exhausted, but determined to do something, even returning to the castle to talk to Rhys. But as luck would have it, Rhys came to me, waiting in my apartment and having a beer with Martin as if they were old friends.

"Gally!" he said, standing and walking over to me. "How was work?"

"Exhilarating," I said with a weak smile. "What are you doing here?"

"Wanted to see my little brother." As if on cue, Martin stood and disappeared into his bedroom, shutting the door behind him.

"Why do I get the feeling I'm in trouble?" I asked, sitting down in the seat Martin had vacated.

"I don't know, maybe because you did exactly the *opposite* of what I told you to do?" Rhys said, placing the beer on the table. "I said not to make a spectacle of yourself. The point was to keep this from Father."

"I had approval from both Kader and Johar. I helped with

whatever..." I paused, considering whether Rhys was aware of why they were there.

"I couldn't give a shit about them and their mission," Rhys said, answering my question. "My first and only concern is *you*. Thanks to your little stunt, you've put yourself back in Father's crosshairs." Rhys sat back and stared at the turned-off television in front of us. "And it's pretty obvious why, after four months of looking like death warmed over, your little girlfriend is suddenly the happiest, cheeriest little escaped prisoner there ever was."

I had to smile at that. "What can I say, I'm good—"

"Galian, for fuck's sake," Rhys said with a hearty roll of his eyes. "I'm serious. Father knows you disobeyed him and went to see your girlfriend just before she gave an impassioned speech about this country's inner workings. He can put two and two together."

"What are you insinuating?" I asked, folding my arms over my chest.

"I'm not insinuating anything. I'm telling you that it looked like you divulged Kylaen state secrets to an enemy agent. I'm telling you that some of the ministers believe you're a traitor and would have you sent to Mael at the drop of a hat." He ran his hands through his hair. "It's a damned good thing the media's in love with you thanks to your rumored engagement."

"And nobody finds it odd that we're discussing my own father?" I asked. "The man would kill his own son to, what? Save face?" I snorted. "Father of the year right there."

"Galian, there's so much more you don't understand—"

"There's no explanation for something like that," I replied hotly. "Just like there's no explanation for why we continue to try to invade Rave day after day—"

"This isn't about Rave, or Theo, or even the war, Gally. This is about you staying out of trouble!" Rhys said before sighing. "Look, man, I meant what I said at the party. I thought you were *dead* for two months, and I never want to go through that again."

"So maybe deal with the person who's going around threatening people's lives."

"I can't argue with you when you're like this," Rhys said, standing up. I let him walk to the door, too tired to fight anymore, but then he paused and said, "How was she?"

"She's...Theo," I said with a small smile. "Keep watch over the airspace on the island, will ya? I have a feeling she might be calling soon."

He waited a breath then responded, "I never stopped."

THEO

I imagined his hand between my legs and his smug smile. Then the way he'd kissed a trail from my knee to the wetness...

I shivered and swallowed hard, wishing the memories of Galian wouldn't visit me when I was sitting in the meeting room in the public relations office. Still, I supposed I should count my lucky stars that *those* memories haunted me and not the ones from Mael. The only danger from these dreams was a goofy, lovesick smile and the inability to pay attention.

Glancing around to make sure I was the only one still in the room, I reached into my pocket and pulled out a well-worn piece of paper with the logo of the Ginger Finn hotel on it. I'd known in my heart when I saw Galian turn and leave that he was going back to Kylae and our brief interlude had come to a close. It had been foolish to think his appearance would go unnoticed by his father, and I regretted not being more realistic about our parting that morning. Then again, if I had been, perhaps I might not have given such an impassioned speech.

When I'd returned to my hotel room, there was a little surprise waiting for me when I lay my head on the pillow to cry.

Theo,

I have been "ordered" back home, so our plans in Jervan will be on hold—temporarily. If it gets too much, just go back to our place, and I'll come for you.

I love you.

Your aymekey

I snorted when my gaze breezed over his pathetic spelling for *amichai.* Then again, there hadn't been much time to teach him how to say the word, let alone spell it.

I saw movement out of the corner of my eye, so I hastily folded the paper up and stuck it back in my pocket. I smiled as Wesson entered the meeting room, but he barely acknowledged me as he placed the meeting material in front of me.

I opened the folder and cringed; my bright, smiling face was on ten out of the ten media clippings. No wonder Wesson was sick of me; *I* was starting to get sick of me. The frenzy of attention from the Raven media had started when I stepped off the plane and at least twenty Raven photographers were waiting for me. Not for Bayard, but for *me.* And they continued stalking me even this morning, photographing me as I crossed the sidewalk to my car.

I couldn't imagine this being my life forever, like it was

Galian's...A smile grew on my face as my memory drifted back to the long night, how his strong chest had rumbled under my fingertips when he laughed, the way his lips felt against my skin, how I writhed under his touch—

"*'neechai*, are you with us?" Emilie's voice shot through my daydream, and I straightened to attention. The room had filled without my knowing it and everyone was staring at me.

"Sorry," I said, opening my folder to the first page.

"As I was saying, Bayard wants Theo's speech to be the theme of all media engagements for the next two weeks, at least. Herrick, Kerico, we'll need to update Minister Breen and Minister Lee's speeches. The full text of Theo's...unplanned deviations is in your folders. Though *'neechai*, next time, please stick to the script."

She winked at me, and I was glad I wouldn't get any further reprimands. Still, I had been too preoccupied with Galian and speaking to even remember anything, and I was curious. I pulled the paper to me and began to read.

"I really said all this?" I said after a moment. Perhaps I should take Emilie's advice and just read from the prepared remarks from now on.

"We've tweaked a little bit for grammar and repetition," she said, beaming at me. "But these are your words. And soon, the whole country will hear them."

I flipped through the folder until I found my schedule for the next two weeks. I'd be with Bayard nearly every day, delivering my speech no less than six times at some of the largest military installations in Rave—including Vinolas and, to my shock, the Raven parliament.

I could scarcely believe my eyes. I was finally at the precipice of the next phase in my career, and within grasp of the power that could change the lives of my countrymen. This was what I'd been working toward all of these months. I'd finally done it.

Emilie's gaze was still on me. "I'm very proud of you, I want you to know. I'm not sure what happened in Jervan, but you've been different. You found your spark. Whatever you did there, keep doing it, because you've become the most interesting person in Rave."

I forced my gaze down to the paper. The thing that I did was Galian, and seeing him again was...

Go back to our place, and I'll come for you.

I wanted to be with him so much it hurt. But at the same time, thanks to this speech, I could help people now. I slid a hand into my pocket and felt the rough edges of the paper. I loved my *amichai*, but I loved my country, too. And right now, Rave needed me more.

The meeting adjourned and, as usual, Emilie asked me to stay behind to have a private chat. For once, I wasn't dreading it.

"I wanted to let you know that Bayard's security team has recommended an increase in your security detail," Emilie said.

I furrowed my brow. "Any particular reason? I'm already pretty well-known in Rave."

"Yes, but now you aren't a silent symbol, you're a speaking one," she said with a smile. "Kylae's weapons don't always come in the form of bombs."

I was well-aware of the talents of at least one special operations officer. "Do you think they would come for me like that?"

"It's doubtful, but we'd always like to be prepared," she replied with a small shrug. "What Bayard is more worried about are the troublemakers in the south end of the city."

I realized with a jolt that I'd never told her about the strange man who'd seen me on the waterfront. I chewed on my lip. "One of them already approached me."

Her eyebrows shot up. "When?"

"A few weeks ago," I said then quickly added, "I told him I didn't want anything to do with him and to leave me alone."

She clicked her tongue against the roof of her mouth. "Theo, the next time something like that happens, *please* tell your security detail. For a group who never leaves Veres, they're awfully hard to pin down."

The memory of the man's enigmatic smile and his too-close-for-comfort words returned. "What will happen to them?"

"Are you kidding?" Emilie snorted. "They're traitors, and they'll be hung. They'd rather cause chaos and disruption instead of banding together during our time of crisis. They walk around the slums, telling the mothers of our pilots that their children have been sold into slavery."

But, my inner voice reminded me, it *was* only those in the slums who were targeted to serve the country. Children like Emilie and other wealthy Ravens paid their way out of conscription. But I shook that idea from my head.

"I know the conscription age is difficult to stomach, but we have no choice," Emilie said. "Our country is at war."

I nodded to agree with her, not trusting my mouth to say the right thing.

"Spreading lies like that isn't just problematic to our citizenry, it's dangerous. We can barely keep our country together as it is, let alone manage a civil war. The Kylaens will sweep in and take over."

Again, I nodded.

"So you'll tell someone the next time one of them comes to you?" she asked with a smile.

"Of course, it was stupid of me not to," I said.

"Good girl."

GALIAN

Not a day after Rhys had stopped by my apartment, Kader informed me I was taking lunch with the queen at the palace. To be honest, I was looking forward to the meeting. I had many questions for my mother, most of which revolved around the *real* mission in Lakner.

More than that, though, I wanted her advice. After all, she was the one who'd introduced me to the horrors at Mael. She knew more about what went on there than anyone else. In fact, she hadn't even blinked when I'd told her about the secret testing facility Theo and I had found on our island. I'd always thought her placated by my father's scientists and their promises of safety, but now I wasn't sure about anything I knew.

My mother wasn't in her residences, nor in her office, but I found her in the small greenhouse off to the side of her library, wearing a pair of gloves and tending to her favorite plants. She looked rather un-queen-like with dirt-stained pants and hair pulled back in a bun. The greenhouse was heated by the sun and also, I suspected, the palace furnace, so while it was a bit nippy, it wasn't too bad.

"The linton bush looks a little rough," she said to her assistant, Filippa, who nodded and wrote in her pad. "See about finding some fertilizer."

"Have you tried adding Father's bullshit?" I asked.

My mother glanced up at the sound of my voice and pursed her lips at me. "Galian, be respectful. Filippa, can you check with the gardener if he has any left over?"

Her assistant nodded demurely and hurried out of the greenhouse. My mother said nothing until the glass doors closed then she dropped her shoulders.

"Galian, watch where you let loose that tongue of yours," she said, much less cheerfully. "Filippa reports to your father."

I glanced behind me, bewildered. "Doesn't she work for you?"

"It's so wonderful to see you," Mom said, walking over and embracing me. She kept an arm around my shoulder and walked me to the small bush she was working on. "Doesn't this look lovely? It was a gift from our friends in Herin. The ambassador told me it would take a miracle to keep it alive here, but here it is, ten years later. Still thriving."

I nodded.

"And this one, do you know where it came from?" She pointed to a flower. "An island off the coast of Jervan." She glanced out the window. "When it gets cold like this, I have to move it inside. It's much easier to keep an eye on things when they're within arms' reach, you know?" She walked over to a small vividly purple flower. "This, though. This is my prize. It's a phoenician plant, native to Rave. Every six weeks, it sheds this beautiful flower and grows a new one. This one I've kept alive for a very long time. I like to believe that as long as it blooms every few weeks, there's still hope for peace between Rave and Kylae."

"Speaking of that," I said, keeping my voice low, "what—"

"Your trip to Jervan was successful, I take it?" Again, she cut me off and I began to wonder if Filippa wasn't the only one listening to her conversations.

"Very, and I want—"

"And I want my son to return home to me," she replied. "But alas, we can't have what we want. Shall we retire to my study?"

I said nothing until we were seated in the bright room overlooking the palace gardens. A thick blanket of snow had covered the castle, but the winter sun and the roaring fire in the hearth made the sunroom cozy. My mother thanked the servant who brought us tea, then closed the glass doors.

"So why is Father bugging your garden?" I asked plainly. "And why hasn't he bugged this room?"

"Oh, your father's bugged my greenhouse, but he knows better than to monitor my private quarters," she said, with a harsh daring that surprised me.

"Why is he bugging you in the first place?"

"He doesn't trust me, and hasn't for many years," she said, placing her hands on her knees.

"I mean, I knew he didn't trust you, but this seems extreme." I glanced around the room.

"Your father is an extreme man." She sat back and surveyed me. "So Theo is well?"

Despite my questions, I grinned. "Very well. I mean, she wasn't, but—"

"A surprise visit from her *amichai*? That would brighten any girl's day."

I don't know what surprised me more: that my mother knew the Raven word for lover, or that she pronounced it as well as Theo.

"I asked her to stay in Jervan, but...thanks to Father's orders..."

"Do you honestly believe Theo would've gone back with you?

After that speech? After all the media attention?" My mother smiled sadly. "From what you've told me about her, even if you hadn't been ordered to return home, I don't think she would've gone. Not when there's so much more work to be done."

"I know." I looked at the brown liquid in my cup. "Which is why I want to end the war."

My mother snorted and coughed, choking on her tea. She daintily wiped her mouth and nose with her napkin. "We *all* do, Galian."

"So what do we do? How do we do it?"

"We have patience," Mom replied. "We don't rush off and do whatever we feel like doing because we're love-drunk with a Raven girl. The right thing gone about the wrong way won't help anyone."

"The right thing not done *at all* doesn't help anyone either," I snarled back. "Do you think you're helping people by sitting and smiling beside the king? How is that supposed to—"

"Galian Neoptolemus Helmuth, you will not speak to your mother in that tone," she barked back. "And just because you don't see activity doesn't mean it's not there." She took a long breath and adjusted her skirt. "Your father has only a tenuous grip on his kingdom, and that makes him a dangerous man to disagree with. To effect change, we must be careful about doing so."

"T-tenuous?" I asked. "I thought he rules this place with an iron fist."

"The only way he keeps the Kylaen public from rising up in total rebellion is that he keeps the barethium flowing, and the consequences of it at a minimum," she replied. "And, of course, the war is simply a chance to remain patriotic while ignoring the total destruction of a foreign country."

I swallowed; we'd come to the topic I was most interested in discussing. "What happens if the barethium stops flowing? Like if Mael were to close?"

She placed her teacup on the saucer. "Galian, you are playing a very dangerous game, one I don't think you're ready for."

"Aren't you the one who taught me that we need to use our status for the good of others?"

"And what use are you if your father has you killed?"

"Is that all you and Rhys care about?" I said. "Why in the world are you putting *me* above the needs of your own people? Why is my life worth more than anyone else's?"

"First and foremost, *you're my son*," she replied, her voice cracking. "As much as I am queen, I am your mother first."

"Mom, we don't have that luxury anymore. We are in a position of power, and we have the ability to change things. We can't let fear hold us back. And it's not fair to the people of Kylae *or* Rave for you not to let me help because you're afraid something might happen to me."

"You don't know, Gally," she said, staring out at the snow-covered castle. "You have no idea what it was like those two months you were gone. Every single morning, I went to your room. I cried until there were no more tears to cry. I could barely find the strength to attend your f-funeral." She looked at her hands. "And to be honest, I'm not sure I'm strong enough to go through that again." When her eyes rose to meet mine, they were glistening with unshed tears. "Gally, I may be queen, but I am still human."

I pulled her into an embrace and felt like a kid again. No matter how long it had been, nothing beat a hug from my mother.

I sat in the front seat of the car, watching the photographers just outside the gate crawl over each other to get a shot of me and Martin in my car. I hadn't said anything to him since I sat down in the front seat, and he hadn't made any move to drive into the chaos outside. I think we were both contemplating our next move.

My mother had begged me to reconsider, even though I hadn't explicitly told her the plan forming in my mind. I trusted her guidance, but at the same time...something had to be done. And I was feeling just brave enough to do it.

In front of us, two photographers got into a shoving match with each other.

"Pathetic, you know?" Martin said with a sniff. "Don't they have other things to worry about?"

"Why don't we give them something to worry about?" I asked with a determined smile. "Let's take a detour, shall we?"

"Cinzia?"

"No," I said, steeling myself. "Somewhere a lot fouler."

THIRTEEN

THEO

I cracked my neck on both sides, rubbing the sore muscles of my shoulders. I had just spent the past week on the road with Bayard, giving my speech (which, surprisingly, I could still deliver with as much passion as in Jervan) half a dozen times. The schedule had been aggressive, which meant a lot of speaking, then driving for hours to the next event. I was grateful I was giving my speech to the Raven Parliament tomorrow; at least I could sleep in my bed tonight.

But before I returned to my apartment, I stopped in at the executive offices to meet with Emilie and get some adjustments to my speech and next week's travel schedule. But when I walked into the offices, no one was at their desks. A quick check of the meeting room found it empty as well.

"Huh?" I said. It was a work day, so where was everyone?

A low mumbling caught my attention, and I wandered toward the sound. As I grew closer, I realized it was the sound of the radio. My heart beat faster—was it a massive attack? Had Kylae done something horrible in retaliation for my words against them? It couldn't have been about Bayard either, he'd been in good health when I'd seen him less than an hour ago.

I broke into a run, nearly passing by the break room where the entire public relations staff, plus another twenty people I didn't recognize, were huddled around the radio.

" *'Neechai*, come here," Emilie said, waving me over. When I came near, she wrapped an arm around me and pulled me close.

"What is it?" I whispered, too afraid to speak loudly.

"Listen..."

My heart stopped beating in my chest as my *amichai's* voice echoed through the radio.

"Today, I call upon my father and the security council to shut down this prison. And I am prepared to stay here until they do so."

"Oh my God, he's in Mael?" I said, covering my mouth with my hands. What the *hell* was he thinking?

"He's been there four hours so far," Emilie said breathlessly. "The entire Kylaen media followed him, and, so far, none have left."

"A very brave Raven spoke at length to the international community about the atrocities committed here. Her impassioned speech moved me to do something. To finally use all this useless media attention for good, instead of gossip. Be sure to take photos of the children, their tumors and sick faces."

I couldn't help the dry sob that echoed out of my mouth and it took everything in me to not break down into tears of relief, joy, worry, fear...Galian had gone to Mael. Galian was standing up to his father and demanding that things change. He was doing what he'd promised me.

"Have we heard what Grieg is going to do?" asked a man to my left who I'd seen around the office.

"So far, nothing," Emilie replied. "But if the Kylaen media is still reporting on this, that bodes well for those in the prison."

"The Kylaen king won't budge. He hates the princeling," Cannon drawled. "Wishes he'd died on that island."

I nodded and used my disgust of Cannon to keep myself from beaming. My *amichai* was standing in the death camp, using the cameras that followed him around all the time for some good.

"I became a doctor to be useful to this country, and now, I am being useful."

"Yes, you are, *am*...Gal...princeling," I said, fumbling over my words.

"You did this, *'neechai*," Emilie said, squeezing me. "You've inspired the world."

I let the smile grow on my face, and for once, I wasn't keeping a secret from everyone in the room. I could show the joy and the relief. I closed my eyes and imagined him standing in front of that horrible place, surrounded by tabloid photographers. My heart swelled with pride as he vowed he wasn't leaving until every last prisoner was gone.

"Empty words." Cannon's voice cut through my daydream, and I opened my eyes to look at him. His gaze was fixed on me, and I withered a little under his scrutiny.

"Relax, Mark," Emilie said beside me. "This is a victory for us all. Even if the prison doesn't close—"

"It'll close," I said with a knowing smile.

"You and the princeling had a chat in Jervan?"

I jumped and stared at him before realizing that he was being his usual self. "Cannon, even you can't be upset by this news."

He snorted, and looked away. Perhaps tomorrow I would worry about him, but for today, I was content to sit in the room with twenty of my fellow citizens, listening to the love of my life finally make good on a promise he'd made to me and save hundreds of lives in the process.

GALIAN

"No more questions," I said, waving my hand in the air. The stench was starting to get to me again, and I needed to stop talking before I said something that didn't make sense.

I hadn't been sure what would happen when Martin and I drove to Mael. The photographers tended to follow me everywhere, and though some peeled off the closer we got to the prison, to my surprise, a good ten or fifteen drove through the iron gates of Mael with us.

The head of the prison had been on hand to meet us, deigning not to wear his gas mask in front of all the photographers. He'd welcomed us, talking about how *pleased* he was at the unplanned visit. The smokestacks were off, and the courtyard had been cleared of prisoners. It looked, to my eyes, the same as when I'd visited with my mother. But I knew what this place was really like.

I demanded to see prisoners, and he'd paraded out a few older, healthy-looking prisoners with light skin, and who must've been there for a few days, tops. I told him to bring out *all* the prisoners, or else I'd go find them myself and take a photographer with me.

That was, I think, when he realized I was serious because he became very sweaty and nervous. He spent a few minutes mumbling about how he wasn't authorized, so I called to the most eager photographer and went on a hunting mission.

Up until that point, all I'd seen of Mael was the large room where they shoveled barethium and smelted it into a workable state. The workers had been chained together at the ankles, moving barethium from a pile in the center to a large fiery put where it would be melted. I'd thought that was the worst part of Mael.

Then I saw the barracks.

I found a large barn-like structure in the back and ordered the two guards to open the large doors. The missing prisoners were huddled together two or three to a bunkbed. I'd even seen that little boy who'd been caught stealing apples from the market a few weeks ago; he looked pale and sick like the rest of them, but he'd waved to me. As the photographer jumped past me to begin documenting every bit of this awful place, I ordered all the prisoners out of their barracks and into the main room, along with all the guards and the media, who now numbered in the twenties.

Then, in front of the media and the prisoners, I publicly fired the prison head (though I didn't really have the authority to do that), and told the media I was staying in the prison until my father ordered it closed and the prisoners removed.

It had been five hours since my great announcement, and the initial fervor was starting to wear off. Most of the original photographers had long since left, the stench and general awfulness of this place too much to bear. Martin, as well, had begun to look green, so I'd sent him back to Norose to get some medical supplies. I figured as long as I was there, I might as well examine the prisoners. At least ten already seemed to be developing the lung cancer that came with inhaling barethium.

My other reason for sending Martin was to find out whether

my message was getting somewhere or if my father had kept it quiet. It wouldn't do me a whole lot of good to remain there if no one in Kylae knew about it.

It was getting dark now, and without the fire of the smelting process, a chill had started to descend. I ordered the guards to find blankets and shelter for everyone, but it was pretty clear that there wasn't enough. Martin still hadn't returned, either, which made me worry that he'd been intercepted by one of my father's people.

"S-sire." The new head of the prison (also known as, "the closest guy to me at the time") approached me. Even with his thick overcoat on, his lips were bluish from cold.

"What is it?" I asked.

"The guards are wondering if we can go home. It's the end of our shift, and—"

"Oh, you want to go home?" I asked, raising my voice. Then I looked out at the rest of the prisoners. "So do they. I thought I told you to go hunt down some blankets."

"We did, sire, but there aren't any more."

I ran a hand over my face. I wondered if this was what Theo had felt with me on our island. "Tell your men to find firewood."

"But—"

"Go, or I'll throw you in jail with the rest of them," I snapped.

I wasn't sure how much longer I could exude authority before someone questioned whether I had any at all. But for now, he did as I asked and conveyed my orders to his men. I made sure the fires were built correctly, stepping in when needed and instructing the way Theo had shown me. Before long, we had three large fires crackling safely.

My stomach rumbled and I glanced out the window. It was now dark, and I'd been there for six hours. Still no sign of Martin or my father. The media, as well, had all but left. It was now me, fifty guards, and some two hundred prisoners.

"You there," I said to the nearest guard. "Go give the order to prepare food."

"T-the prisoners usually do that," he replied meekly.

I stared at him. "Are you serious? After you make them slave all day over this poisonous shit, you force them into the kitchens to cook?"

"T-they take shifts—"

"*Go into the kitchen and get food for these people*," I said through clenched teeth.

He nodded and with a little bow, grabbed two of his friends and disappeared. I watched the door, praying I hadn't just given him the go-ahead to run off, but they returned with bags of rolls, which they began to hand out to the prisoners. I was surprised they didn't all rush to get the food, but then again, they looked barely strong enough to stand.

My heart lifted to the dark sky when I saw two headlights approach. I told the head guard to maintain calm as I rushed out into the cold and waited. Kader, not Martin, stepped out of my car, a grim look on his face.

"Where's Martin?" I asked, hoping my teeth weren't chattering.

"Back at your apartment, where I'm going to take you," Kader replied.

"I'm not leaving. Did you bring the medical supplies I asked for? Blankets? Food? Anything?"

He shook his head. "You need to come home."

"Kader, I can't leave," I said quietly. "This place is even worse than I thought. If I leave, then this all gets turned back on, and these people, who knows what happens to them?"

"And who knows what happens to you, Galian?" Kader replied. "Your father said that if you come home tonight, he will give a speech tomorrow calling for a review of practices at the prison."

I blinked. "A r-review? Not closing it down?" I shook my head. "No way. A *review* is what they told my mother. And, hey, look at that, they did *nothing*."

"I figured you might say that," he said with a heavy sigh. He reached into the car and, for a moment, I thought he might pull a gun and threaten me, but instead, he retrieved out my thickest winter coat and a brown paper bag. "Rosie wanted me to make sure you stayed warm tonight."

I took the coat, but didn't put it on, and peeked into the bag—leftovers. "As much as I appreciate this, I have two hundred people inside who need food. I can't possibly eat until they do."

Kader took the bag back and tossed it in the front seat.

"W-what did Father say would happen if I didn't come back home?" I asked.

"He didn't," Kader replied. "But the longer you stay here, the less control he has over the story, and the more this looks like a true revolt on your part." He glanced above my head, then back at me. "Are you willing to accept the consequences?"

"Are they mine?" I asked. "Is he threatening anyone else?"

"Not at the moment, but you never know with him."

"Then yes, I'm willing to accept the consequences," I said firmly. I had nothing to lose at this point. Nothing except the respect of the woman I loved if I walked away when things got difficult.

"Figured as much," Kader said, pulling out his keys. "Well, good luck to you."

"You aren't going to stay here with me?" I asked, stepping

forward. I wasn't sure why I wanted him around. Maybe I thought his imposing figure would keep the guards in line more than my royal title would. Maybe I needed a little assurance that I wasn't making a colossal mistake.

"Unlike you, your father has leverage over me. This is your fight, Galian." He opened the car door then said, "But for what it's worth, it's a good one."

I spent the night pacing the floor of the smelting room, checking vitals of the smallest prisoners and keeping the fires stoked. Weeks of night shifts had trained me to be alert, and to keep pushing until the first rays of the sun poked through the grimy windows. I sent the guards to hunt down breakfast, but they informed me that their shipment of food had been due yesterday, and thanks to my unplanned appearance, they'd been unable to restock.

For a brief moment, I considered whether there were any rabbits around for me to skin, but then I realized that I had bigger problems. I was now responsible for two hundred prisoners and twenty guards, none of whom I'd allowed to go home. I was nearing the one-day mark on my stay in the prison, and was surprised that the guards continued to listen to me.

But I was growing tired. I ducked away into one of the offices. Leaning against the closed door, I sighed loudly and released all the tension and exhaustion. My head swum with the barethium smell, still pungent even after nearly a day of inhaling it. I spied a discarded gas mask on the desk and tripped over my feet to retrieve it and yank it over my face.

I slouched down in a chair, the gas mask on my face, and my mind took me back to our island and that disgusting laboratory. The photos of the test subjects were eerily similar to the faces I was seeing just outside this room. Kylaen leaders had known what exposure to this poison would do, and they'd ignored the dangers. I tried to wrap my head around the reasons why my father, hell, even my *brother* could've stomached this.

There was a knock at the door. I pulled the mask off and the full punch of the barethium odor hit me again. "Come in."

"It smells like shit," Rhys said, walking into the room.

I nearly collapsed in relief. "*Oh, thank God, you're here.*"

"Thank me later," he said, closing the door behind him. "I've brought supplies, as you asked. Blankets, food, water. Dr. Hebendon is arriving in a few hours with support staff from the hospital to check on the injuries at the prison."

My jaw fell to the floor. "A-are you serious? Why?"

"Because if we do nothing, Father looks like a heartless bastard," he said dryly. "He's spinning this that he was completely unaware of the horrible treatment of the prisoners here. He's thrown the head of the prison, the one you supposedly fired, in jail for probably the rest of his life. There's a call for his execution, too."

I winced. "I didn't mean for that to happen."

"Well, what did you expect? Father's not going to take responsibility for this place. Not after you've splashed photos of child prisoners all over the news. He's pulled me off everything else— including the Jervan trade agreement—to deal with this mess."

"I'm so sorry that saving hundreds of lives is such an inconvenience to the crown prince of Kylae."

Rhys seemed unconcerned with my sarcasm as he rubbed a

hand over his face. "It really does smell terrible here. I don't know how you can stand it."

"Imagine being held here against your will," I replied. "Also, did you know that breathing in this toxic fumes for just one day increases your cancer risk?"

"Yes, I heard your interview," he said. "This is really bad, Gally. Father is...well, he's *livid*—"

"Good."

"No, it's *not* good. He's completely lost control over the media, and now the ministers are in an uproar! There's talk about deposing him—"

"What a horrible idea," I deadpanned.

"Gally, I'm serious—"

"No, I'm serious. Are you worried you'll lose your riches? Your place on the throne?"

"I'm worried Father may have to do something drastic to regain control over his country," Rhys said. "He's already been fighting back against pressure from the hawkish ministers. You know, *the ones who think we should be more aggressive against Rave.* If Father gets knocked off his throne, *they're* the ones who'll step up in his place."

"How much worse could they be?" I asked.

"Try bombing Veres, where your girlfriend lives," Rhys replied. "Hasn't been bombed in fifteen years. Neither have any of the major Raven cities. Most of the attacks have been on Raven armories and weapons to stifle their production so they don't retaliate against *us*. Some of the ministers think it's time to launch another major offensive." He ran a hand through his hair. "But if Father does that, he risks alienating the ministers who want peace, as well as Jervan and Herin. They're just as eager to see him deposed."

"So let's depose him and put *them* on the throne," I offered. "War over."

"Sure, and the Kylaen economy will go into a tailspin from the sudden drop in revenue," Rhys said. "The war puts almost a third of our country to work, and another third indirectly. If we just *stop*...the country will implode. And then the citizens will revolt, and the ministers will be the least of our problems." He slumped down into the desk chair. "So now we have to close the *second* biggest employer of our people because you decided to go rogue. Without barethium, our building and weapons industries will collapse."

I paced in front of the door, glancing out at the guards who had no idea what they were doing. "Rhys, we'll figure it out. That's what we do as leaders. We make tough decisions. Keeping this place open just because it's politically difficult...go out there and tell those kids that."

"Trust me, I'm with you on this. But you need to consider the consequences of just *acting* without talking to someone first. You aren't some nobody who can move in a vacuum. You've got more eyes on you than you know."

"Well, I'm not leaving until this place closes," I said. "And I don't regret my actions."

"You'll be pleased to hear that I've been authorized to give the order to stop production, and begin the process of moving prisoners," Rhys said, holding up a hand to silence me. "We'll review files and release those with minor crimes, and transfer others."

I closed my eyes in relief. "I did it."

"You certainly did something," Rhys replied. "Mom wants you back in the castle. *Tonight.*"

"No way," I said, shaking my head. "I can get more done when I don't live under the same roof as him."

"And he can do more *to* you," Rhys replied. "This isn't over between you and him. You've won this battle, but he's planning on winning the war."

"Yeah, well, he hasn't won the Madion War in fifty years, so I'm not holding my breath," I replied with a smile before my low blood sugar washed over me. "You don't have any food with you, do you?"

He reached into his pocket and tossed me a bag of peanuts. "Have you grown soft, Gally? Didn't you and Theo used to go days without eating?"

I inhaled the bag and tossed it aside. "You think she's heard about this?"

"I think *everybody* has heard about this." He held his hand out to me. "Come on. Let's go have our photo op and make the announcement so I can get the hell out of here."

Fourteen

Theo

Grieg Shuts Down Death Camp

Two tears slipped down my face and I pressed my fingertips to the grainy photo of my *amichai* and his brother, standing in front of Mael and announcing that it was closing for good. Galian looked pale and tired, but happy, and I just hoped his brother had been truthful in his agreement to shut down the prison. This newspaper article seemed to indicate it was another empty promise, but...Galian wouldn't have left otherwise.

His speech had been on replay, and I kept my radio on to listen to it until I fell asleep. Hearing his voice, knowing that he was talking about *me* to the world, I was giddy with excitement. And to know that he was fulfilling his promise to me just made my heart swell so much, I might've floated all the way to Kylae. I hadn't had any events for the last two days, so I'd been able to revel in the privacy of my apartment.

But it was time to return to reality, so I dressed in my jumpsuit and prepared for the deluge of photographers who now camped outside my apartment. I'd thought they would grow tired of waiting, but they

187 | S. USHER EVANS

photographed me with a great deal of excitement. For my part, I actually smiled at them.

"Where to, today?" I asked my driver.

"*Platcha*," came the reply from the front seat. "You've been going there so much, you might need an office, huh?"

I grinned, but didn't reply. I'd been spending a lot of time with Bayard since my speech. Although we hadn't really gotten into policy discussions, we'd shared a few short personal conversations in a few of our trips we had ridden together. But now that I'd been partially responsible for the closure of Mael, I expected we'd begin talking a lot more. After all, if Cannon could figure out how to weasel his way in with absolutely no experience in policy or politics, so could I.

Agustin, the same aide who had seen to me at my last visit to *Platcha*, was waiting for me at the front of the house and he looked more interested than usual. Predictably, Bayard's schedule had shifted after two weeks on the road, so my meeting with him would have to be squeezed in.

This time, however, Agustin led me to a small office down the hall from Bayard's. It was empty save a desk, chair, and lamp.

"I'm not sure when President Bayard will be able to see you today, so you can work from here," Agustin said, flipping on the light. "I'll come get you when it's time."

I took a seat at the desk, wondering what work Agustin expected me to do, or if he was simply trying to keep me out of the way. I swiveled in the chair and looked out the window, which faced the close-in wall of another wing of *Platcha* then drummed my hands on the desk.

"Don't you just look right at home."

I glanced up to see Cannon in the doorway. He looked more

sour than usual; probably because he hadn't been invited along on any of Bayard's appearances. I never really wanted to celebrate someone's defeat, so I smiled and said, "Good morning."

Cannon did not return my smile as he sauntered into the room. He held a folder in his hands, which he made a big show of flipping through before placing it in front of me. I noticed my name on the outer tab.

"What's this?"

"Your medical file."

My heart fluttered anxiously. "Why do you have my medical file? Aren't those private?"

"When you're in the spotlight, *nothing* is private."

My worry that he'd seen something in Jervan returned. Would he really sit on something this long? Why would he let me flit around the country if he knew? Was he just waiting for the opportune moment?

"Why do you have my medical file, Cannon?"

"I was curious about something," he said, lazily scratching his hairless chin. "I never quite understood the particulars of how you ended up in Mael. Would you care to share them with me?"

"Kylaens were attacking the armory at Vinolas, we realized that the princeling was amongst them. I went after him and my engine redlined." I paused for just a moment. "The Kylaens found me and took me to Mael. I don't see what this has to do with my medical file."

"You spoke so *passionately* about the dangers of Mael," Cannon said. "And yet, you don't seem to suffer any lingering ailments. No cancer, not even a cough. Your medical file shows that, besides a lower leg injury and being a little malnourished, you were quite healthy."

"I sustained the leg injury in the crash."

"You spoke about chains and long hours," Cannon said thoughtfully, "so if your leg was injured in the crash, how could it have healed properly? Two months of manual labor..."

"I don't know, Cannon. I'm not a doctor."

I didn't like how his smile widened, and I hoped it wasn't the inadvertent reference to Galian.

"And about that crash...your plane went down and you were taken prisoner by the Kylaens."

I nodded. It was mostly the truth.

"Why go through the trouble of finding you at all? Why not just let you drown?"

I narrowed my eyes. "Any particular reason for the investigation? Mael is closed now. Who cares?"

"Because I don't trust you, that's why," Cannon said. "I've had my doubts about you, *kallistrate*, since the moment you washed up on our shores. There are too many unanswered questions, too many coincidences. And now Bayard wants to bring you into the cabinet because you gave a speech?"

"H-he does?" I said, sitting up straighter.

"Oh, yes, he's all excited about you now. Thinks we could use you to leverage lower wheat tariffs from Jervan, or even get in on some Herin contracts," Cannon said, his tone making it perfectly clear how he felt about my involvement.

"Cannon, I don't know what you think, but all I want to do is..." I looked beyond him. "End the war so our country can finally start to heal."

"And see, *that* is why I'm so interested," Cannon replied. "Why so eager to end the war, *kallistrate*?"

"Because we are sending children to *die*. Because every time I go to these commissioning ceremonies, the pilots look younger and younger. Because it needs to end."

"And what, pray tell, are you willing to do to end it? Return to Kylaen rule?"

My mouth fell open. "What gave you that idea?"

"Did the Kylaens offer you a deal? You would spy for them in exchange for your freedom?"

"No," I said as firmly as I could. "I escaped."

"How?" Cannon pressed. "Because to my eyes, the evidence doesn't add up."

Luckily, a soft rap at my door interrupted my interrogation, and Agustin poked his head in. "Excuse me, Major? Minister Wolfe would like to meet with you for a moment."

"T-thank you," I said, standing and nodding to dismiss him. Then I turned back to Cannon. "I am no spy for Kylae. But believe me when I say that my goal for being here is to bring an end to this war *and* to maintain a free and independent Rave. You might want to consider why you're here, *Cannon*. Because to *my eyes*, it looks like you're here for your own personal gain. Now, if you'll excuse me, I have meetings to attend."

Cannon's interest in my medical file sat in the back of my mind as I met with three of Rave's parliamentary ministers. Each of them wanted the same thing: to have me appear with them at their next press conference and to vocalize my support for their initiatives.

Minister Wolfe was petitioning Bayard and the parliament to increase funding to an air base in his district on the west side of the country. I asked him why he felt that the least-attacked portion of the country deserved to get more money over the western front, and he gave me an excuse about jobs and the economy and then I tuned him out. When he pressed for my support, I told him he would have to check my schedule with Emilie and also made a mental note to tell Emilie to decline his invitation.

Minister Neb was trying to secure funding for one of the only boarding schools left in Rave, as the roof was in need of repair. While I assured him that I valued education, I told him I'd rather that money go toward building a school in some of the poorer cities, like the one I'd grown up in. When he mentioned how the poorer children would end up being conscripted anyway, I left the meeting without another word.

The third meeting was the best, though that wasn't saying much. Minister Ula's initiative was to introduce green beans into the military food staples. After pressing him, I found that his good friend had a cannery that was looking to expand his business. Tired from saying no all day, I told him I would seriously consider his offer before leaving to join Agustin in the hall.

"What's next?" I asked wearily.

"Bayard's ready for you," he said.

"Thank God," I said, hoping my chat with him would be void of anything having to do with money or favors.

Instead of waiting, this time, Agustin led me right inside. Bayard was reading at his desk, and told me to take a seat at the ornate table. Before he left, Agustin reached into the small drawer in the table and helped himself and me to a chocolate.

"So, Theo," Bayard said, putting down the paper. "Great news about Mael."

I nodded and swallowed. "Have you heard if it's...really

closed?"

"Our sources tell us it's a ghost town now," Bayard replied. "They released sixty percent of the prisoners, and the other forty were transferred to regular prisons."

Despite being in the office of the president of my country, I slumped in relief.

Bayard chuckled and stood, crossing the room slowly to join me at the table. "I'm sorry that I had Emilie cancel all your appearances over the weekend. But with Mael closed, it didn't make sense for you to be delivering your speech about a place that's no longer a threat."

"To be honest...I would rather not speak and have it be closed," I said with a bright smile.

He winked at me and rolled another chocolate ball down toward me. "But now we have a conundrum. Theo, you are the symbol of Mael, and with Mael closed, what do we do with you?"

I nearly choked on the chocolate, not bothering to mask my worry. "Sir?"

"Oh, dear, dear, don't worry. We aren't going to send you back to Vinolas. But I did want to hear your thoughts on your next steps, career-wise."

I swallowed the bulk of the chocolate. I considered the meetings I'd already had that day, and how each of the ministers had jockeyed for my favor. My voice had weight now, and I intended to use it. "I want to get involved. The Kylaens are showing that they're willing to budge on some major issues—they've closed Mael, they've reduced the number of bombings. I think now might be the time to approach the negotiation table. Try to come to a peace agreement with them. The p-princeling said—"

"You feel very strongly about peace between Rave and Kylae?"

I remembered what Cannon had said, and considered my response. "I want a free and independent Rave, but we aren't free as long as we're fighting off the Kylaens. I'm sure that the people of Kylae are weary of war, too."

"They don't know war," Bayard said with a sigh. "They know nothing of daily bombings and the struggles of this nation."

I could've argued that many of the people in Veres were the same, but that wouldn't have gone over very well. "But they've been enlightened to Mael. They're closing it. The whole country is in an uproar."

"Not as much as you'd think."

"But enough that maybe we could start treaty negotiations," I replied. "I'd love to be involved—"

"I'm sure you would," Bayard said, reaching into his desk and pulling out a chocolate. I now assumed this was a sign for me to shut up and agree with him. "And I love this new Theo I'm seeing. Unfortunately, I don't think we could use you to help relations with Kylae. You did escape their prison, even if it is now closed, and I'd hate to send you back there just to find yourself in danger."

I chewed on the chocolate instead of arguing with him. I might not be able to do much in Kylae by myself, but with Galian, we might be able to change some minds. But now probably wasn't the best time to inform Bayard of my relationship with him.

"Instead, I'd like you to return to your appearances. You did so well boosting morale at the bases, and I'd like to see us capitalize on that." I didn't bother to hide my distaste at that idea, and Bayard chuckled. "We need a new story for you, though. One that will sell as well as Mael did. Have you given any thought to marriage?"

I blinked at him. "Excuse me?"

"You're twenty, in the prime of your life. What better way to show your Raven pride by taking a husband and having more Raven citizens?"

I barked a laugh. "I...don't think that's how I want to be marketed."

"Cannon might make a suitable match," Bayard said. "Both of you are becoming stale. A wedding might be just the thing to reinvigorate your brand. Then, of course, you can continue—"

"With all due respect, *sir*, I'm not going to get married just so I can be a media spectacle," I replied harshly. "I am a major in the Raven air forces. I've survived seven years in the front lines and two months...in Mael. I'm not here to chase down the 'next big thing' for my brand. If I'm going to be used, I want to be used to *help* people—and not to give them something to gossip about."

Almost immediately, I regretted my outburst. But to my surprise, Bayard's smile hadn't faded a bit; in fact, it grew.

"I do love this new, *passionate* Theo. Tell you what, how about we make a deal, hm? If you'll do me the honor of attending a few more ceremonies and helping bolster our Raven morale, Emilie and I will knock our heads together and see where we can stick you that would make the most sense."

Having to go back to ceremonies was disconcerting, but I nodded. "Yes, sir."

"Buck up, Theo. I have a feeling we're not quite finished with you yet."

GALIAN

"I think you'll be fine after a few days, but please lay off the hot peppers," I said to the young man who'd come in complaining of stomach pains. He nodded to me and groaned as I wrote him a prescription for some heavy-duty antacids.

It was my first day back at the hospital since leaving to close down the prison, and it had taken me a few hours to get into the swing of things. After tending to prisoners who could barely stand on their feet, wealthy Kylaens who complained of small ailments and self-inflicted wounds were a bit hard to stomach. I was also a bit moody; I couldn't keep the smell of barethium out of my nose, no matter how many showers I took.

But it was hard to be too upset. Rhys had kept his word, and most of the prisoners were in the process of being released. I'd witnessed more than my fair share of tearful reunions as parents were reunited with their kids, most of which my father had kept out of the press. The sooner the story died, Rhys had said, the sooner he could reclaim his popularity in the polls. From what I saw on the news and what I heard at the hospital, not many people believed that he'd been completely unaware of conditions there.

I left the patient room with Mr. I-ate-too-many-hot-peppers-on-a-dare and padded over to the nurses' station. "I'm discharging room twenty. Can you take care of him for me?"

The nurse snorted and took the folder from me.

"What's wrong?" I asked. It wasn't that I expected everyone to be nice to me, but I didn't think I'd done something to offend this particular nurse before.

"Did you really think it was a good idea to release hundreds of prisoners into the streets?" she asked.

"Because all those poor kids are such a danger to society," I replied lazily. I suppose I should've expected this, but the sentiment took me by surprise.

"They were in jail in the first place. *Obviously* they belonged there."

"Do you honestly believe that?"

"If they followed the law, they wouldn't have been in jail."

I pinched the bridge of my nose. "That's not..."

"Excuse me, Doctor." She stood and left, with a disgusted look on her face.

"Thanks...for nothing," I said.

"Dr. Helmuth, are you annoying my nurses?" Hebendon asked, appearing behind me.

I swallowed a comment about how they weren't exactly his nurses, they were Maitland's, but I didn't think that would help my case.

"Just asking her to help me discharge a patient," I said, not wanting to have a long, drawn-out conversation with him. He might schedule me for another night shift, and I was *so* happy to be working a day shift for once.

"I just wanted to let you know that I appreciated what you did last week," Hebendon said. "I thought it took a lot of courage."

That surprised me. I thought Hebendon worked for my father. "Are you serious?"

His face darkened. "Of course I'm serious. I'm a doctor, and that place...the human toll is not worth it, whatever your leadership— excuse me, your father, might say." His sallow skin grew redder. "I do hope that won't get back to him."

"You tell me. You're the one working for him."

It was his turn to look surprised. "W-work for him? The endowment comes from the royal treasury, but the hospital is run by the board of directors."

"You know what I mean," I replied. "When Maitland left—"

"Dr. Maitland and I go back forty years, to when we were in medical school together," Hebendon said. "He wanted a break from Norose and offered to let me bolster my resume as the temporary Chief of Medicine here."

I glanced around for anyone who might be listening. "And my father hasn't been telling you to give me all the shitty shifts?"

"Dr. Helmuth, you're a resident. It's the nature of the beast that you receive the worst shifts." He patted me on the shoulder. "Rite of passage."

"Huh," I said, rocking back on my heels.

"But perhaps I gave you a nicer schedule this week after all of your work last week," Hebendon said with a sparkle in his eye. "Speaking of which, I'd like to do a quick examination and make sure there's no adverse effects from all the barethium you inhaled."

"I'm sure I'm fine," I said, waving him off. "The smoke stacks weren't on."

"Yes, but I've got a direct request from Dr. Maitland to make sure I at least do a chest x-ray on you," Hebendon said.

I found myself smiling. "Maitland asked you to? What else did he say? And what was Maitland like in medical school?"

"Let's have that x-ray and we'll talk all about it."

Now that I didn't think Hebendon was a dirty spy for my father, I accepted that he was a fairly decent physician, and an excellent teacher. He talked me through his review of my x-ray, which had come back clear, and quizzed me on whether I thought I should be prescribed medicine for the wheezing in my chest (he and I both agreed we'd monitor it).

When we'd finished, it was about time for my shift to be over, and since I didn't have any patients, Hebendon and I went to the cafeteria and swapped stories about our own medical school training. I think he was surprised to hear how dedicated I was, and that most of the stories he'd heard about me and partying had been false.

"I confess, I thought perhaps it was your time on the island that changed you," he said. "The nurses said you came back different."

"I was different," I said, looking at the dregs at the bottom of my paper cup. "Wish I'd gone to Mael sooner, though. How many more lives could I have saved?"

"But I thought you were inspired by that Raven girl's speech?"

I smiled. "I was. But it shouldn't have taken her speech to get me to do something." I glanced at the clock on the wall. "Oh shit, I have to get going. My ride's here. Thanks for the coffee."

"I'm just sorry it took us this long to have it," he said. "But don't get any ideas. Next week, it's back to impactions and night shifts."

I laughed, and although I knew he was dead serious thanks to all the crap *he'd* been put through as a resident, I didn't mind the torture anymore. Hebendon was in my corner, and I could handle whatever shitty cases he threw my way. Pun intended.

I left him in the cafeteria and strolled around to the back parking lot of the hospital. There, at least, I could stand outside without the threat of having my picture taken. I inhaled the moist, cool air that seemed, if possible, a little warmer than usual. Perhaps spring wasn't too far off.

I heard my car before I saw it, turning the corner around the back and parking right in front of me. Martin rolled down the window, flashing a smile at me. "Are we headed back to Mael today?"

I glanced at the sky and shook my head. "Let's take a night off."

"Good, because that place depresses me. Why don't we get shitfaced tonight?"

I reached for the car door, but a knock behind me drew my attention. A red-haired nurse popped her head out. "Dr. Helmuth, room twenty has a question for you before you go."

I groaned and closed the door, turning to the nurse to answer her. But the blow from the explosion behind me was the last thing I heard before everything went black.

Fifteen

Theo

"...Prince Galian assassination...car bomb..."

The pen dropped from my hand. I couldn't even remember what I'd been reading. I flew out of my dining room into the living room and grasped my radio, turning it up in horrified panic.

He couldn't be.

I must've misheard.

There was no way my *amichai* was...

"...Yesterday morning, a car bomb was detonated in downtown Kylae near the Royal Kylaen Hospital. The intended target was Prince Galian, although he was not in the car at the time—"

"Fuck," I cried, sinking to my knees.

I lay on the floor of my apartment, breathing in the scent of the carpet and breathing out the heart attack I'd nearly had. I wasn't sure how long I stayed prostrate against the ground, calming myself down, but when my heartbeat had almost returned to normal, I lifted my head.

Someone had tried to assassinate Galian.

I flipped onto my back and finally began to listen to the white noise of the radio. The Raven news had moved onto something else, but they would circle back around. In the space between listening to Bayard's appearances to a story about a squadron on the southern coast of the country, I began to speculate the details of an attack until I was beside myself with worry.

"In case you missed it, breaking news out of Norose. Yesterday afternoon, a car bomb intended for Prince Galian detonated near the Royal Kylaen Hospital. The royal family is not releasing details, citing a need to conduct a full investigation. While the prince suffered minor injuries, one of his guards, David Martin, perished in the blast."

Martin, he was the young man I'd seen with Galian in Jervan. The one who'd been flirting with the girls around the pool. Galian had moved in with him, and said that they'd become close friends. He was young too, around my age.

I closed my eyes and said a small prayer for him, and another for Galian, that he might find some peace amongst all this tragedy.

GALIAN

Martin was dead and it was my fault.

If only I'd listened to Rhys and my mother. They'd been warning me that testing my father was a bad idea, but stupidly I'd thought he'd only go after me. Never in my wildest dreams did I think he'd kill Martin.

I vaguely remembered my mother coming to visit me in the

hospital, where Hebendon was treating me for a mild concussion and shock. She'd said it wasn't safe in my apartment anymore, and that I needed to come home where she could better protect me. I almost told her she had nothing to fear from me anymore, that my days of risking lives that weren't my own were over. Instead, I told her I would return to the castle, but on my own terms and in my own time. I needed time to grieve in private, and the only place I wanted to do that was Rosie's couch.

I lay there for two days, staring at the ceiling fan and wondering if I'd ever have the guts to cross the hall into our old apartment. I found myself recalling every single moment of my short time with Martin, wondering if I'd been kind enough to him, if I'd been a good friend. If I'd known that his time was limited to twenty years, I might've spent less time moping over Theo and more having beers with him.

One morning, I overheard Kader telling Rosie that Martin's family was having a private funeral, and that woke me from my stupor. Martin had been dishonorably discharged after I'd helped Theo escape, and was therefore not allowed the full rights of a military funeral. But since he'd died in the line of duty, protecting me, I thought he deserved better.

So I peeled myself off the couch and went to see my brother at the castle. He hadn't been surprised to see me, but he had agreed to pull some strings to give Martin the honor he deserved.

The day of the funeral was so cold and bitter. Kader, Rosie, and I drove to the military cemetery where the most esteemed Kylaen military heroes had been buried—including my ancestors and my brother, Digory. I felt a bit guilty that I hadn't come to see Dig since his funeral. He'd been an asshole, but he was still my brother. I promised myself that I'd start regular visits to him and Martin...

Martin.

Martin was dead, and it was my fault.

"You all right back there, son?" Kader asked.

"Yeah," I said hoarsely.

Rosie turned around to look at me, but I couldn't meet her gaze. I didn't want to start blubbering in front of Kader.

When we arrived at the gravesite, a crowd was already assembled around the coffin. Thankfully, there were no tabloid photographers around. I didn't want Martin's funeral to turn into another propaganda event for my father.

Kader and Rosie made their way to two empty seats, but I stayed apart from the rest of the crowd and stared at the photo of Martin next to the dark wooden casket. A few flurries had begun to fall, which seemed fitting.

I'd never met Martin's parents, but they were easy to spot, as was his younger sister. She looked just like him, with dark black hair that disappeared onto the black coat she wore. But the most telling were the distraught looks on their pale faces. They'd expected their nineteen-year-old son to outlive them. Yet now they were burying him. Because of a decision that I'd made.

I heard footsteps approaching. Kader had left Rosie's side to stand next to me, his hands behind his back at attention.

"You should say something to them," he said softly. "They want to meet you."

"I don't know if I should," I replied, wishing I sounded a little less emotional.

"Steady, son," he said, placing a hand on my shoulder. I thought he was offering support, until I heard the excited whispers from the funeral attendees.

A cadre of ten cars had pulled up in the center of the road, and my father and brother had stepped out of one of them. They'd brought their top generals, a few ministers, and, of course, photographers and reporters to capture every scene.

My somber mood turned furious in an instant. "What is *he*—"

"*Steady*, Galian," Kader said, his hand tightening on my shoulder. "Just get through this. It will be over soon."

I couldn't believe my eyes as my father, the man who'd ordered Martin's death, strolled up to Martin's father and shook his hand then grasped his mother's in solidarity. Rhys caught my eye and gave me a small shake of his head as he followed behind my father to offer his condolences.

"You would do better to honor Martin's memory by not defiling his funeral with a temper tantrum," Kader whispered, his hand still on my shoulder. "There are other ways to achieve your goals. Keep that in mind."

"This isn't about goals," I said, wrenching my eyes away from the scene. "He shouldn't be here. He has *no right*—"

"Martin was killed while protecting his son. It would look stranger if he weren't here."

My father remained next to Martin's mother, holding her hand and looking for all the world like a man in mourning. My brother broke away from the group, joining me and Martin.

"When I asked for your help, this is *not* what I expected," I said through clenched teeth.

"Galian, you know as well as I do that I couldn't have stopped him if I'd wanted to," Rhys replied, standing at military attention beside me.

"Could you have stopped the assassination attempt?" I asked.

"Because we all know who gave the order."

Rhys and Kader were silent for a moment. Then Rhys spoke, "I don't know who gave the order. But it wasn't him."

"As if he'd tell you."

"He wouldn't, but I have my sources," Rhys replied. Out of the corner of my eye, I saw him lean behind me to look at Kader. "Anything on your end?"

"So far, nothing," Kader replied, not breaking eye contact with the funeral, which had begun. "But what I'm hearing is that Rave—"

"Do you really expect me to believe the Ravens did this?" I said, feeling the warning glare from Kader on the other side of me. "I go to Mael, and suddenly there's an assassination attempt. Pardon me if I'm skeptical. Especially considering His Highness' track record."

Silence descended between the three of us and we watched the funeral. The priest stepped aside and my father took the podium. I was too far away to hear his words (a good thing), but I caught wisps of talk about Kylaen pride and service to country. It sounded the same as the speech he'd given at Dig's funeral, and probably had been repeated at countless others'.

This war had taken too many people already and yet it went on without end. How many of the gravestones around us were casualties of a war that never should've been started in the first place? And how many Ravens had died?

Today, though, this death was on my hands.

We bowed our heads in prayer, and the funeral was over. Martin's parents stood and received their well-wishers, pale-faced and shaky.

"Are you going to greet them?" Kader asked.

"Once the circus has moved on," I said, glaring at Rhys. "I don't want an audience."

"Gally..." Rhys closed his eyes and shook his head. Then he clapped my shoulder. "I'll tell Mom you'll be home for dinner."

"Tell her whatever you want."

Rhys left me to join my father, who made no move to speak to me or even acknowledge my presence. He made one more pass at Martin's parents, then took his contingent of bodyguards and photographers with him. Most of the funeral's attendees went with him, more interested in the king than the young man they'd just mourned.

I left Kader and approached Martin's parents for the first time. Up close, I saw he had his mother's nose and chin and his father's kind disposition.

"Your High—" Martin's father began.

"No need for that nonsense," I said gently. "Martin was...he was a good man and one of my very best friends."

His mother's eyes softened, and she gently took my hands. "He spoke a lot about you. He was very...very impressed by you. Especially after your ordeal on the island. He was honored to have been assigned to you."

I nodded. "I'm so..." Emotion welled up in my eyes. "God damn, I'm so sorry. I'm so sorry that I got him...that he was mixed up in my..."

"Martin was never as proud as when he was discharged," his father said. "He came home and told us what you had done, saving that girl. Going back to the hospital. Working to better this country." He grasped my shoulder. "We're honored that he could give his life to protect you."

I gnashed my teeth together and nodded, needing to get away.

We dropped Rosie off at the apartment building, but I didn't get out of the car. As angry as I was that my father had come to the funeral, I knew it was time for me to return to the castle. Even if I'd wanted to, I was just too emotionally drained to fight anymore.

But the drive was taking longer than usual. I wrenched my eyes away from my hands and realized I didn't recognize this part of town.

"Where are we?" I asked. "I thought you were taking me back to the castle."

"I will, but not yet," Kader replied, parking the car in front of an old building. "First, you need to blow off some steam."

Curious, I closed the car door behind me and followed him inside the grungy building. The room was small, and smelled of old alcohol and body odor, but it was empty save a group of people seated around tables smashed together in the center of the room.

"Eli!"

"Oi, Eli!"

Kader passed me and shook hands with two men. I spotted Johar; she raised her tankard to me and offered me a seat next to her.

"Galian, the men of the 101st Special Operations Unit," Kader said. "You know Johar, but this is Cyra, Gibbs, Piplu." One by one, they introduced themselves. Each were middle-aged like Kader, rough-skinned and weathered. Their eyes held a similar detached pity, like they knew how I felt, but had experienced it too many times to be really affected anymore.

"Sit down, son," Johar said, grabbing me by my shoulder and sitting me down next to her. She placed a glass mug of sudsy beer in front of me. "Drink."

I took a long sip, and it tasted really, *really* good. But I couldn't be happy about it.

"Talk," Kader said, taking the seat across from me.

"About?"

"You've been holding it in," Kader replied. "You need to let it out. Talk about it. You're a doctor. You know that's not healthy."

I did know; it was the same guidance I'd given Theo in Jervan. But she was the only person I felt comfortable breaking down in front of, not fifteen of the most badass people I'd ever seen. I sucked down half the beer.

"We're looking into who put that bomb in your car," Johar replied after a moment.

"It wasn't Rave," I snapped. "And my father's going to use it to bolster the war. Again. Because that's what he does. He kills people then uses it as justification to kill *more* people. First Dig, then me. Now M...Martin."

"That wasn't a justification, that was a warning," Kader replied. "And I'm not sure it came from your father. There are a few powerful businessmen who stand to lose millions when the barethium runs out. They're not above using dirty tactics to get what they want. And they want the prison turned back on."

My heart sank. "You can't be serious. After all that—"

"Grieg has dispatched his own minions to soothe them," Johar replied. "They have at least two years' worth stockpiled—more if we slow down production of some weapons. That's plenty of time for them to start investing their considerable fortunes elsewhere."

I couldn't believe my ears. "So you're saying that a bunch of businessmen killed Martin because my father closed Mael? Because it impacted their bottom lines?"

"Life would be so much simpler if we could blame everything that goes wrong on your father, Galian," Kader said. "Unfortunately, it's not."

"But Rhys and my mother, they said...they told me not to be a target. Grieg *left me on the island*."

"He's done his fair share of things, sure," Kader replied. "But we're pretty sure that this episode was a message *to* him, not from him."

"And that's it then," I said, sitting back. "Martin's dead, but message received. Does his life even *matter*?"

"Do you know what matters?" Johar replied harshly. "The fact that two hundred prisoners are out of a toxic death camp. Do you even understand what you've done? People knew about Mael, but they didn't *know* about Mael. You don't hear about it in the papers, but the Kylaen people aren't too happy with your father right now." She nodded to me. "That's because of you, son."

"You've kept your promise to your girl," Kader said. "That counts for something."

The mention of Theo was at once uplifting and devastating. I needed her there with me so much it ached. She'd gone through loss before; she would know exactly the right thing to say to me. But more than that, I needed the safe haven she'd created for me, where I could let everything out. Without her, I felt ready to explode. I clenched my jaw.

"Son, there's no shame in it," Kader said, putting a strong hand on my shoulder. "Martin was a good kid. We've all lost one of our own before."

"Romola Simec," Johar said, raising her glass.

"Alastair Friedland."

"Charley Elm."

Around the room, they raised their glasses and honored those they'd lost in the line of duty.

"You get through it by honoring them the best way you know," Johar said. "I drink only Nikle whiskey for Charley."

A grin broke out on Kader's face. "Man, he loved that shit."

"How did he die?" I asked.

"Classified mission," Johar said. "But bottom line was that the Ravens knew where we were and dropped a couple bombs on us." She shook her head. "Which, in effect, did what we were there to do. Place was decimated."

I wrapped my hands tighter around the mug. "Where in Rave?"

"Nowhere near your girl," Kader said.

My hands relaxed, but not much. "But he died on a mission? Not because of anything that you...anything that you did."

The group grew more solemn and focused on their beers as Kader spoke. "We were going to shut down a power plant on the north end of the island. We thought it supplied power to a secret facility we'd been hunting for a few years. But our intel was wrong, and, thanks to the Ravens, we cut power to a nearby city and hospital." He inhaled deeply. "I made the call to go on the mission even though I had a question. And therefore..."

"But you said the Ravens bombed it?" I said. "So isn't it the Ravens' fault? They would know what they were doing—"

"By the same logic, how can you claim guilt for Martin's death?" Kader asked.

The table went deathly silent. I glanced around at the faces of the men and women who'd given their lives and friends to my father's cause. Not one of them disagreed with Kader.

"So what do I do about it?" I asked. "What did you do?"

"Requested a transfer out of Special Operations into your mother's private security," Kader said, sitting back. "We all did."

"She keeps us busy," Johar said with a sardonic grin.

"Your mother is more than meets the eye," Kader replied. "And although you might think going back to the castle is a terrible idea, it actually puts you in a better position than drinking beer with Martin in your apartment."

A fresh wave of grief washed over me. I'd never drink beer in the apartment with Martin again. He'd never try to pass me off as his cousin Jem or give advice about Theo. The nights of hearing him rummaging in the fridge for a midnight snack, the evenings of coming back from the hospital and seeing him on his second bag of chips, the mornings of waking up and hearing his loud snores from his bedroom— they were gone.

He was gone forever.

"Let's toast," Kader said, picking up his beer. "To Martin."

"To Martin," came the reply from the group.

I raised my glass as a tear slid down my cheek. "To Martin."

Sixteen

Theo

For most of Rave, news of an assassination attempt on Prince Galian was met with a shrug and a commentary on how the princeling continued to give death the slip. Days passed, and the story died down in the Raven papers, though it still dominated the weekly meetings with Emilie. Galian himself had disappeared, returning to live at the castle and only leaving at night to work at the hospital. Selfishly, I was glad he was under lock and key. I didn't know what I would've done with myself had the assassination been successful.

I did know he was hurting. He'd told me about Martin and Kader during our night in Jervan, and how Martin had become his good friend and confidant. To make matters worse, I was sure moving back into the castle was salt in his wounds. I wanted, more than anything, to gather him up in my arms and comfort him.

But I had my own problems. Cannon still watched my every move, and I was starting to get the feeling Emilie was as well. With Mael closed, I was no longer delivering my speech, and was thus back to attending commissioning and promotion ceremonies. There'd been no

213 | S. USHER EVANS

more talk of marriage to bolster my reputation, so that, at least, was a blessing. But I still needed to make myself useful to Bayard, if only to remain close at hand.

One week after news broke of the assassination attempt, I'd returned late from a promotion nearly four hours' drive away, and stopped in to drop off my report at Emilie's request. She informed me that the next morning, I would be needed at the executive offices at 0500 hours. When I asked her where I'd be going, she said she didn't know, but the look in her eyes said otherwise.

Bleary-eyed, I arrived at the executive offices before the first rays of sunlight even broke the dark sky. Emilie was nowhere to be found, but I was ordered into a car with Cannon and several other aides I didn't recognize. The lot of us looked ready to go back to sleep, and I even caught a few minutes of a nap as we sped through the city.

We arrived at the nearest military base, where we were then shuffled onto a pair of large helicopters that held all ten of us. There we sat, shivering and blinking in the night, until another set of cars rolled up. Bayard and Ministers Lee and Breen stepped out, and walked to the second helicopter.

"Where are we going?" I whispered to myself as the helicopter engine roared to life above us.

Cannon had taken the seat behind me, and I caught his eye. His gaze on me was studied and alert now, as if every breath I took was confirmation of some greater secret. I spun in my seat and leaned my head against the cool window. I didn't feel like getting into a pissing match this morning, so I kept my mouth closed and my gaze straight ahead.

The chopper had landed in an airfield I'd never seen before. After disembarking, I realized it wasn't so much an airfield as a large, concrete plain. Dry grass rose up through cracks in the cement, as if this place hadn't been used in years. The concrete plain stretched all the way to a line of dark trees in the distance.

I turned to look behind the helicopter and took a step back in surprise. I recognized the smoke stacks, the grimy windows, the acrid smell crawled into my nose. I shook my head to clear it, inhaling deeply and reminding myself this place wasn't a Kylaen death camp. The smell was just in my mind. There was no danger.

"Come now, Theo, look sharp," Cannon said, coming to stand next to me. "Look familiar?"

"Where *the hell* are we?" I spat, not even bothering to mask the panic on my face. "Is this...this isn't Mael..."

"No, no," he said, looking a little disappointed. "A precursor to it, though. Here in our own country."

"P-precursor..." My sleep-addled mind raced through what I knew of Raven history until it landed on the glaringly obvious option. "M-Malaske?"

I was now wide-awake and full of nervous adrenaline. Bayard had invited me on a tour of the secret facility to see the secret project. Perhaps whatever was being built in Malaske was my new "brand."

Again, I looked at the smoke stacks, hoping the dread I felt was due to memories of Mael, and not what I was about to encounter.

I trailed at the back of the group, which included more ministers and aides than I'd seen before, as we met a full colonel in front of the dilapidated buildings. Her hands were clasped behind her back, her steely brown eyes visible underneath her cap. Her gaze slid over me—first at my capless head (a violation of Raven uniform code) then at my pants, which seemed worn and haggard next to her crisply ironed ones. I was happy when she surveyed Cannon in the same way, and her lip curled even more.

"President Bayard, sir," she said, when Bayard joined us. She saluted him, and he waved his salute back. "Colonel Hilda Willet, Malaske commander."

"Very good, Colonel," Bayard said. "I've very eager to see the project. Minister Breen has been very complimentary of your efforts."

Willet didn't acknowledge his praise. "If you'll follow me." She performed a perfect two-step turn and marched inside the building, leading us down a long, skinny hallway. There were near twenty of us by my count, so we had to file in two by two through the small entry hallway. I was paired with Minister Lees, whose head nearly scraped the top of the low ceiling.

The long hallway ended abruptly at a pair of double doors.

"President Bayard, we'll need to split the group up," Willett announced. "The lift can hold eight."

Cannon made sure to push himself into the first group with Bayard, smiling at me as the doors closed. The lift took a while to return, but when it did, I flattened myself against the wall so the rest of the group could climb in. We'd been stuck with a few of the more rotund ministers, so it was a tight fit.

A chill ran up my spine as the lift dropped like a stone, hurtling down the shaft with a speed I hadn't expected. I gripped the handrail against the wall and closed my eyes, feeling the car slow and then, finally, come to a stop.

The group exited the car and cold air hit my face. I stepped out and gazed upward at the cave we now stood in. Giant rock formations pointed down at us from high above.

"Welcome to Malaske Cave," Willett said, her sharp voice echoing through the space. "This was the site of the first Kylaen barethium processing facility."

Several of the ministers covered their mouths with their handkerchiefs, but I took a deep breath and couldn't smell the odor anymore.

"Fear not, the barethium in here is in its natural state and is completely safe." Willet's eyes slid over my face, and I thought I saw a flash of pity in them. She cleared her throat. "If you'll indulge in a little history lesson, this cave and the processing plant at the surface level were the prize of King Thormond and," she chuckled, "the first that our Raven forefathers destroyed."

A murmur of approving comments echoed from the group as the older ministers shared triumphant glances.

"What was once the death knell for thousands of our countrymen is now the pride of our nation," Willett said. "Please direct your attention to the future of Rave."

She opened her arms to a large plane in the center of the cave. I glanced at the ministers, reading their faces. They were as confused as I was. To my eyes, it appeared a similar model to the one which had brought us to Jervan.

"Fellow Ravens," Bayard said, walking the group closer to the plane. "Much like our great Major Kallistrate is made of stronger stuff than she appears, I implore you to wait to form your opinions until you see what our plane has inside."

I bristled at the unwelcome attention, and hung at the back of the group. Up close, the airship was massive, with four turbines and a cargo bay that could've fit my whole fighter plane. The Raven symbol was painted on the side.

Willett gave the order, and the back of the plane lowered into a ramp, groaning and squeaking.

"Oh!"

A bulky object sat in the center of the cargo space, so large that it nearly took up the entirety of the space. Bayard and Willett climbed the ramp to stand in front of the object, Bayard placing a hand on the edge of the dark metal casing.

"What is that, Tedwin?" Lee asked.

"This, my friends, is a warhead," Bayard said. "Capable of leveling over one hundred square miles of land."

A collective breath left the group.

"But that's..."

"Tedwin."

"Yes, enough explosives to level the entire city of Norose." Bayard's voice echoed across a silent audience.

I became aware of my own breathing, fast and nervous, and closed my mouth. Bayard was planning on bombing Norose? Over half a million people lived in that city, we couldn't possibly be considering doing what Bayard was saying.

"We've tried to bomb Norose," Lee said, his old voice breaking through the silence. "We can't get past their defenses."

"This time, we've got a bit of help," Bayard said. "You see, thanks to our intelligence division, a few years ago, we solidified an alliance with Herin and Jervan. They, too, are tired of Kylae's iron grip on their economies. We proposed a joint venture—with Raven firepower, Jervanian funding, and Herinese technology that makes us invisible to their radar, we built a bomb so large it could destroy Norose with a single blast. The Kylaens won't know we're coming until we're right over their shores."

My hand desperately wished to cover my mouth, but I gripped my pants to keep it in place. I heard my own voice call out, "But this is a last resort, right?"

The group turned to stare at me. "We are at a last resort, my dear," Lees said.

"N-no," I said, glancing around at their solemn faces. Their initial surprise had turned to grim acceptance. "No, they're getting better! They shut down Mael—"

"For now," Bayard said with a wave of his hand. "But Grieg will simply open another in a few years. His less-than-savory business partners have made that message clear with their attempted assassination of his son. There is no other option. In order for us to maintain our independence, we must destroy Kylae."

I couldn't believe what I was hearing. More than that, I couldn't believe that the Raven ministers weren't arguing with Bayard, telling him this was a horrible idea. Rave had already lost hundreds of thousands of people, how could we justify killing the same number in Kylae? We were supposed to be *stopping* the bloodshed, not doubling it.

There was never going to be an end to this war, not when Bayard was in power. I'd thought all our problems lay with Grieg, but Rave was just as guilty.

There was no denying it now.

I had to run.

If only to warn Kylae about what was coming their way.

GALIAN

For once, I was thankful for a long set of night shifts.

Hebendon had asked which I'd preferred, and I told him that I wanted to forget where I was for a while. I found it much easier to overpower the guilt and sorrow to sleep after a long night at the hospital.

Mael had closed, but other than that, everything seemed to have reverted to before I'd crashed on the island. Faced with the consequences of my own actions, I was less eager to make waves. I'd stopped checking on the prisoner transfer at Mael, less willing to put Kader in danger by drawing attention to myself. I could barely look at Martin's family; how would I be able to face Rosie if I'd killed her husband?

I was living in the castle, but I was quite good at avoiding my mother and brother, especially with my strange hours. But Mom, at least, was tuned into my schedule, because my first day off, I found a summons in my breakfast tray.

So, at two o'clock, I put on a clean shirt and pants and hoped that "tea" included "coffee" because I was already in need of another nap.

The guards at her door opened it for me and the left guard passed on her condolences for the loss of Martin. I didn't respond, but nodded with a tight smile. Kader's impromptu bar run had made it a little easier to bear, but not by much.

I found my mother in her sitting room, reading a book. She was on her feet the moment she saw me, rushing over to pull me into a tight embrace. I returned it wordlessly and let her hold me.

"Gally, I am so sorry."

"Me too."

She stepped back and her brow furrowed. "For what, son?"

"Not listening to you," I said.

"Come, let's have some tea," she said, putting her arm around me and guiding me to the small sitting table. Filippa appeared with the tea tray, setting it in the center before touching my arm comfortingly.

"I'm so sorry about your loss, Your Highness."

"Thanks," I said, patting her hand.

"Ma'am, will there be anything else?"

"No, dear," Mom replied with a genuine smile. Then her eyes lit up, as if remembering. "Actually, could you run to Rhys' office? He had a letter for me that I wanted to get answered today."

Filippa blinked for two seconds, then smiled and nodded, disappearing out the door.

"Well, that should keep her gone for a bit," Mom said before leaning forward to take my hand. "Son, how are you doing? I might send you back to Rosie's apartment, if only to get regular updates on you. For some reason, you're harder to talk to when you live three doors down from me."

"I'm..." I shook my head. "I don't really want to talk about it, Mom."

"I know you don't, but you will eventually. And when you do, you know I'm here for you."

"Is that why you asked me to come see you today?"

"No, actually." She picked up her tea and blew on it. "I wanted to apologize to you."

"For what?"

"You asked me to include you, and I let my emotions get the better of me. I wanted to keep you out of everything because I was afraid..." She took a sip. "I was afraid of what might happen to you. And you, rightfully, pointed out that I shouldn't coddle you simply because I love you too much."

"Mom, it was my choice to go to Mael—" I closed my eyes,

thinking about Martin.

"But if I'd involved you sooner, the outcome might've been different," she replied. "One of my many ongoing projects was to get the barethium processors involved in shipbuilding. With the new port city in Duran, Silas Collins was going to need a brand new fleet, and the barethium processors had the machine equipment to make the ships. Of course, ocean-faring vessels don't need reinforced steel." She gave me a knowing look.

I swallowed. "You were already trying to phase out barethium..."

"Very slowly but...yes. As I'm sure Kader told you, they were a hard sell. Part of the trade agreement with Jervan was to allow them to expand their business there, too, but...well, that seems to have been put on hold."

I squeezed my temples. There were so many interconnected parts.

"Of course, that particular effort has been done in conjunction with your father's assets. Believe it or not, he saw the value in closing Mael."

"Value." I snorted.

"As evidenced by your great media storm, he knew that Mael was an embarrassment waiting to happen. The sooner we weaned Kylae off it, the better prepared we'd be for the inevitable collapse of that part of the economy. But..."

"But we weren't weaned off it yet," I said, nodding. "And that's why—"

"That's why a particularly nasty businessman thought that he'd remind your father how powerful he was," she said, with more than a little bit of venom.

"Can't you do something about him?"

"We're...trying," she said, in that same strained voice. "But that's neither here nor there. The fact of the matter is, had I told you we were close—within a year—of closing Mael, you might not have gone with the cameras."

"And Mael would've been open for another twelve months!"

"And Martin might still be alive."

I nearly dropped the cup. "Mom..."

"I'm sorry, son." She placed her cup gently down on the saucer. "But the fact of the matter is, your actions have consequences far beyond what you see."

I stared at my teacup.

"Which is why I want you to know...well, everything," she said. "You asked me to involve you, and since you obviously won't take no for an answer, I'm going to involve you."

"A-are you serious?" I said, suddenly burning with questions. "What else don't I know? What was Kader doing in Jervan?"

"Ah, that." She smiled. "I confess that when Kader asked me if it was all right to bring you along on the mission, we both agreed simply because we were tired of seeing you so upset over losing Theo."

I quirked an eyebrow. "*Kader*?"

"Yes, son, he actually cares for you quite a bit. I thought that it might cheer you up, but he thought that if you met up with Theo and she rejected you, it might help you find some closure. I won a lovely bag of Jervanian coffee in that bet." Her eyes twinkled as she smiled.

My mom making bets with Kader was one thing, but I asked, "So which bedroom was Johar breaking into?"

"Bayard's," she replied. "Rave is moving beyond simple defense, and soon may escalate using some sort of super-weapon. So far, our attempts at finding out exactly what kind of offense have come up short. We know Bayard's been gathering international support, both money and technology. We know whatever he's planning has the Herinese and Jervanians eating out of his hands. And since your father has reduced the number of bombs sent to Kylae—"

"Because he's trying to wean us off barethium."

"Yes, son. But since there's been less need to defend the shores, Bayard has routed the surplus somewhere else."

"Mom, you know I'm as pro-Rave as it gets but...really? They can't even seem to get their people fed..."

"Who told you that? Theo?"

"Well, yeah..."

"You know I think the world of your *amichai*," she said, the word rolling off her tongue. "And while all our intelligence reports suggest she's one of Rave's *best* pilots, she's woefully out of her depth in Veres and hasn't been allowed into Bayard's inner circle. She, like your father, has no idea what Bayard is planning."

"Father's not doing anything about all this?" I asked, incredulous.

"In the first place, he refuses to admit that the Ravens are capable of such a thing. He, like so many others in this country, see Ravens as lesser beings, to his own detriment. Beyond that, he's more concerned with keeping the Kylaen economy afloat and keeping his warring ministers from starting a civil war."

"So Kylae squabbles amongst itself while the Ravens build a superweapon?" I let out a long breath.

"I, for one, am not going to let that happen," she said firmly.

"Me neither!" I sat up straight. "Mom, I want to help."

"I know," she said. "Which is why you'll be tending to a new patient. He'll arrive at the hospital at midnight and his name is Gerard McMullen. He will give you a message."

"What do I do with the message?"

"Kader will make sure it gets into the right hands," she said.

I slouched. "So I'm not really involved. I'm just the messenger boy?"

"Unfortunately, with your face so well known in Kylae and with the media following you, there's not much you can do unnoticed. But your place in the hospital, with so many faces coming and going, well, son, it makes you an ideal messenger...man."

Her attempts to soften the blow didn't help. "So this is all I can do? After all that, all I do is relay messages?"

"The first step in any negotiation is communication," she replied simply.

"Wait...who am I meeting with exactly?"

"The less you know, the less you can be questioned about. Just know that Mr. McMullen may provide us a means to a mutually agreeable end."

SEVENTEEN

THEO

I had to get to Kylae as soon as possible, but thanks to my outburst at Malaske, I was now being watched even more closely. Flying was going to be my only option, but with my transportation into and out of Veres provided by the military, I couldn't just ask for a special trip to the nearest airfield. Besides that, if I flew to Kylae, they'd shoot me out of the sky—and the same went for Jervan and Herin, who were apparently in on this half-cocked plan to murder half a million people.

Laying awake the night after visiting Malaske, the idea came to me in a brain wave. Galian had promised me if I went back to the island, he'd come for me, and then, at least, he could help me warn his nation. Although the safest option, I still needed to get to a plane, and also, land that plane on said island. The last time I'd tried that, I ended up with a broken leg and a Kylaen blood transfusion.

Three days later, I began to fear time was slipping away. Every day Bayard grew closer to giving the order, and every day I sat on my hands, afraid to act and arouse suspicion.

"Theo?" Emilie's voice drew me back into the meeting room and away from the thoughts running ragged in my brain.

I glanced around at the faces staring at me and cleared my throat. "I'm sorry, I missed the question."

"I was asking if you would be willing to travel to Fontnel next week," she repeated, giving me a curious look. "Bayard will be meeting with the local city government and discussing their latest proposals on funding improvements to the base there. We'd like to have you on hand."

"Of course," I said with a smile.

She nodded and continued on with the meeting. If Bayard was planning on meeting with a local government next week, that meant he hadn't decided to blow up Norose yet. But I couldn't stand to wait much longer. I had to give the Kylaens enough time to mount a defense, if there even was one. Maybe they could bomb Malaske, maybe—

"Theo, are you with us today?" Emilie asked.

Again, I apologized for my inattentiveness, and told her I'd provide my leave schedule for the spring. That was the last item on the agenda for the meeting, and Emilie dismissed the attendees with a smile and curt nod.

When I rose to leave, she placed a hand on my arm. "Is everything all right, Theo? You've been...preoccupied since your return from Malaske."

Something cold slipped down into my stomach as I considered who else might've noticed a change in my demeanor. I scrambled to think of an excuse. "I just...President Bayard...thinks that my brand has gotten stale. I've been worried about what that might mean for me."

"Yes," she said, releasing my arm. "I've been meaning to talk with you about that. Have you given any thought to your next move?"

Getting the hell out of here? "Bayard mentioned that he'd like to see me..." I grimaced. "Married with children."

Emilie smiled and shook her head. "I told him that wouldn't go over well with you. You're not the maternal sort, Theo."

"I'm not going to get married and have a baby for spectacle," I replied, glad that we were talking about something other than Malaske.

"I agree with you. For a few years, Bayard tried that tactic with the general population. It didn't work then and it sure won't work now. Rave doesn't want to be reminded that it's sending children off to war." She tapped her pen to her chin thoughtfully. "But we still need something new for you. What are your interests?"

"Vinolas," I replied, a quick plan forming in my mind. One that could get me out of this conversation with Emilie and maybe, just maybe, to Kylae.

"Theo, it's not prudent to shine a light on one of our most heavily attacked bases."

"I know, but..." I swallowed. "Do you know why I was so much better in Jervan?" I said, hoping I sounded wistful and thoughtful and not nearly as excited as I was. "I went back to Vinolas. I worked on the engines. I talked with the kids there. Met with Lanis. It reminded me of the importance of that place. Why I got into my plane every day. Why I...came home."

"But it will be very tricky to craft a message that doesn't show Rave unfavorably."

"Let me go back there," I said, a little too hastily. "Not as an official trip with the photographers, but just me. I'm sure...if I spend some time there, I can figure something out. I know there's something in Vinolas that Bayard can use."

She considered me for a moment then released the tension

between her brows. "Fine. I'll arrange a car to take you out there tomorrow. But if you don't think of anything, I do want you to consider the alternative. It might be a nice distraction to have the country preoccupied with a wedding."

I smiled. "Absolutely."

Now entering
Vinolas Forward Operating Base

My hands sweated as we drew closer. I had a semi-formed plan in my mind, but one that relied on a great number of unknown variables. I'd second guessed everything Galian had told me in his letter. How could he be watching the island? What would happen if I crashed there and no one came for me? I could survive, sure (this time I was going to bring a parachute), but all of this would be in vain because I couldn't tell Kylae about the bomb.

Lanis was waiting for me, as usual, and looking at him, I realized this might be the last time I ever saw him. I thanked my driver and left the car, watching my old chief mechanic for moment before greeting him warmly.

"What is it?" he asked, gripping my shoulders.

"Can we talk?" I asked quietly. "Somewhere private?"

"Sure, the mess hall is empty this time of day. I'm sure you remember where that is."

I grinned, but it felt plastered on. We walked through the old, familiar hangar to the back hallway that connected several of the main buildings of the base. We passed by the locker rooms, and a memory surfaced.

"Hey, Lanis, what happened to Zlatan?" I asked.

"Shot down a few weeks ago," he replied quietly.

I looked down at the ground, feeling guilty for how I had treated him the last day I'd seen him.

"Don't be sad. He was a jerk," Lanis said, opening the double doors leading to the large mess hall. Five long rows of tables stretched the length of the room, but, as predicted, the room was empty. Meal times were 0600, 1200, and 1700 every day, no midday snacks for us.

We settled at the end of one of the tables, Lanis sitting across from me. "So, Theo, what's on your mind?"

I stared at the plastic coating on top of the table, sticky from cleaner. "I have to go to Kylae."

"I'm sorry...what?"

I didn't lift my gaze, knowing if I looked at Lanis, I'd lose my nerve. "I have to go to Kylae."

"Any particular reason?"

"I have to warn them about what Bayard's going to do."

"What is Bayard going to do?"

I swallowed and considered that what I was about to say was grounds for treason. "He has a bomb in a plane that can't be tracked on radar. He's going to blow up Norose and kill half a million people."

Lanis didn't respond so I finally looked up. He was staring at me as though I were crazy, and I was inclined to agree with him.

"Lanis—"

"What did they do to you in Mael?" he said.

"They..." I closed my eyes. Well, since I was telling the truth... "I wasn't in Mael for two months. I was there maybe...six hours."

He blinked once, twice, then shook his head. "Then where

were you?"

"On the island with Galian." His name rolled off my tongue, sounding unfamiliar in this space. But I'd known Lanis' reaction before the words came out of my mouth.

"G-Galian!" He ran his hands over his face. "The prince?"

I nodded. "I followed him all the way to an island in the north. I shot him down, but then my engine redlined. I was badly injured...he saved my life..." I chewed the inside of my lip. "We survived together for two months. Then the Kylaens found us and I was sent to Mael. Galian and his guard helped me escape." I swallowed. "And now I have to get back to the island so I can warn him what Bayard is planning to do."

"Theo..." Lanis said after a few moments of silence. "If I didn't know you so well, I'd have thought you'd lost your mind."

"I have lost my mind," I said with a small chuckle. "He's my....my *amichai*."

The weight of the word settled on Lanis, and he nodded. I trusted he knew it wasn't a phrase I would use to describe a crush, as some besotted kids did.

"If there was any other way, I'd do it," I said. "But Bayard isn't interested in ending the war, and all the Raven ministers care about is money, and who owes whom favors, and lying and keeping the poorest Ravens on the front lines while they send their own children to fancy boarding schools in Herin—"

Lanis covered my hand with his to stop my angry tirade. "*'neechai*. You're starting to sound like those rebels."

"Maybe they're on to something," I said. "After all, if Bayard cared anything for ending the war, he wouldn't have wasted all that money on a bomb. He'd rather retaliate against Kylae than try to come to a peaceful solution."

Lanis squinted and shrugged, as if that didn't sound like the worst idea to him.

"*Lanis,*" I hissed. "We are not that country. That is *not* what we stand for. And besides, all that'll serve to do is reinvigorate Kylae. They'll come after us even worse than they have been. You said yourself that their attacks haven't been as frequent."

" *'neechai.*" He took my hands and squeezed them.

"I didn't give up nearly my entire life in service to this country just so we could become like Grieg," I said. "I refuse to let Bayard sully our name like that."

"What are you going to do?"

"Galian told me that if I ever...if I ever got tired of all this bullshit, I was to go back to the island. He said he's got people watching that sector, and he'd come get me." I looked up at him. "Got a plane and a parachute I could borrow?"

"How sure are you that your princeling will come for you?" Lanis asked.

"He'll come," I whispered.

"Let's go then. I've got a friend in the tower who owes me one," Lanis said, standing.

I snapped my head to look at him, mouth open. "Are you—?"

"I may be an old man," he said with a twinkle in his eye. "But I still know how to fly. Besides, we're low on planes as it is. Can't afford for you to crash another one on that island."

GALIAN

I never thought being a messenger boy would cause me so much stress. By nine, I'd already nearly given two patients the wrong medicine and checked another for a rash instead of a lung infection. Thank God for my nurses, who patiently suggested that I might need a stronger cup of coffee and took over for me. I was even luckier that they didn't inform Hebendon, who showed up around ten to check on my progress.

I had no idea what to expect, so my mind ran wild with different scenarios. I imagined a Kader-like man in a dark cloak handing me a manila envelope, or a Raven child speaking riddles I would have to memorize. I even imagined Kader himself a few times.

At a quarter to midnight, I started skulking around the nurse's station, listening for his name. I had no idea how he'd come in—as a patient, a visitor, or what—so I wanted to be prepared. My hovering had begun to piss off the head nurse, who swore, with two minutes until midnight, that if she saw my face in the next hour, she'd flay me alive.

Luckily, just as she finished her threats, I heard the name in question come out of an approaching nurse's mouth. I made some flimsy excuse and bowed my deference to Nurse Rima before rushing down the hall toward my patient/message-bearer.

I slowed as I drew closer to the room and straightened up. I was a prince, a doctor, and, above all else, a pretty badass human being. What was I getting so worked up over? A meeting? A message? I'd survived two months on an island eating nothing but rabbits. I'd broken my girl out of a death camp—*that I'd then closed down.*

Amped up on my own ego, I stood in front of room forty and

233 | S. Usher Evans

swung open the door.

Gerard McMullen was a short, squat man with fire-red hair encircling his bald head. He wore the hospital gown, his bare legs swinging against the table he sat on. My mouth twitched, and I closed the door behind me, staring at him for a good minute.

"Well?" he asked, folding his arms over his chest.

"Er...do you have...a message for me?" I said, keeping my voice low and dangerous.

"Yeah, I need a full panel to check my cholesterol," he said. "And you're terrible at this."

I slapped down the clipboard and glared at him. "It's my first day. Give me a break."

"Hope you're better at sticking needles than espionage."

"For your information, my nurses... You know what? Never mind. What's the message?"

"Tell yer mother I got shut down," he said, holding out his arm. I walked toward him, realizing that he did, in fact, want a blood panel. I took the blood pressure sleeve off the wall and wrapped it around his meaty forearm, pumping it up.

"In what way?"

He heaved a sigh. "Your mother asked me to talk to some of our dark-skinned friends across the sea. Find out if there's any viable candidates looking to unseat Bayard."

My stethoscope nearly fell out of my hand. "Are you...serious?"

He glanced at me. "Don't tell you much, do they?"

"I told you, it's my first day—"

"Well, it don't matter because the few contacts I had shut me down. They said no matter how much money I said I had, they wouldn't trust no Kylaen. Couldn't even barter transport into the damned country."

I glanced at his red hair. "You'd stick out like a—"

"Yeah, well, ain't nobody else agreeing to go," he snapped. "How's my blood pressure?"

I looked down at the sleeve and realized I'd forgotten to check.

He made a noise and ripped off the sleeve, handing it to me. "If you want my advice, stick to doctoring."

There was a knock at the door, and the nurse poked her head in. "Sorry to interrupt, Dr. Helmuth, but there's an urgent call for you."

"I think we're done here anyway," I replied, picking up my clipboard from the table. "Make sure Mr. McMullen gets a full blood panel."

I followed the hall to the main nurse's station, where I was directed to the doctor's lounge to take the call. I opened the door and took a step back. "Rhys?"

"Gally," he said with a tense smile. "A Raven plane just flew over your island."

THEO

There weren't many two-seater planes in the Raven fleet, but one of the other squadrons had two at their disposal. Lanis sought out its young captain, finding him on his bunk. He was barely twenty years old, and mumbled his responses to the chief mechanic. But when we asked to borrow one of his two prized planes, he was clear that was a no-go.

So, I pulled rank and told him to sit down and shut up. As we left him stammering in his bed, I promised myself that would be the *last* time I ever did that.

Once we'd checked the plane, Lanis called in that favor to the air tower, saying he was giving me an aerial tour of Vinolas. If the air control chief had any questions, he kept them to himself because he gave us the all clear to depart.

The two-seater plane was larger than my girl, and much slower, which was why it was rarely used during attacks. The second seat had the gun-mount on it, versus the normal Raven planes where flying and shooting were handled by the pilot. I toyed with the trigger a bit, glad I no longer had to worry about that side of piloting.

Nearly two hours after we left Vinolas, Lanis' voice came through my helmet. "Hey, Theo, we're approaching some islands ahead. How are you gonna know which one is yours?"

"I'll know," I said, unhooking my seatbelt to sit on my knees and look over Lanis' shoulder. Ahead of us, a few mounds of land rose out of the dark waters of the ocean below. Those couldn't have been our island, because there wasn't anything else around us.

I scanned the horizon, knowing that the sun was setting and there was only enough fuel to do a quick search before Lanis would have to head back to Vinolas.

Then, I saw it. "There."

"Are you sure?"

"Very." I had no idea how I knew it was our island, except that I felt it in the same place that had told me it was Galian's plane I was shooting down. It hadn't steered me wrong before.

Lanis circled around to fly lower over the island as dusk colored the sky a mixture of purple and pink. But the wreckage still visible on the beach was unmistakeable.

"One final chance to change your mind, Theo," Lanis said.

"Thanks for everything, Lanis," I replied, turning and hooking in my restraints. "Pull it."

It happened in a burst of wind and the exhilarated rush of being launched out of the plane. Cold air froze my hands as they moved to pull the parachute release. The whiteness billowed around me, and I watched Lanis' plane disappear into the purple sky.

"Thanks," I said, hoping that my helmet radio was still connected to his.

I wafted down, carried by the breeze, toward the place I'd called home for two months. My feet landed on the soft sand of the beach, and I unhooked the straps to release myself. The moon was bright and full, casting an eerie blue glow as the sun disappeared below the horizon. I took a moment to drink in the sounds and the feel of the wind on my face.

"I'm home," I whispered to the salty air. The only thing missing was my *amichai*.

Shouldering my pack, I walked to the forest, pressing my hands against the familiar trees and feeling for the marks Galian had left in them.

The dark outline of my mangled ship greeted me. A ghost of pain ached from the back of my right leg and the calf of my left.

This time, I was a bit more prepared, as I pulled a flashlight out of my pack and shone it over the campsite. A white tail disappeared into the bush, and I had to smile. I had some rations; I wasn't planning on killing any more rabbits any time soon.

Instead, I found the old stones we'd used to start fires and quickly made one with some nearby kindling. I'd brought an extra jacket, which I wrapped around myself, but it was still chilly. And I wanted Galian to know where I was when he came for me.

The fire crackled and popped, and I settled back against my familiar tree. Our mattress was still in our cave, about an hour's walk away. In the morning, if Galian hadn't made it, I would venture there.

More pressing was what I would say when I arrived in Norose. I knew Galian would believe me, but would the rest of Kylae? Would his father? And if, by some miracle, I could convince them, would it be in time?

Was I walking to my own death?

I exhaled a long breath. When I'd last been on this island, I'd been so convinced that Kylae was the villain. From my limited perspective, everything had seemed so cut and dried. But now I was committing high treason against the very country I'd given seven years of my life to protect.

I considered what might happen if I was successful and Norose was saved from almost certain doom. I obviously couldn't return to Rave—a thought that caused an awful ache in the bottom of my chest. And although Kylae was much safer for Ravens with the closure of Mael, it had been made clear that anyone who disagreed with Grieg was in danger of finding themselves blown up.

Herin was probably too closely aligned with Rave to offer me asylum. Jervan could be an option. The Jervanian president hadn't seemed so sure about murdering Kylaens; maybe they could be reasoned with.

And if that failed...

I glanced around the still trees and smiled to myself. Well, we'd lived here before...

A cackle escaped my lips and I settled against the tree, pulling my coat tighter. We'd need to build a house and perhaps bring in some livestock and try to make the rocky soil into something I could grow food in. Not to mention figuring a way to pipe in water from the vile laboratory on the north end of the island...

I yawned and closed my eyes, dreaming about making a new life with my *amichai*.

And, just as quickly, a loud sound woke me. It lacked the buzzing of a passing propeller plane, and was more the whirring of a helicopter. I stepped to attention, gazing at the black sky above my head. Yes, I was sure of it—there was an aircraft approaching. I stood and closed my eyes, trying to pinpoint the direction it was coming from.

I grinned and pulled on my pack, rushing toward the beach. The fire I'd made was bright enough, but I wanted him to see me. I doubted he would've come alone and I was all-too-familiar with how trigger happy Kylaen guards could be.

The helicopter landed a way down the beach. I broke into an all-out run, my calves burning from the shifting sand under my feet. Despite everything, I was beyond excited to see him, to have him hold me in his arms like he'd done in Jervan. For that brief moment of sublime happiness before we had to get to the business of saving our countries from themselves.

I saw his dark form standing in front of the ship, and my heart raced. He started walking toward me, and I cried, "*Amichai!*"

"*Amichai?*"

Where I'd expected Galian's sweet voice, came the cold, heartless voice of Cannon, and a contingent of Raven soldiers.

EIGHTEEN

GALIAN

"So you drag me out of the hospital, and you *aren't* going to let me go get her?" I scowled, crossing my hands in front of my chest. "What the actual fuck, Rhys?"

"I didn't say you couldn't go," he said with a dismissive wave of his hand. "I just want to gather the facts before I approve this mission. Lochan, report."

Lochan, a one-striper barely out of basic training, nervously gripped his cap, staring between me and Rhys as if we'd behead him at any moment.

Behind me, Kader cleared his throat, and the boy jumped. In a shaky voice, he said, "Sire, about three hours ago, we had a report of a Raven plane leaving the forward operating base at Vinolas, flying over the island where Prince Galian had been found then returning to the FOB."

"So that means nothing, Gal," Rhys said, sitting back.

"I have to check," I said. "Send me. I still know how to fly."

"You can crash a plane," Kader replied. "But in order to get on and off the island, you'll need a VTO."

"V..TO?"

"Vertical take-off," Rhys snapped without looking at me. "I'm not pulling a VTO out of the fleet on a lark. Take the Ledsi. Do a flyby. If you see signs of life there—"

"You won't know unless you're on the ground," I snapped.

"Really? You think Theo wouldn't have thought to get a flare?" Kader replied.

I reddened slightly. She was always more prepared, so she probably did have one.

"How long will it take to get there?" Rhys asked.

"With the Ledsi? Three hours, if we punch it," Johar replied.

"*If* she's there," Rhys said with a pointed look at me. "We'll take a team with a VTO. I'm not convinced this isn't some big trap."

"Theo wouldn't—"

"Theo wouldn't, but her country would," Rhys replied.

My pulse quickened. "You don't think..."

"Let's not jump to conclusions until we know what we're dealing with," Kader replied. "Johar and I will take the Ledsi and report back."

"I...don't want this to get out," Rhys said with a little fear in his voice. "This sort of thing would require...approval."

"Understood," Kader said, bowing and disappearing through the door with Johar in tow.

"Guess that means I'm on duty tonight," Rhys said, slouching into the radar operator chair. "Wonder if this'll count for my quarterly assignment."

"Rhys..." I said, taking the seat next to him. "Thanks for this. You don't—"

"Don't thank me until we know what we're dealing with," he said with a stern look. But he placed a comforting hand on my shoulder and squeezed. "Congratulations, you're now officially off reserve duty and back in the force as a radar operator. You want some shitty coffee?"

THEO

"*Amichai?*" Cannon said, his smug voice audible over the sound of the helicopter. "I didn't think you liked me that much, Major."

"What are you doing here?" It was all I could do to keep my voice normal. I didn't know what he knew, and I didn't want to give anything away.

"Catching up with an AWOL soldier, it seems." The gleam in his eye was visible even in the darkness. I considered running, but one look at the guns hanging from the Raven soldiers told me I wouldn't get very far. "Of all the places I expected you to go, this island wasn't one I would've picked."

I swallowed. "I wanted to get away from it all."

"And yet you landed the exact same island where Prince Galian of Kylae was marooned."

"Is it?" I said, and then shrugged. "Coincidence."

"At first, I thought so, but there were so many unanswered questions about you." Cannon stood a mere foot from me, wearing a self-satisfied smile. "You crashed here, too, didn't you? The princeling didn't survive on his own, *you helped him.*"

I clenched my jaw but didn't deny his claim.

"That, in itself, is grounds for a treason charge," Cannon said, but I knew he wasn't here to drum up some false charges against me. "And yet, you said *amichai*."

I couldn't hold his gaze any longer, choosing to give him the win versus showing what that word meant to me.

"To be frank, I thought the Kylaens had offered you some sort of deal. Spy on us in exchange for your freedom. I told Bayard as much, but he didn't believe me. So we tested you and allowed you to accompany us to Malaske, just to see how you'd react."

I closed my eyes, ashamed at my own foolishness. In hindsight, it had been strange that they'd sent me to such a highly secretive place out of the blue. I hadn't even attended a cabinet meeting.

"But now I see that we had it all wrong," Cannon said. "All the pieces have finally come together."

"Cannon, you don't understand—"

"You *fell in love* with him, you stupid woman." Cannon sounded like his birthday had come early. "Did you think that you could run away to Kylae and be a princess?"

"I thought if I could *end* the war, I could save the lives of hundreds of thousands of our countrymen!"

"Oh Theo, you are an idiot, aren't you? This war isn't killing people. It's *saving* our country!"

I couldn't believe what I was hearing. "And how's that?"

"By giving us a common enemy," Cannon said. "If we suddenly stopped our war with Kylae, Rave would tear itself apart. You've seen the rebels, they've gotten much stronger in the past few years. The only thing keeping them from taking over is Kylae's constant bombing."

"If you don't stop this war, there won't be a nation to take over, Cannon," I said. "There might be a chance to reason with Kylae.

They could provide help—financial assistance. Jervan might be onboard, too—"

"Did you hear that when you were fucking the prince in Jervan?" he asked with a sneer. "Honestly, Theo, I expected much more from you. Falling for a Kylaen?" He tutted. "I suppose you'll be reunited with him soon enough."

My heartbeat quickened. "What are you talking about?"

"I offered Bayard a new spin on your public story and, thanks to your little stunt here, it'll be an *explosive* last chapter."

GALIAN

"If you don't stop tapping your foot, I will cut it off."

"I'm sorry," I snapped back at my brother, wondering for the thousandth time how he could remain so calm. Then again, he wasn't about to see the love of his life.

It wasn't just that—there were questions. Why now? What had happened to make her to go to the island? Did it have anything to do with the mystery weapon the Ravens were planning? Had she just gotten sick of it all? With Mael closed, did she think it safe—?

"I have a knife, and I'm not afraid to use it."

I placed my hand on my knee to cease the movement.

"What's going to happen when she gets here?" I asked. "You aren't going to...do anything to her, are you?"

"Nowhere to send her anymore, Gally," Rhys replied, glancing at the radar screen in front of him. "Remember, we don't even know if she's there."

"She's there, I know it," I said, rubbing my stomach that was doing flip-flops. "But even if Mael is closed, she could still be in danger." Martin was evidence of that. "I want to take her to Jervan. Start over and make a new life there."

"Godspeed."

I turned to look at him. "You aren't going to stop me?"

He yawned and glanced at his empty cup of coffee. "To be honest, you being out of the country saves me a hell of a lot of work. Ever since you got back from the island, all I've been doing is following behind you and making sure you don't get yourself killed. Besides, I like Jervan. It'll give me an excuse to come crash on your couch."

"I don't think Father, Mother, or the royal guard will let you...*crash on my couch*."

"And I don't think any of the aforementioned people will let you just uproot and move to a different country with your Raven girlfriend." He wore a tired smile, and I flicked him off. Laughing, he went to refill his coffee from the pot in the small kitchenette area of the radar tower and brought me a fresh one as well.

"So you just sit here and it counts as military duty?" I asked, before shaking my head. "Man, me and Dig got the raw end of the deal."

"Dig wanted to go out there." His eyes stared into the distance the way he always did when he talked about Digory. "Even as a kid, he was always eager to put himself in danger."

"Put me in danger is more like it," I muttered.

"You were always the quiet one, you know?" Rhys said with a brotherly smile. "I'm glad you got out from under Father's thumb."

"Careful, you'll be arrested for treason," I scoffed.

"You know, sometimes I think he forgets he's not going to live forever," Rhys said.

"And—"

A loud beeping interrupted our conversation. Coffee in hand, Rhys rushed over and swiped the microphone out of my hand.

"This is tower zero four seven. Aircraft, identify yourself."

"It's Kader."

My heart leaped to my throat.

"And?" Rhys asked.

"She's not there."

"W-what?" I said, leaning over Rhys' shoulder.

"Return to base, Eli," Rhys said, pushing me out of the way.

"Already on our way. Should be landing in an hour."

Rhys acknowledged his message and placed a comforting hand on my shoulder. "That doesn't mean she won't come—"

"She did come," I said. "I know she did. Why else would a Raven plane be in that airspace? It's too far—"

"Maybe Lachlan read the radar movements incorrectly."

"How hard is it to read a dot moving from Rave?" I asked, throwing his hand off my shoulder.

"It's okay. This was good practice for when she does come," Rhys replied.

"Thanks, Mom."

"I'm serious," he said. "Look, go home. Get some rest. I'll talk to Kader when he gets here and give you the full report."

I swiped his coffee off the table and downed half of it. "If it's all the same to you, I'll wait here. I want to hear *exactly* what Kader found."

She was there, I knew it. So why hadn't she shown herself?

THEO

I woke to blackness and my arms and feet bound with itchy rope and my memory slid back over me. Shortly after Cannon had found me on the island, he'd put a black hood over my head and everything had gotten hazy. Based on the raging headache, I assumed they'd drugged me.

I heard voices and stopped moving, hoping to fool them into thinking I was still unconscious so I could devise an escape. From the pressure in my ears and the vibrations under my seat, I knew we were long gone from our island, so any hope of my *amichai* stumbling upon us was, too. If I wanted to survive, it was, yet again, up to me.

I wasn't sure how long I sat in absolute stillness, but I knew when we'd landed. With the overhead propellers off, conversations which had been muffled became clearer. I heard Cannon, and some other voices I didn't recognize. I strained my ears trying to make sense of what they were saying, but I couldn't.

"Get her," came Cannon's voice. Disembodied hands grabbed my arms and pulled me to stand, walking me off of the airship and onto solid ground. They ripped the hood from my head along with a fistful of hair and I blinked in the bright light.

"Ah good, the traitor is awake."

I blinked a few more times before the stench of latent barethium hit my nose. I was in Malaske cave, standing in the center of the room with two guards holding me upright. Bayard and Cannon stood before me, both with disgusted looks on their faces.

"Tr-traitor?"

"I'm disappointed, Theo," Bayard said, and looked genuinely so. "I thought that after all we'd been through together, Cannon must've been wrong about your loyalties."

"I am loyal to Rave!" I said, my words coming out slurred as the effects of the drug wore off.

"Then why were you on your way to Kylae?" Bayard asked. "To warn your...*amichai*."

"You can't bomb them," I said. "It's wrong."

"They must've done a good job brainwashing you if you value Kylaen lives over those of your own countrymen," Bayard said. "If we don't show Kylae that we can stand on equal footing with firepower—"

"This isn't equal footing. This is an annihilation," I said with more control. "Did you even *try* diplomacy?"

"And who would we send? You?" He chuckled. "We might as well sign the surrender papers."

"I want a free Rave," I said, wishing the cotton would clear out of my head so I could argue my points better. "I love this country."

"Then you have two options, *kallistrate*," Cannon said. "We'll expose you as the Kylaen-loving traitor you are. Hang you in front of *Platcha* for the world and your *amichai* to see. Forever associate you with treason to the country you *claim* to love."

"Or," Bayard said, "you will get on our plane."

I wasn't sure which option drove more fear into my heart. "You want me to fly the plane to Norose?"

"The plane can—and will—fly itself straight into Kernaghan Castle," Bayard replied. "We are simply giving you the option to go out a Raven hero instead of a turncoat traitor. Think of it as a small token of our appreciation for your seven years defending our country."

I glanced between him and Bayard for a moment. Bayard's face was unreadable, but there was no kindness there. He wouldn't stop either outcome. He thought this was just. And since I was a lot better at aircraft than breaking out of a prison, I chose my strength.

"Put me in the plane."

Bayard nodded solemnly to the two sergeants at either side of me, and they marched me toward the aircraft that was to be my tomb. I didn't bother to look back at Bayard or Cannon, but I felt their eyes on me. I sensed Cannon's smug satisfaction that he'd effectively vanquished another obstacle between himself and the presidency. I sensed Bayard relishing in his short-sighted victory this bomb would bring.

My boots clacked on the metal onramp but I remained silent. They walked me past the warhead that would obliterate my body before I knew what hit me. They sat me in the only seat on the plane, in the cockpit, handcuffing both of my wrists to the chair. I supposed they wanted to give me a front-row seat to my own demise.

I glanced up at the young women. Both barely older than I was, both with stoic, dead eyes. Still, perhaps I might appeal to their humanity.

"If you don't want this war to escalate into a total annihilation of Rave, leave the key," I whispered to the woman on my right.

She stared at me for a moment, her eyes dancing back and forth. Then, her face screwed up and she tossed the key into the back of the plane.

"Traitor," she spat.

I said nothing else to them, made no other move, except to shudder when the ramp sealed shut.

There was a loud rumbling noise and the earth shook. The

sound wasn't the plane engine though, and the plane wasn't moving on its own. I craned my neck as far as I could with the handcuffs; the plane must've been on a platform that was being raised to surface level.

"Okay, so this is really happening," I whispered to myself, tugging at my cuffs in a vain hope that they hadn't been properly secured. I glanced behind me to the empty space where the key had been thrown; I wasn't going to get it back any time soon.

The plane broached the surface of the large concrete plain, and the mechanized lift shuddered as it stopped moving. The large engines on either wing rumbled to life, the computer in front of me began to beep, and the controls moved. The gauges rose in preparation to take off, and I prayed with all my might that the plane would be too heavy. That this whole thing would end in a fiery crash and that no one but me, Bayard, and Cannon would be the victims.

The brakes released, and the plane rolled forward.

"Don't take off, don't take off," I whispered, my knuckles white against the armrests. But as the speed increased I felt it: the slight bounce, the change in pressure, and then, the plane was in the air.

I screamed my curses as the plane ascended into the clouds. I didn't care if Bayard and Cannon were listening. I wasn't going down without a fight. Gritting my teeth, I yanked as hard as I could on the handcuffs. I pressed the right cuff into the metal armrest and jammed my leg against it, trying to slip my wrist out of it. I pulled harder, willing to break my hand, but it wouldn't come out.

I screamed in frustration, standing up as far as I could go with both hands cuffed to the chair. I thrashed, and I yanked and—

One of the poorly-attached armrests came flying off, nearly clocking me in the head. I lifted my now-free right hand with the cuff still attached to it. I couldn't go very far, but at least I could now reach the dashboard. I leaned over and stared out the window, horrified to see water underneath me. I wasn't sure where exactly Malaske was, but if I was over water, I was quickly running out of time.

I attempted to orient myself with the controls, but other than the gauges, most of them brand new to me. This technology was either Herinese or Bayard had been keeping it pretty close to the vest. My left hand dangling helplessly behind me, I kicked the facing under the dashboard to expose the wiring beneath it.

Along with a radio.

Nineteen

Galian

The early morning shift had shown up to take over, but Rhys had dismissed them with a casual smile and a promise that he'd deal with whatever issues arose from missing their shift. Then he returned to sit beside me in silent companionship.

Kader and Johar arrived just as the sun was peeking over the horizon. The plane landed on the runway, and their small figures walked towards the tower where Rhys and I sat. I didn't look up when they walked into the room.

"So?" Rhys asked.

"Nothing." Kader shook his head. "We flew low enough that the roar of the engine would've woken her if she'd been asleep. We saw no sign of her—no fire, no flare gun."

I shook my head and ran my hands over my face. "This is all wrong. It makes no sense. I want to take a VTO out there."

"Gally," Rhys said.

"I don't disagree," Kadar said. "A Raven plane leaving that base? It's too far away to be a coincidence. I'd like to take my team up there and scout around."

"A whole team?" Rhys asked.

"I'm going," I said,

"No, you're not," Kader said over Rhys' shoulder. "I think this may be a test on Rave's part to see if Kylae is watching that island. They might've stationed a team there and are planning an ambush if Galian were to go there."

"And if they are, you'll clean them out?" Rhys replied.

I slouched on the seat and thumbed the paper edges of the coffee cup. All I wanted to do was get my Theo back, and now they were talking about killing more Ravens. Ravens who wanted to kill me in the first place. It was all so...cyclical.

"Galian, I know you had your heart set on this," Kader said gently.

"Don't do that bullshit with me," I growled, standing up. "Stop *patronizing* me. I know that there was a reason a Raven plane went up there, and damn it, I'm going to—"

The words died in my mouth. Perhaps it was a hallucination or sleep deprivation, or maybe I just desperately needed to hear it, but in that second, I could've sworn that I heard Theo's voice.

But by the curious looks on everyone else's face, so had they.

"...Hello...this is...somebody...seeking Kylaen contact..."

I spun around and faced the radio the voice was coming from, my jaw slack and my eyes wide.

"Move aside," Rhys said, shoving me out of the way. "This is Kylaen Tower zero-four-seven, identify yourself."

"Oh thank God...thank God..."

The terror in her voice was clear. I took two steps forward, but Kadar and Johar grabbed my arms and pulled me back.

"What are you doing?" I snarled.

"Let him talk," Kader said.

"Identify yourself," Rhys repeated.

"My name is Maj...well, I guess just Theo Kallistrate now...I am...was...a pilot in the Raven air forces. And I need you to do something really drastic."

"Oh yeah?" Rhys said, glancing at me. "What's that?"

"What I'm about to tell you sounds really, really unbelievable, and coming from a Raven, I'm sure that it's even less believable but...I'm in a plane flying over the Madion Sea right now, and there's...a really big bomb in here that can level Norose if it gets there. So I need you to get some planes together and..." I heard the sharp intake of breath. *"Blow me out of the sky."*

My voice died in my throat. She couldn't...she couldn't be...

Rhys pressed the button to speak. "That does sound awfully unbelievable, Major, especially considering I have no such Raven airship on my radar screen."

"Please! You have to believe me. It's using Herinese technology that hides the ship from radar, so you wouldn't see it but...this thing...if what they tell me is true...it could kill thousands...hundreds of thousands of Kylaens."

"And why would a Raven care about that?"

"Because I can't let Rave do this. We can't do this—the war will escalate, people will die..."

Rhys turned to look at Kader, but Theo continued.

"And there's someone I love very much in Norose." Her voice cracked and something twisted in my gut. *"I couldn't bear it if... You have to stop this thing. Please believe me."*

"Stand by," Rhys snapped, turning off the radio and looking at

Kader. He glanced at my arms still pinned near my ears by Kader and Johar and smiled. "Can I trust you not to talk to your girlfriend if they let you go?"

I bared my teeth at him.

"Fine, then stay there. Kader, thoughts?"

"I believe her," Johar said before Kader could speak. "This could be the weapon Bayard has been building at Malaske."

"But why put Theo in it?" Rhys asked.

"Does that really matter?" I barked. "She's in there and she's going to die if we don't do something—"

"Did you not hear her?" Rhys said. "We're *all* going to die if we don't do something." He looked at Kader again. "What do you think, Eli? A trap, maybe?"

"It could be a trap, but I doubt it," Kader said. "In any case, we've got the Ledsi already fueled up. It's the fastest ship we have, and we can take down whatever's out there." I made a noise, but Kader's look silenced me. "After extracting the girl. We can bring along the tether."

Rhys stared at him, face unreadable. "Do you really think it's worth it to risk yourself and Johar for a single Raven life?"

"With all due respect, even if she wasn't your brother's girlfriend, she's still just as important as any other human," Kader said, surprising me. "To boot, she told us she was coming. She's ready to sacrifice herself. Least we can do is go get her."

"What if it's a trap?" Rhys said. "What if there are twenty people on that ship waiting for you and no bomb?"

"I'm willing to take that risk," Kader replied. "Give the order and it will be done, Your Majesty."

Rhys swallowed, and I knew he was thinking of the

consequences of authorizing military action without express permission from the king.

"Rhys—" I began.

"Do it," he said suddenly. "I'll take the heat. Just go...get that thing out of the sky. I'd rather risk my father's ire than have the blood of our people on my hands. But please, *be careful*." He looked at me. "Go with them, Galian."

"Y-you're letting me go?"

"Yes, because I want to stay and see what else I can glean from her, and I don't think I can stand you prowling around here."

Kader chuckled beside me. "Come on, lover boy. Let's go see what kind of mess your girl's gotten into this time."

THEO

They'd stopped talking, but I didn't care. Someone had heard me. When they came back on the line, I would scream and plead until they understood me, but for now, I took solace in the silence.

I cried softly, allowing myself the sorts of morose and selfish thoughts a person has before they die. I'd considered my mortality before, but it had always been in the context of chancing it. If I'd survive, it was because I was meant for something greater. There seemed to be no way I'd survive this, and as much as I tried to accept it, I couldn't stop the sad tears from falling down my face.

The most surprising was my worry for Galian. He'd recently lost Martin, and I wasn't sure how losing me would affect him. I wanted to tell him not to mourn me, to move on and marry that Collins girl. Perhaps it would be a blessing to cleave me from his life.

Blessing or not, my soul ached at the thought of never seeing him again. I should've been grateful for the few precious moments we'd spent together, but I wanted more. I grew angry at the pure unfairness of life. I'd given up so much in my twenty years; I deserved more than I'd gotten with Galian.

My silent tears turned into heaving sobs that shook my whole body, I almost didn't hear the voice on the radio calling my name.

"Theo?" The dispatch voice echoed through the speakers. *"Theo, are you still there?"*

I leaned forward and pressed the comm button. "Yes. I'm here. Please tell me—"

"We will destroy the weapon."

Relief and anguish mixed in my stomach as I slid down to the ground. My hand was still cuffed to the seat, and it was starting to hurt.

"Theo?"

"Yes?"

"It's going to be all right."

I stared at the radio, quite sure I'd heard incorrectly. "What?"

"I said, it's going to be all right. I can tell you're crying."

I sniffed and brushed the tears out of my eyes. "You would too if you knew you were going to die."

"This can't be the first time you've faced your own death."

"It never gets easier," I said, thinking about all the close calls and near misses. "I've never waited for death, though."

"Why don't you allow me to keep you company while you wait then?"

I laughed. "And why would you be interested in that?"

"Same reason you told the enemy you were coming."

"Fair point." I pulled the receiver toward me and leaned against the seat. "Well, what do you want to talk about?"

"Why don't you tell me more about this love you're willing to die for?"

I snorted. "You wouldn't believe me if I told you."

"I've believed you so far."

This was true; or he could've been lying. There could've been no plane. But his voice was kind, and I wanted to believe he wouldn't lie to me.

"Theo?"

"The man I love is..." I sighed, letting myself think about him. "He's...himself."

"Not a very apt description."

"You'll have to forgive me. I've never been able to talk to anyone about him before," I said, realizing how true that was.

"Because he's Kylaen and you're Raven?"

"Part of it," I said, clenching my fists then releasing them. If I was going to die, might as well come clean with the whole truth. "I am in love with your prince."

"Rhys?"

"No, the other one," I said with a small laugh. "I am in love with Galian Helmuth." It felt good to say it out loud to someone.

"You and every other girl. Galian gets all the chicks."

"Well, I am a special chick, I guess." I closed my eyes and took myself back to that first day I met him. "You know how he was marooned on an island for two months?"

"Yeah?"

"He wasn't alone."

"You were there, too?"

"Do you really think someone like the princeling could've survived for two months on his own? Idiot couldn't even make a fire. Didn't know how to make drinking water. Couldn't skin a rabbit..." I blew air out of my mouth. "Totally helpless."

"So how did you end up on the island?"

"We'd been in a battle together, and I knew it was him." It had been such a strong gut feeling. "So I took off after him. I shot him down, but unfortunately, my engine redlined and I went down, too."

"Sounds like you got what you deserved."

I barked a loud laugh, almost dissolving into giggles. "That's what he said!"

"The prince is a smart man, then. So what happened after that?"

I smiled and told him about how I was injured, and how Galian's selflessness and medical expertise had saved my life. I told him about those first few days of tense moments and blow-up fights. It seemed so strange to me that I'd ever hated him, but my feelings for him then were anything but loving.

"So what changed?"

"I don't know," I said, realizing I'd never considered it. "Maybe when we found that lab. I was relieved that we finally had shelter, and his first thought was...me. He was worried about my injuries and wanted to make sure they weren't infected." That night we'd slept across from each other in bunks, and I'd had the first flashes of wanting to be more than survival buddies with him.

"What lab?"

My mood darkened. "We had the misfortune of crashing on an island that used to serve as the Kylaens' barethium testing site." I closed my eyes. "Thank God Mael is closed now."

"Closing Mael caused a lot of problems," the voice sounded a little annoyed, but then added, *"but I'm glad the prince was strong enough to do it. Not many men would be."*

I was silent for a while, thinking about Galian and how much I was going to miss him. I didn't know what was beyond death, but I knew that if Galian wasn't there with me, I'd be lonely.

"There's one thing I can't figure out. After you'd gotten your bearings on that first day, why didn't you kill him?"

I smiled to myself. "I couldn't. It's one thing to shoot someone down when they're shooting at you, but to kill in cold blood?" I shook my head, then laughed. "Definitely wanted to, though."

"You wanted to kill him?"

"Have you ever heard him make a joke?" There was barking laughter on the other side. "I take it you know him." I didn't know how I knew, but there was an affectionate tone to all the questions.

"Very well. And yes, he has the worst sense of humor. And timing."

"And he's reckless," I said, the voice agreeing with me fervently. "I can't tell you how many times he gave me a heart attack on the island. First, he's nearly blown up in the lab while he's fetching blankets, then he's dangling off a rock because he wanted to go fishing. Then he's showing up in Jervan, unannounced, climbing balconies, sneaking into my room..." I trailed off and closed my eyes. "Watching me give the speech..."

"Wait, he watched you give your speech?"

"Yeah," I said quietly. "I don't know how he got in, but he did. He did because I told him I needed him." I clenched my jaw. "And because I specifically told him *not* to."

"He doesn't listen very well when it concerns you, I've noticed."

A tear fell down my cheek. "Did he talk about me?"

"Constantly."

"Please tell him to get over me," I said, the words tumbling out before I could stop them. "I don't want him to mourn me, or...just..." I looked at the shimmering blue ocean in front of me. "Maybe just don't tell him I died. Perhaps he'll just forget about me after a few months."

"I wish I could say he would do that, but we both know he won't. He never stopped thinking about you, no matter what anyone told him."

I let out a sob, mourning the future we would never get a chance to have. "He was the only good thing that ever happened to me. So optimistic. He always thought we'd just find a way to be together."

"Maybe you will."

I smiled. "Thank you."

"For what?"

"Filling my last moments in this world with kindness."

"I'm honored to have spent them with you." A pause. *"But somehow I don't think these are your last moments."*

GALIAN

My heart was in my throat as we took off faster than I'd thought possible in a plane. Johar was at the helm, expertly managing the controls with an ease I'd never mastered in my brief stint as a pilot. Kader sat in the co-pilot's seat, saying nothing and barely moving. He'd ordered me to sit in one of the four jump-seats that lined the cargo-bay.

Johar's whistle drew my attention and I unhooked my restraints to stand behind them. The airship in the distance was massive, appearing more like an innocuous cargo plane than a weapon of mass destruction.

"That's not showing up on any of our radars," Kader said, glancing at the screen in front of him.

"Those Herinese sons of bitches," Johar replied with a snarl. "I hope we turn around and bomb them."

"Do you think we'll be able to get her out of there?" I asked.

He looked up at me and actually smiled. "Piece of cake."

"Are you just saying that, or do you mean that?" I asked. "Have you ever done something like this before?"

"Boarded a plane with a bomb on it and rescued a Raven? Can't say I have."

"I'm so glad you can joke at a time like this," I snapped as Kader stood and brushed past me.

"Joking's a good sign," Johar replied.

I followed Kader back to the small cargo bay and watched as he donned a black suit made of thick material.

"Go sit up front and take my seat," he said.

"No," I said, holding onto a nearby handle when the ship trembled under turbulence. "I want to go with you."

"Son, I'm going to be dangling a thousand feet over the Madion Sea. I don't think you want to do that."

"I do."

Kader sighed and put a black helmet under his arm. "You have two options: I can save her, or I can save you. Which is it gonna be?"

"Don't worry, lover boy. She won't care who plucks her off that ship, just as long as she ain't on it when it goes down," Johar said from the front seat. She held up a pistol, and Kader crossed the cargo bay to take it from her. She gripped his hand and said, "Just in case this is another Kapila."

I had no idea what that was, but Kader grimaced and pointed the barrel of the gun at his shoulder. "Still hurts when it rains."

He turned, but I stood in his way, a serious look on my face. "You aren't going to shoot her."

"Son, go sit down before I *make* you sit down."

"Promise me you aren't going to hurt her."

Kader grabbed me by the shoulders, lifted me off my feet, and put me behind him with ease. Too stunned that he could actually lift me so easily, I didn't follow him to the back of the ship.

"You're gonna want to put on your seatbelt," Johar said, turning two keys and pressing a button.

My ears popped, and a rush of wind took the air from my lungs. The door in the cargo bay slid open and I felt the tug of air pressure toward it. I climbed over the seat and fastened my seatbelt as instructed, but immediately turned to watch Kader.

He was hanging onto one of the overhead grips, a large gun in his other hand. He lifted the gun onto his shoulder and aimed it, adjusting the sight and his stance.

"Hang on," Johar replied, gripping the joystick of the plane tighter. "Give me the signal, Eli."

"On my mark," he called back.

"I thought we were going to get her!" I cried, glancing between the two of them.

"Will you calm down already?" Johar barked. "Kader?"

"A little closer, Sayuri."

Johar guided the plane closer, then I heard Kader say, "Now!" before a loud crack echoed through the plane.

Terrified, I waited for the Raven plane to explode, to go down, but it remained in the air. Only now it was connected to ours by a thick, black cable. I heaved a sigh of relief, but Kader and Johar were still tense.

"What's next?" I asked Kader, who was attaching himself to the cable via a harness around his waist.

"Now, we hope I don't have to use this gun," he replied wryly. "Keep 'er steady, Sayuri."

"Be careful," she called.

Kader met my gaze and shrugged, lifting himself up onto the harness. "Like I said, piece of cake."

Then he was gone.

TWENTY

THEO

Bang!

I screamed and gripped the edge of my seat, awaiting the agony of being burned alive. When no pain came, I opened my eye and took deep, gulping breaths.

"Sounds like they got there."

"They who?" I asked, still shaking.

I flinched when another loud crashing sound echoed through the cabin, and the air pressure changed rapidly. The door opened, and a black-clad man in a helmet stepped onto the airship.

"W-who are you?" I said, gripping at the dashboard. But I refused to appear weak in my final moments, so I straightened my shoulders. "If you're here to kill me, please make it quick."

"Oh, your boyfriend would be pretty pissed at me if I did that," said the man as he pulled off his helmet. Bald head, tall, with a tense expression. Galian's guard, Kader.

"You!" I collapsed to my knees in relief, pressing my hand to my face and taking sweet gulps of air. I'd nearly come to my death too many times in the past year, and I would never tire of the relief when it never came to pass.

He whistled loudly, placing a hand on the bomb. "You weren't kidding, Theo. This thing's a monster."

I was still reeling from his appearance, so I didn't respond until he knelt in front of me.

"Are you all right?" he asked.

I nodded blankly, and a devilish smile crossed his face.

"You want to get off this bucket of bolts?"

"Yes, please," I said with a smile.

He reached into his pocket and pulled out a small pin. In two clicks, my wrists were free of the handcuffs and I absentmindedly rubbed them. Then, before I could stop myself, I launched myself at him, wrapping my arms around his solid frame.

"Thank you. Thank you so much," I whispered into the folds of his jumpsuit.

He placed a comforting hand on the back of my head. "Thank you for warning us. Now, we have to put this in the ocean quick."

I nodded and looked at the dashboard. "It's Herinese and it's on autopilot. I can't—"

"How's this for autopilot?" he said, lifting a pistol from his pants. I tensed for a moment, but he kept the barrel pointed away from me. "I can aim it at the processor and guidance systems, but we're going to have to get off quick. You okay with that?"

I nodded and followed Kader to the open door. A long black cable connected the airship with another Kylaen plane.

"C'mon," Kader said, opening his arms.

I stepped closer to him and he wrapped a harness around my waist and between my legs, then slid his helmet over my head and asked, "You ready?"

I glanced behind me at the sea beneath us and nodded.

He picked me up as if I weighed nothing and held me up to the black cable, where he instructed me on how to attach myself. I dangled over the ocean, trying not to look down as he did the same for himself. When we were both secure, he pointed the gun at the inside of the plane.

"Wait!" I cried. "I want to do the honors."

"You sure?"

I nodded. "It's my country. I want to take care of it."

He handed me the pistol and I raised it the same way he had. My finger slid around the trigger and I said a prayer for the two of us as I squeezed it.

As soon as the gun went off, Kader unhooked the cable from the plane, and we began to fall toward the ocean. I screamed and my body smacked into Kader's, and somewhere amongst my fear, I registered his arms securing around me.

Our bodies jerked up from the force of reaching the end of the cable, and we hung suspended over the water.

"You okay, Theo?" Kader asked, sounding much too unconcerned for the danger we found ourselves in.

"No!" I shook my head, but glanced at the Raven plane, still flying in the distance. I began to worry my shot hadn't been true, but the plane began to tilt to the right, then the nose dove downward.

"K-Kader!" I said, looking back at him. "If the warhead detonates when it hits the water—"

"Ahead of you, Theo," Kader said. "They should be pulling us up any—"

Our bodies were yanked upward, and I left part of my stomach at the lower altitude. I squeezed my eyes shut, preferring my heights in the safety of a plane under my control. Kader's throaty laughter against my back eased my nerves somewhat, and I heard him say something about how I was a battle-hardened pilot. If I could've opened my mouth without fear I'd vomit all over myself, I would've shot back.

The roar of the Kylaen plane was actually comforting, and before I knew it, we were climbing into the small plane. I collapsed onto the floor, yanking the helmet off and thanking God that I was on something solid.

GALIAN

I watched Theo stare at the ceiling of the plane for a minute before saying anything to her. Her face was pale, her lips chapped, but she was alive. The outside door suctioned shut and all I could hear was her gasping breaths and whispered thanks.

"Hey," I said with a grin.

She sat upright, staring at me as if I were the last person she'd expected to see. Then she turned to Kader, who was barking orders to fly away as fast as possible.

"*What in God's name were you thinking, bringing the princeling here?*" she bellowed. "This... We are *seconds* from being blown up and —"

"Talk to him," Kader said, deflecting her rage with a flick of his wrist. "He was insistent."

"Talk to him *later*," Johar barked from the cockpit. "We've got to get the hell out of here. Strap in."

I had my arms around Theo in two steps and pulled her back to the seats along the wall, buckling her in before doing the same to myself. I grasped her hand and gave her a quick kiss before I heard the secondary engines roar to life.

"Hold on!" Johar called, and then she punched it.

I'd never flown so fast in my entire life, and based on the green look of Theo's face, neither had she. A loud rumbling echoed through the metal, and the plane began to tremble and bounce with the air turbulence. This was the fastest ship we had, but was it fast enough to outrun the blast?

"Kader?" I called, pulling Theo tighter to me.

He didn't answer, but he was gripping the outside of Johar's headrest with white knuckles. His unease was enough to shake me to my core. I'd never known Kader to be worried about anything.

I wrenched my eyes away to look at Theo. She stared back at me, eyes wide with fear, and a strange calm settled over me. Yet again, we'd beaten the odds and found our way back to one another. Holding her, feeling her tremble beneath my fingers, knowing I'd made it back to my girl against all odds, somehow dissipated any worry I had that we weren't going to make it.

Despite the way Johar yelled and Kader cursed as the ship shook even more violently than it had before, I smiled.

"W-what?" Her mouth moved, but I heard no sound.

"I love you," I said, closing the gap between us and kissing her.

She leaned into it, hungrily and desperately moving against my mouth. I threaded my fingers through her hair and pulled her closer, needing to taste every inch of her. Her voice rumbled low in her throat where my hand pressed against her neck, and I deepened the kiss even further.

"Nice to know you two can still make out while we're about to die." Kader's droll voice popped the euphoric bubble.

Theo wrenched her face away from me, and my awareness returned. Kader's already pale face was even paler, but the worry was gone.

"I thought we were going to die," Theo said, but a red blush tinted her cheeks.

"I didn't," I said, grinning at her. "That was an I-missed-you kiss."

Theo's eyebrows shot upward and her mouth grew slack. "You knew we weren't about to be obliterated?"

"Of course," I said with a shrug. "I mean, we didn't go through *all that* to get blown up, did we?"

Kader stared at the space above my head as if he were considering bodily harm, but instead he turned and disappeared in his chair.

"You never change, do you, princeling?" she asked, her eyes shimmering with love and amusement. Then they shifted and grew wet. "I can't believe that I just... You just... *Oh my God.*"

She collapsed across my lap, pressing her forehead into my thigh and gulping down air while she mumbled incoherently.

"Theo?" I asked.

She shook her head against my thigh. Chuckling, I removed the hairband from around her bun and let her black tresses fall around her, rubbing her scalp and waiting for her to finish processing her latest near-death experience. After a moment, she pushed herself upright and her face was wet.

"I thought I was done for," she said, staring at some unseen point beyond my face.

"Did you really think I was going to let that happen?" I asked, wiping her cheeks. "I promised you I wasn't going to let you die. And I make good on my promises."

A ghost of a smile crept onto her lips. "You really do, don't you?" She leaned over and captured my lips with a sweet, gentle kiss. "That was for closing Mael." She kissed me again, this time even more gently. "That was for Martin. *Amichai*, I am so, so sorry..."

I inhaled deeply. "I feel guilty. He shouldn't have died—"

"And Bayard shouldn't have placed me on that bomb, either," she snapped. "Unfortunately, our respective leadership *sucks*."

"Wait...*Bayard* put you on the bomb?" I didn't know why that surprised me so much. Maybe because I'd always thought the Raven president to be bad, but not as bad as my father.

Kader made a noise to Johar and unhooked himself from his seat, coming back to join us. "What else can you tell us about this weapon?"

"She doesn't have to say anything," I said, tightening my hold on her. "As far as the Raven government is concerned, she's dead. And as far as Kylae is concerned—"

"*Amichai*," she whispered. "It's all right. I don't know much, but I know that this...it was built at Malaske. Bayard was hoping it would put a stop to the war once and for all."

"What, by wiping out the royal family and half the city of Norose?" I blanched.

"That's one way to end it," Kader said. "Were there any other ships?"

She shook her head. "None that I saw. I'm afraid my trip there was nothing more than a test to see where my loyalties lay. I know their facility is underground—"

"Ah, that's why we could never see it," Kader said with a nod. "And of your loyalties?"

"Cannon found me on our island," she replied. "Bayard said it was either be tried and hanged in the public square or get on the plane." She lifted her shoulder in a half-shrug. "I figured my odds were better in the plane."

"Did you know about the plane before?"

"I found out about a week ago," she replied, looking at her hands, still clasped in mine. "I knew I had to stop him, so I asked Lanis to..." Her eyes widened, and she looked away. "Oh God, I hope they didn't do anything to Lanis."

"Is there anything else of value you can tell us about Malaske?" Kader asked.

"The Herinese were in on it, as were the Jervanians, but I don't think the Jervanians were as sold on the plan," she said. "Herin, though —they provided the plane-hiding technology. I think...perhaps the plane was a prototype or proof of concept. I don't know if...now that it's been destroyed—"

"And we know about it," Kader finished for her. "We can set our intelligence group to discuss these new developments with Herin and Jervan."

"Oh God, you aren't...you aren't going to bomb them, are you?" Theo asked, her brown eyes wide as saucers.

"Grieg will probably order a strike on Malaske," Kader said and she nodded in solemn acceptance. "But as for Jervan and Herin, we have other ways of keeping them in line."

"And us keeping them *in line* is what moved them to work with the Ravens to bomb the shit out of us," I snapped.

"Which is why this information is going to your mother, not your father," Kader said. "We'll be landing in Kylae in about an hour."

She went stick straight. "Kylae?"

"Yeah," I said, rubbing her back to calm her. "It'll be fine. Nothing to worry about."

"Wait," Theo said, unhooking her restraints. She stood in front of Kader as if he were a superior officer. Shoulders squared, she extended her hand. "Thank you, Kader. For saving my life. Tw...three times now."

I smiled. Theo hated being in someone's debt.

"As far as I see it, Major, by telling us about that bird, you've saved my life, my wife's, and all of my dear friends back in Norose," Kader said, crossing his hands over his chest. "So I'll call us *niec*, if that suits your Raven *miall*."

Her mouth twisted into a smile. "How does a Kylaen sergeant know about Raven traditions?"

"What's that?" I asked.

"*Miall* is a very old Raven tradition amongst our warriors. A life debt," she said, glancing to me. "I didn't tell you about this?"

"You were very upset that I'd saved your life, as I recall."

"Ravens like to be *niec*, or square," Kader said. "And as far as I'm concerned, Theo, we're *niec*."

"See?" I said, pulling Theo back down to sit next to me. "I told you that you and Kader would get along."

THEO

All I wanted was to have a stiff drink and curl up with my *amichai* and sleep for the next ten thousand years. I settled for resting in the crook of his neck. Galian, of course, was more than willing to hold me and explain his plans for us once we left Kylae for our new life in Jervan.

"I'll find us an apartment. Penthouse with a terrace overlooking the lake," Galian said, tracing the lines of my palm. "I found a few...just in case."

"Were you thinking I'd be calling you to come rescue me sometime soon, then?" I asked, tilting my head up to look at him. "You know we're woefully out of balance now."

"Not neck, are we?"

"N...*niec?*" I stifled a giggle. His accent hadn't gotten any better.

"But I thought we were a little closer," Galian said, thinking to himself. "There was the crash, then the wolf. Then you saved my life when I fell off the cliff. You scared off the pack of wolves the second time."

"You saved me from Mael." A smile grew on my face. "*Amichai*, I'm so proud of you. It took a lot of courage to stand up to your father like that."

"Luckily I have a good role model," he replied, bringing my fingers to his mouth and kissing them. "You make me want to be better, you know."

I swallowed, guilt replacing giddiness. Galian had done his part, and there I was, about to run away.

"What?" he asked.

"Is it really that simple? Just leave all this behind?"

"I think it's pretty clear that neither side wants peace," Kader said, standing in front of us. "It might be wiser to just disappear. At least then, I won't have to watch this sickening display."

I frowned, unsure what about me had made him sick, but Galian huffed loudly and glared at him. "Please, I've seen you with your wife. You've no room to talk, you big softy."

"Oh, Rosie!" the pilot I now knew as Johar replied with a coo. "You shoulda seen this idiot the first night he laid eyes on her. I'd never seen him trip over his own two feet before."

I laughed as Kader grumbled, but the back of his neck was as red as my face.

"I came back here to tell you two idiots to strap in. We're nearing the airfield," Kader said. "Try not to get slobber all over my plane, please."

Galian tossed Kader a dirty look and wrapped his arms around me as if to prove a point. Personally, I didn't mind it, and I curled in tighter under his chin as the plane bumped to land. I wished that being back on solid ground made me feel better, but it only restarted my nerves. My heartbeat was in my throat when the plane rolled to a stop and the engines quit. Kader brushed by us to open the door and release the ladder down to the ground.

"I promise nothing's going to happen to you," Galian said, unhooking my restraint and then his own. "I've made provisions this time."

"Oh?" I said, letting him pull me to stand.

"Is that her?"

My attention snapped to the back of the plane where the crown prince of Kylae stood, smiling at me with his hands in his pockets. I barely recognized him in plain clothes.

"Rhys, this is Theo," Galian said, putting an arm around me.

"Theo, this is my brother Rhys."

"I..." I couldn't find my tongue, unsure what to say.

"I have to say, it's *wonderful* to finally get to talk face-to-face with you," he said.

And in that instant, I recognized his voice and my nerves turned to mortification.

"Oh my God," I whispered to myself, turning to press my face into Galian's shoulder. "He was the radio dispatcher."

"Theo?" Galian asked. "Rhys, what—"

"Theo and I just had a little chat while you guys were off on your heroic rescue," Rhys replied.

I peeled my face off Galian's shirt and glared at him. "A little chat?"

Rhys' smile widened as Galian's face grew angry. "Rhys, what did you *do*?"

"What?" He waved his hands in the air and came closer. "It's not every day you get to question your little brother's girlfriend when she thinks she's about to die."

"*Rhys!*"

"I just wanted to...hear her side of things," Rhys said, holding up his hands in defense.

"And you let me prattle on like I was going to die!" I barked at him. "You could've warned me someone was coming!"

"I wasn't sure you were alone!" Rhys said, holding his hands up, but I didn't quite buy it.

"That was a real shit thing to do, Rhys," Galian growled, holding me closer.

"Oh, stop being such a baby. I got your girlfriend back, didn't I?" Rhys said, holding out his arms. "Now come here before we have to rescue you from some other death-trap."

I didn't move; I'd spoken so plainly about Galian to him that I suddenly felt shy.

"Go on," Galian whispered, nudging me forward. I could tell I was being watched, and I kept my hands firmly at my side, lest they think I had any intention of harming—

Rhys pulled me into a hug, and I stiffened, terribly afraid that something bad was going to happen.

"Relax," he said with a toothy grin that strongly reminded me of Galian. It softened my nerves to see something so familiar. "We just went through all that trouble to save you. We aren't going to send you back to Mael. Not that it exists anymore."

I barked a laugh, and in spite of my fear, a smile broke out on my face.

"It's nice to meet you..." His title hung on my tongue. As a proud Raven soldier, I couldn't call him 'your highness' or any of the other titles bestowed upon him as prince.

"You can call me Rhys." He winked, again reminding me of his younger brother. "After all, *Gally*'s been whining about you for the past few months, so you're practically family now."

"*Gally*?" I immediately turned around and chuckled at the way my *amichai*'s face turned a bright shade of red. Though I wasn't sure if it was because of the pet name or because of the insinuation that we were family now. "I think I prefer princeling."

"I think I prefer neither."

"And speaking of family," Rhys said, releasing me back into Galian's arms, "we might have a slight problem."

TWENTY-ONE

GALIAN

"I love that you're a fiercely loyal Raven woman," I said to her. "But I am begging you, *please don't piss off my father*."

"I'm not planning on it," she replied shakily.

That little weasel of a radar operator had gone to his supervisor about the anomaly. It had taken a few hours, but my father had become aware of everything—starting with the sizable tidal wave that had washed away six months' of work in his shithole port city of Duran.

"Yes. For my sake, please don't piss him off," Rhys said from the seat parallel to ours.

"He wouldn't...kill you, would he?" Theo asked.

Rhys shook his head, but then grimaced. "But it won't be pleasant. Collins is *pissed*."

"Collins? Olivia Collins?" Theo asked.

Despite himself, Rhys smiled. "Oh, you know about her?"

"She knows that she was a favor to...Oh." Realization dawned on me. "Mother asked me to go out with Olivia to get dirt on her father, didn't she?"

"Why?" Theo asked.

"There's a whole, big political chess match going on between my parents," I explained. "One that, after tonight, we won't have to worry about. We'll just have dinner, be pleasant, then get on our plane to Jervan."

"Father's not—"

"I smuggled myself into Jervan before, I can do it again," I replied with an overly cheery smile on my face. "Besides, what could he possibly want from us? He hates me, and he's at war with Theo's people. I don't know why he's even asked for dinner."

"Maybe he wants to meet your girlfriend?" Rhys offered.

"Right, the same one he sent to Mael," I growled, placing a protective arm over her shoulder. She leaned into me and closed her eyes. I could tell she was exhausted, and I was as well, so I just wanted to get this over with as soon as possible. "Maybe we'll just sleep in my room tonight then go to Jervan."

"Sleep sounds good," she mumbled.

"You know what? Go to Jervan," Rhys said, throwing up his hands. "Because if I have to watch you two get handsy all day long..."

"It gets old, doesn't it?" Kader barked from the front seat.

"Is this what it's like to have a family?" Theo whispered against my skin.

"Yeah," I replied, tucking her in tighter. "Do you like it?"

"As long as you're the target, it's perfect," she said with a grin.

"So here's the plan," Rhys said, as Kader pulled the car around to the back of the castle gardens. "I don't want anyone to know about Theo until we've got a story, so we're going to go in through Mom's private entrance. Her guard won't talk, and we're having dinner in her private dining room. Even so, let's not...say anything to anyone."

Theo nodded and I squeezed her hand. "It'll be fine."

My mother must've been in agreement with (or concocted) our plan, because we saw no one between the two guards stationed at her entrance and her private dining quarters. Rhys and I walked briskly, but I noticed Theo's wide-eyed absorption of the castle. Had things been different, I might've enjoyed showing her all of my favorite places. But for now, I just wanted to leave.

When the door closed on my mother's dining space, I finally let out a relieved sigh. Rhys immediately left through another door to look for Mom, leaving me and Theo alone.

She wandered around the lavishly decorated room, trimmed with red and silver, before turning to smile at me over her shoulder. "This is where your mother eats dinner? This place could feed my country for a year."

"It's a bit of a misnomer," I said, lounging on one of the chaises in the corner. "We used to have family dinners in here when we were younger—without His Highness."

"And with?"

"He'd drag us into the grand dining space to entertain some minister or diplomat," I said, patting the cushion next to me. "But here, we could be three rowdy boys and give our mother hell by throwing peas at each other."

She sat down and crawled into my arms. "You mean they were throwing peas at you?"

"Usually." I glanced at the ceiling, feeling her breath against my skin. "You're gonna meet my mom, Theo."

"Yeah?" She lifted her head. "I thought—"

"No, I mean, you're gonna meet her. You're actually *here*." I shook my head. "I didn't think this would ever happen."

"To be honest? Me neither." She cocked her head to the side. "Today's been a bit of a whirlwind. I don't know how much more I can take."

A soft knock at the door interrupted our conversation, and my mother swept into the room, grinning brightly.

Theo's eyes had grown large again, and her hand was sweaty in mine, so I moved quickly to show her that Mom wasn't someone to be afraid of. "Theo, this is my mom," I said, pushing her forward. "Mom, this is—"

"The Raven girl." My father appeared through the other door, Rhys on his heels, looking neutered and miserable.

THEO

The king of Kylae bore down on me, swimming in a fur-lined cloak fastened by solid gold pieces at each shoulder. His gold crown (*did he always wear a crown?*) was perched on his balding head. Like Bayard, he seemed much older in person than in photographs, but every bit as imposing.

He swept toward Galian and me, and I fought the urge to hide behind my *amichai*. I saw nothing of Galian in his father, but I didn't know why I expected to.

"Does she not bow?" Grieg asked, his malicious eyes sweeping over my *amichai* as if he were dirt.

"I believe only your subjects do that," he snarled back. "And as she's not, she doesn't have to."

I found myself wondering if this was the first time Galian had seen his father since he'd left the castle and, based on their body language, I assumed it was. The tension crackled between them, and I was sure that one of them would throw the first punch.

"Grieg. Galian. Let's sit down and have dinner." The queen's dulcet tones broke them from their stalemate, and they begrudgingly moved toward the table. I pretended to be invisible, repeating to myself that as soon as we got out of this dinner, we could be on our way to Jervan.

As often as I considered what life might be like with Galian, never in my wildest dreams had I imagined eating a four-course meal on golden plates with the king, queen, and crown prince of Kylae. The absurdity of it all kept my attention away from the sparks flying between Grieg and Galian, who said nothing as they poked at their creamy soups.

"Is the food all right, dear?"

The queen of Kylae was asking me a question. I looked up at her, my tongue sticking to the roof of my mouth.

"Speak, Raven," Grieg barked at me.

My face heated, and Galian's clammy hand slipped through mine, giving me strength. "It's very good, thank you."

"You haven't touched it," Grieg snapped.

"I'm sure, *Father*, that after events of the day...she's probably lost her appetite," Galian answered for me.

I nodded in agreement, but picked up the golden spoon that probably cost more than my entire year's salary and dipped it into the soup. I felt as exposed as the day I'd given my speech in the Jervan parliament, with as many eyes on me.

I hadn't even realized I was shaking until the pad of Galian's thumb brushed against the underside of my palm and he winked at me. At least now I wasn't alone.

"So the question is, what do we do with you?" Grieg said, breaking the silence at the table. "We've got a port city half underwater, and a group of soldiers who need an explanation for why two princes decided to go on a rogue mission. And now I hear that Bayard's gone and built himself a bomb."

Despite my fear, I faced the king. "You aren't...going to retaliate, are you?"

"Damn right I'm going to retaliate," he grumbled. "Can't have those creatures thinking they can get away with building a bomb."

Creatures? My mouth fell open.

"And with what money? Those bastards over in Jervan are going to hear it from me. First they invite the animals from Rave, as if it's a real country."

Galian's grip tightened on my hand, but there was a buzzing in my ear.

"These Ravens think they know war, they've got another thing coming. I've been content to let them flounder, but I've had enough. After all, it is *my* damned country—"

"It is *not* your country," I said, my voice a deathly whisper.

His Kylaen arrogance had awoken my Raven patriotism, long dormant since I'd witnessed all the faults of my country. But although my love was Kylaen, I, myself, was Raven, and I would be until the day I died.

And no king, Kylaen or otherwise, was allowed to speak about my country that way.

"Oh?" he asked, sitting back and examining me as if I were beneath him. "Got something to say on the subject?"

I felt the warning glares of everyone in the room, but I'd been too silent for too long. "Rave never has been, and never will be yours."

Before I knew what I was doing, I'd dropped Galian's hand and left the room through the nearest door. My boots—Raven-issued boots I'd been wearing since I'd left with Lanis the day before—echoed on the pristine tile floors.

I stopped against a wall to try to collect myself, and to stop the shaking. I heard someone approaching and I didn't bother to look at him.

"Go away, princeling."

"I am neither a princeling, nor am I one to be ordered around."

My blood ran cold. Queen of Kylae stood before me, beautiful in her gown and terrifying in her countenance. She'd followed me? I turned to look for guards or soldiers, or those who would arrest and execute me for impudence against the precious king. But the queen was alone.

Why was that scarier?

She approached me without hesitation, coming close enough that I could smell her expensive perfume. I was rooted to the spot, terrified by what horror my words had wrought.

To my surprise, she simply looped my arm through hers and gently guided me through the maze-like corridors of the castle.

We walked in silence, the only sound was the quiet *clack-clack* of her shoes on the floors, and the bowing and murmured hello of passing servants. It was apparent that they loved their queen, and she them, as she nodded her head in a pleasant greeting to every one who offered her the same. I might as well have been invisible for all the attention she paid to me.

I wasn't sure how long or far we walked before my curiosity

got the better of me.

"What are we doing?" I asked, my own voice sounding foreign.

"My darling, we are taking a walk," she replied. There was no malice or anger in her voice, simply observation. She reminded me very strongly of Galian with her gentle nature.

"Oh," I said simply. "Why—"

"There are things you need to understand," she said, interrupting me. "First and foremost, you should watch your temper around the king."

I tensed, my curiosity about the queen suddenly turning to hatred. How *dare* she—

"He is not a forgiving man, and I would hate for Rave to lose such a valuable ambassador because she lost her temper one too many times," she continued, and her words defused my anger almost immediately.

"A-amb... What?" I sputtered.

"You are the first Raven citizen to walk freely in the king's castle in over fifty years," she replied, looking forward. "You have the ear and heart of the king's third son, and the respect of the king's successor, and at this moment, the arm of the king's wife. You are in a very powerful position for your country."

"I'm not here to..." Did the queen think I was only here on behalf of my country? The thought of her not knowing how I felt about Galian made me sick. "I love Galian—"

"Oh dear, that is apparent, and he is most deeply in love with you." She smiled, patting my arm lightly. "And as his mother, I wholeheartedly approve of anyone who my son is willing to go to such great lengths to be with." She cast a quick glance at me, affirming that she was truly happy to see me there, yet I saw the trace of regret on her face.

"But?"

"As queen, my first priority is my people, who have been locked in a fifty-year war with another nation. Hundreds of thousands have died because peace is out of our grasp." She stopped to look at me in the eyes. "You and Galian built a bridge of trust and peace on that island. I only ask that you consider how best to bring more people across."

I was stunned into silence. Korina *wanted* me here. She *wanted* me to use my position to advance the cause of peace between Kylae and Rave.

If only I had a position. "I wish I could help but I'm nothing but...Bayard won't listen to me. He put me on that plane. He thinks I'm a traitor—"

"There are others within Rave who would listen," she responded. "A small rebellion has been fomenting in the slums of Veres for some time. They have a good cause, but are in dire need of money, and money is something I have plenty of. What I do not have is a person to extend the olive branch."

My heart skipped a beat, but my suspicions were raised. "And what is Kylae's interest in the Raven rebels? To what end would I be working?"

"An end to the war, however that may happen. To bring the two countries to the table to work out their differences and come to an agreeable solution. But first they have to want to come to the table. Kylae is weary of war, and Grieg may be amenable in the way his father and grandfather weren't. But we need someone we can work with in Rave until we can get better leadership in place here."

"Better le..." My voice died in my throat, and I stared at her in wide-eyed astonishment.

Rhys.

Korina Helmuth had been singlehandedly trying to stop the Madion War since she married Grieg. Rhys seemed much more gentle than I'd imagined him to be. He'd cared for whether I lived or died on that plane. The same way Galian had cared when we'd landed on that island. I'd considered it a fluke, or perhaps just his nature, but I'd never considered that the heir to the Kylaen throne would share the same kindness.

But his voice on the radio had been calming. He'd been interested in what I had to say. He'd valued my life. He'd even given the order to save it. For someone like that to take over in Kylae...

Korina paused in front of a door where two soldiers were stationed, and I realized our walk had come to an end.

"Where are we?" I asked.

"We are at the back entrance of the castle," she said. "Elijah, Galian's guard, is waiting for you. He will take you to his apartment where you can stay until you can secure passage back to Rave."

The air left my chest as I realized what this meant for me and my *amichai*. In order for the Raven rebels to trust me, I would have to continue to keep my love for him a secret. They wouldn't trust me otherwise.

"If you don't want to go, nothing would make me happier than to see my son happy. But," she touched my cheek, "I have a feeling you will want to delay your happiness for just a bit longer."

"If it means all this could stop—"

"*T-Theo!*" Galian's voice took me away from his mother as he came running down the hall breathlessly. "Oh, damn it, Theo, you really—"

"I will take care of your father, Gally," Korina said, and I couldn't help but enjoy the way he bristled at the name. For as much as I loved him, it amused me to see others love him as well. She nodded her goodbye to me and asked the two guards to take a walk with her.

And then it was just me and my *amichai*.

GALIAN

I watched her face as she warred over whatever my mother had just told her.

"What did my mother say to you?" I asked, pulling her into my arms.

Instead of answering, she buried her head in my shoulder, wrapping her arms around me and shaking her head.

"What?"

"I won't do it. I won't put my life on hold again," she whispered. "We're going to Jervan."

"Why wouldn't we?" I asked, gently lifting her chin until she looked at me. "What did my mom want you to do?"

"S-she wanted me to go back to Rave. To...to make contact with the Raven rebels and..." She scrunched up her face and shook her head. "No. I won't do it."

I held her to me, but my mind returned to my meeting with Gerard McMullen in the hospital. He'd said that no one would meet with him because he was Kylaen.

"Why does she want to work with the rebels?" I asked.

"She wants to depose Bayard," Theo replied. "She wants to put someone in power who will come to the negotiating table when...when your brother takes over."

Her words were barely audible, but they seized me with so much hope and terror that I crushed her tighter to me.

"But I won't do it," she repeated. "I can't...because it means we couldn't be together—"

"You should go."

The words came out of my mouth before I could stop them. My mother was right; Theo would never have willingly left Rave behind. Even now, as she said she wanted to leave, I could see guilt mixed in with the relief. She was a Raven woman, and as much as she loved me, she would always be Raven. She loved the shores and the dried plains of the country, the dingy cities and the crowded slums. Even when her government turned its back on her, she still remained faithful to the people.

I knew it wouldn't be easy. Finding peace between Raven and Kylae was about as probable as the Madion Sea freezing over. Their president was willing to massacre half a population rather than come up with a real solution, and my father was already intent on avenging all those who would've been killed had Bayard succeeded. It would be damned near impossible to bridge the river of blood already spilled.

But just as she saw my potential for greatness, Theo knew the potential in Rave. She wasn't willing to give up on it just yet. And I would never give up on her.

I cupped her face and brushed away her tears. "I love you, Theo. But I love you enough to know that if I take you to Jervan, you'll never be able to forgive yourself."

Two more tears slipped out of her eyes, but there was

resignation and a silent gratitude in them.

"Six months," she whispered. "I will try for six months, and if I don't succeed—"

"You're mine," I said, knowing we would be having this same conversation in six months. But I didn't want to think about that now.

"I'm always yours, *amichai*."

The word shivered through me. I yanked her closer, covering her mouth with mine and pouring all of my anger, my frustration, and my love into the kiss. My hands clutched the back of her neck and I seared everything into my memory for the lonely months to follow. The smell of her hair, the sound of her soft moan, the taste of her tongue as it slid over mine, and the saltiness of her tears.

I lifted my lips and stared at her without a word, too afraid to say goodbye.

Then I let her go.

As always, thank you, dear reader, for going with me on this adventure. As an indie author, I rely on my awesome folks like yourselves to help share the word about my work. Please consider leaving a review on Amazon, Goodreads, or any other fine book retailer. I am so excited to hear what you think—even if it's a short review. And don't forget to check out my other work below and subscribe to my newsletter to get all the latest info from yours truly.

THEO AND GALIAN'S ADVENTURE CONCLUDES IN
THE MADION WAR TRILOGY BOOK 3

THE
UNION
THE MADION WAR TRILOGY

VALENTINE'S DAY 2017

ALSO BY S. USHER EVANS

The Razia Series

Lyssa Peate is living a double life as a planet discovering scientist and a space pirate bounty hunter. Unfortunately, neither life is going very well. She's the least wanted pirate in the universe and her brand new scientist intern is spying on her. Things get worse when her intern is mistaken for her hostage by the Universal Police.

The Razia Series is a four-book space opera series and is available now for eBook and paperback. Download the first book, Double Life, for free.

empath

Lauren Dailey is in break-up hell, but if you ask her she's doing just great. She hears a mysterious voice promising an easy escape from her problems and finds herself in a brand new world where she has the power to feel what others are feeling. Just one problem—there's a dragon in the mountains that happens to eat Empaths. And it might be the source of the mysterious voice tempting her deeper into her own darkness.

Empath is a stand-alone fantasy that is available now free for Kindle Unlimited subscribers and also for paperback and hardcover.

ABOUT THE AUTHOR

S. Usher Evans is an author, blogger, and witty banter aficionado. Born in Pensacola, Florida, she left the sleepy town behind for the fast-paced world of Washington, D.C.. There, she somehow landed jobs with BBC, Discovery Channel, and National Geographic Television before finally settling into a "real job" as an IT consultant. After a quarter life crisis at age 27, she decided consulting was for the birds and writing was the bee's knees. She sold everything she owned and moved back to Pensacola, where she currently resides with her two dogs, Zoe and Mr. Biscuit.

Evans is the author of the Razia series, Empath, and the Madion War Trilogy, all published by Sun's Golden Ray Publishing.

Check her out in her internet home
http://www.susherevans.com/

Or on Twitter
@susherevans

Want to know the latest from S. Usher Evans? Sign up for her newsletter.

CPSIA information can be obtained
at www.ICGtesting.com
Printed in the USA
LVOW05s1102030616

491098LV00001B/2/P